Silent Blue Tears
Strong Women Unite
By
Detective Ron Bateman (Ret.)

Silent Blue Tears © 2021

The characters and events in this book are fictious. Any similarity to real persons, living or dead, is coincidental and not intended by the author.

Copyright © 2021 by Ronald Bateman

All rights reserved. The scanning, uploading, and distribution of this book without permission is a theft of the author's intellectual property. If you would like permission to use material from the book (other than review purposes) please contact ronwood655@verizon.net. Thank you for your support of the author's rights.

This book is published by SBT Entertainment LLC and found at ronbatemanbooks.com. The publisher is not responsible for websites or their content that are not owned by the publisher.

ISBN 9798468508473

Cover designs by Zoe Neely

Printed in the United States of America

Dedicated to those honorable men and women who passed before us and impacted so many lives.

Doctor William Jones

Major Bill Donoho

Judge Bruce Williams

Ray Bateman

Steve Bateman

Chapter 1

The air brakes made a hissing sound just before the aging Greyhound bus came to a halt. The doors swung open, making a shrill noise in the crisp January air. The early evening's bitter cold greeted the patrons as they filed outside, dark already and only a few minutes after 6:00 p.m., men and women returning from work, stepped from the public transportation to begin their walk home.

One of the occupants, Suk Kim, standing a mere 4'9", weighing only 105 pounds, was a hard-working 44-year-old Korean mother of two teenagers. Married since the age of 17, she worked 12 hours a day, seven days a week, at her husband's family dry cleaners, a few miles from the townhome they rented. Dressed in tan polyester slacks, a light blue sweater and a warm jacket, Suk re-adjusted the purse on her shoulder and clutched onto her canvas bag, partially filled with her uneaten lunch and tattered bible.

Suk started the mile-long walk to the community known as Pioneer City in Severn, Maryland. The impoverished community is speckled with all races, comprised of everything from hard-working, law-abiding citizens, to drug dealers and street criminals who suck off the government subsides like leaches. The city of Severn is the proud home of the Fort George G. Meade Army base and the National Security

Administration. Most of the area communities are made up of middle-class families, many of which are members of the military or government employees.

A small portion of the route Suk walks each morning and evening is owned and under the jurisdiction of the United States Army. The adjacent neighborhoods and streets remain within the confines of Anne Arundel County. The law enforcement and emergency services on the federal property remain the exclusive responsibility of the Military Police and Fire Department, and everything else belongs to the Anne Arundel County Police and Fire Departments.

Briskly walking home to prepare dinner for her family, Suk scurried down the sidewalk next to the heavily traveled Reece Road. With her head down, she approached the vacant elementary school, still owned by the military. The immediate areas before and after the school are illuminated with dull streetlamps, casting only a glimmer onto the barren school property.

Suk didn't care much for this part of the walk, especially during the evening hours, in fact, she made it a point to quicken her short strides to get through faster. With her senses heightened, she could hear footsteps rapidly approaching from behind. Before she was able to turn, a man breathing heavily wearing an Army hoodie whisked by at a fast pace. The soft soles of the jogger's shoes silenced his impact and startled Suk. Relaxing once more, she continued for several more steps when she felt her head violently jerk backwards from the callused hand that gripped over her mouth. The attacker's hold silenced her attempts to scream. Her hair was being used as a leash as she was pulled from the sidewalk.

    Frantically, Suk dropped her bag while her purse slid from her shoulder to the ground. She tugged on the wrist of her assailant, but the grip was far too powerful. Horrified, Suk was unable to yell for help. Her body was manipulated like a ragdoll to the rear of the school. Losing consciousness, she managed to see the dark area where she was being drug. Thoughts of her husband and their children raced through her mind. She went limp and fell to the ground. Using both hands, she pulled at the large hand covering her face to no avail. Her cold small hands weakened as she felt herself fading from lack of oxygen. Her limp body was forced across the asphalt to a basketball court behind the school. Lying on her back with the controlling grip now released from her hair and face, she began to come to. Struggling to focus, she got the first glimpse of her assailant. He was a white man in his 30's, dressed in dark clothes, round glasses, with a horrid look on his face. She peered into his eyes with a look of helplessness and sheer fear. His eyes were dull, focused like a lion who was about to devour his catch. The accoster dropped down, straddling her waist with his knees on the ground. Forcefully, he squeezed her neck and again placed his other hand across her mouth.

"If you say a word cunt, I'll kill you," he said through his gritting teeth.

The man removed his hand from her throat, unsnapped his jeans and lowered his zipper. Suk knew his evil intentions but was unable to scream because of his hand pressing over her mouth. Reacting on her will to survive, she bit down on the man's fingers.

"OWW, YOU FUCKING WHORE," he yelled, jerking his hand from her penetrating teeth. He clenched his fist and struck her face. Blood poured from her nose and severed lip. His forehead tightened with wrinkles and his eyes squinted. "You must want to die, you little bitch," he said, punching her again in the face.

The man grabbed the polyester waistband of her pants and violently yanked downward, causing them to tear. He pulled sadistically at her underwear until it tore in half. Knowing she was about to be raped, she was fearful he would kill her. Her life flashed like a motion picture before her. Vividly, she could see her children and husband. Thoughts of the shame her culture would cast upon her rushed through her mind. She knew she had to fight, perhaps for her life. With the man's pants down Suk could see his erection exposed. In an instant she lunged forward, grabbing a handful of testicles and squeezed down on his sack.

"AHHHH, you bitch!" the man screamed. His voice echoed off the old school brick walls. The excruciating pain radiated through him like an electrical shock.

The weakened attacker pulled Suk's hand from the relentless grip on his genitals. While he groaned in agony, he flipped Suk onto her stomach like a piece of meat. "You little bitch," he shouted.

In a fit of rage, he mashed her face into the cold asphalt. Suk struggled, kicking her legs, trying to grab the man with her free hand. Enraged, he took hold of her right wrist and twisted her arm behind her back. He wrenched her arm toward her head until the bone in her forearm snapped like a branch. Suk's scream from the unbearable pain was drowned out by the road noise. She gasped for air while tears gushed from her eyes mixing in with the blood on her face. She was unable to summon for help. The man jumped from her battered body, leaving her on the cold surface, destitute and hurt. Crying in agony, she waited for the next round of assault. Her adrenaline overtook her body, masking the pain she was soon to feel. As quickly as it began, the brutal occurrence ceased, and the man disappeared into the night.

Suk pushed herself upright with one hand, while she gingerly attempted to bring her broken arm to the front of her body. The shattering pain was immense, making her nauseous from the agonizing sensation that jolted through her. With her arm now in front, she could see the compound fracture through the sleeve of her coat. It looked abnormal, almost fake. Still fearing another barrage of assaults, she forced herself from the ground and stumbled toward the road where she could see traffic passing by. Her torn slacks fell to her ankles and her underpants drug from behind. With dirt and stones embedded in the soft pale skin on her cheek and forehead, she made her way closer to the road, waving her hand to get anyone's attention. Blood oozed down her chin from the incisions on her lip. Nearing the roadway, she collapsed to her knees, giving in to her demise. Now lying on the curb, cars continued by. No one would stop. Finally, a passing military paramedic caught glimpse of the near lifeless body lying motionless on the sidewalk.

The personnel in the ambulance activated their emergency lights before they stopped. The male paramedic passenger, Zach Garten, jumped from the ambo and ran to Suk's side. "Ma'am, ma'am," he shouted, quickly assessing her injuries. He reached into the pouch strapped around his waist and snapped open an ammonia inhalant. He placed it beneath her nose causing an immediate reaction. Awakened, Suk shook her head side to side from the putrid vapors. The atrocious pain spiked through her body once more. "My arm. My arm. Help me," she moaned.

With the aid of surgical scissors, the female paramedic, Heather Fox, carefully lifted the sleeve of Suk's jacket and began slicing through the material. Suk screamed. Her radius bone protruded from her blood-soaked blouse. The pain intensified each time the severed bones shifted. The two worked in tandem to cut the shirt from her arm, fully exposing the fracture. Heather looked down at

Suk's pants. She could tell something horrible had happened from the sight of her underwear barely attached to her ankle. Sadden, Heather removed her thick warm jacket and draped it across Suk's waist to cover her private parts.

Fighting back her own tears, Heather held onto Suk's wrist and looked into her crying eyes. "Don't move ma'am. We need to stabilize your injury. I know this is going to hurt but try not to move." Suk could see the hint of tears in the eyes of the stranger helping her. Suk nodded her head, squeezing her face muscles together in anguish. Zach slid a support board under her forearm while Heather wrapped the wound snug with gauze and tape on both ends. With blood still dripping from her lip, Suk opened her eyes. Overcome with pain, she looked helplessly at the medical staff hovering above her. Their headlamps and emergency lights flashed in the darkness and the sound of sirens could be heard nearing their location.

"Can you tell us what happened?" Zach asked Suk, oblivious to the observations his partner had made of the victim's pants and undergarment.

Tears flowed harder from Suk's eyes. She turned her head toward the school. "He tried to rape me."

Both medical personnel looked back toward the grassy section in front of the vacant elementary school. They could see a purse and a carrying bag on the ground with many of its contents spilled about.

A few minutes later, an Anne Arundel County police officer and her sergeant were on the scene arriving simultaneously with two Fort Meade Army Military police officers.

"Ma'am, we need to put you on the stretcher to get you to the hospital. We'll help you. Are you ready?" Heather asked.

"What about my husband?" Suk cried out.

"The police officers will get that information from you at the hospital ma'am. Are you ready?" Heather asked.

Wincing in pain she moaned, "But my family is expecting me."

"What's your name?" Heather asked.

"Suk. Suk Kim," she mumbled.

"Mrs. Kim. When we get to the hospital, I'll make sure we get in touch with your family. I promise," Heather assured her. Suk nodded her head while the tears cascaded down her cheeks.

The two military police officers and paramedics assisted Suk onto the stretcher, taking extra care with her badly injured arm. She moaned as bolts of pain shot through her. Once in the ambulance, the dumpy looking county police sergeant spoke. "Does anybody know what happened to her and where?"

Zach joined Suk in the rear of their unit as Heather secured the rear doors. "Yes sir. We have an Asian female named Suk Kim with a compound fracture to her right arm and facial injuries. She said a male tried to rape her. From the looks of her pants and underwear, it looks pretty serious. Her purse and bags are lying on the grass over there," Heather said, pointing to the front of the school.

"Ok. Thanks. We'll go take a look," the sergeant exclaimed.

The frumpy grey-haired county police sergeant and a veteran female officer joined the two military police officers now standing near their jeep. "Hello gentlemen. How are we this fine cold January evening?" the sergeant asked sarcastically.

"Fine Sergeant. I'm PFC Dan Dinko and this is my partner, Specialist John Astle."

"I'm told we have an injured female that was attacked on the school grounds. Some type of sexual assault. If that's the case, it belongs to you fine soldiers," the sergeant said pulling his droopy pants up from the sides using his gun belt.

"It looks like her personal belongings are lying on the grass near the front of the school," PFC Dinko pointed out.

The four walked over to the brown canvas bag lying on the grass. They could see most of its contents on the ground and the grass and dirt had noticeable scuff marks where it had been freshly disturbed.

"Go get the camera and tape measure. We got a crime scene here," PFC Dinko ordered Specialist Astle.

"Ok, that's all I needed to hear. We're out of here. Come on officer, these fine gentlemen have this under control. This case belongs to the United States Army. Have a nice evening guys," the cantankerous sergeant blurted over the blaring siren of the ambulance leaving the scene.

Dinko keyed up the shoulder microphone clipped to his fatigue uniform. "MP7 to Communications."

"Go ahead with your transmission," the dispatcher answered.

"Notify the on-call CID special agent to respond to the Anne Arundel General Hospital for an assault of a civilian at this location."

"Roger MP7."

Specialist Astle began photographing the bag and purse lying on the grass. They shined their flashlights across the school ground, attempting to determine exactly where the attack had occurred. Each took an assortment of measurements to pinpoint the location of the victim's belongings for the crime scene drawing.

"From the scuff marks in the grass it looks like they stop at the edge of the pavement," Astle indicated. Dinko pointed his flashlight in the direction where the grass was disturbed. "Astle,

I'm going to the jeep to get some evidence bags. Check behind the school."

Astle moved toward the rear of the school, slowly scanning ahead with his bright light. With each step he felt like he was entering a tunnel. It was total darkness. His flashlight revealed the faded marks on the basketball court asphalt. He shined his light to the corner of the building and noticed a black flat soled shoe. The surface near the shoe had been disturbed, evident by the way the pebbles and sand were brushed away. He knew this was the scene of the attack.

Dinko collected the items from the purse, bagging them separately, then made his way back to Astle. "See anything back here?"

"I got a small woman's shoe near the building, and you can see by the pavement that something happened in this general area. Let's get some pictures and measurements of that shoe. Hold your light on it for me," Astle said.

Astle took photos of the shoe and the markings on the ground, while Dinko measured the distance from the shoe to the rear corner of the school and the support pole attached to the rusty backboard. Dinko picked up the shoe to place it in an evidence bag, when something hidden by the shoe caught his eye.

"Holy shit. Check this out," Dinko shouted. "Well, fuck me running."

"What is it?" Astle asked.

"Keys," Dinko said, bewildered from his find.

"Ok. They probably belong to the lady they just carted off to the hospital," Astle said, dismissing the discovery.

"Umm, I don't think so. These are Army issued," Dinko said, dangling the ring of the specialty keys from his hand. "The CID agent is going to love this. I wonder who they belong to?"

Just as Army CID Special Agent Lenny Athas arrived at the Anne Arundel General Hospital, his cell phone rang. "Athas here."

"Agent Athas, this is PFC Dinko. I am at the scene where the lady was attacked sir."

"Thanks for the call PFC. What happened?"

"Well sir. We found something very interesting here you should know about."

"Go ahead. I'm listening."

"Sir, I found a set of keys with U.S. Army stamped on them. They belong to our stockade."

"What?" Athas raised his voice.

"That's correct. Unless these were already here, it looks like one of our own is involved in this one."

"Dinko, do you have the keys with you?"

"Yes sir."

"Look under where it says U.S. Army Fort Meade and tell me what number is stamped on each key."

Dinko opened the evidence bag. "The number 1095 is on each key sir."

"1095 you said?"

"Roger that sir."

"Thank you. What else do you have there?" Athas inquired.

"We had a small Asian lady taken to the hospital with a severely broken arm and some cuts to her face. It looks like whatever happened started in front of the old Van Bokkelen Elementary School and continued to the basketball court. The school doesn't have any lights, so it's much darker in the back."

"Besides the keys, was there anything else?"

"Just the victim's purse, a handbag and her shoe. Specialist Astle and I took photographs and measurements of everything sir."

"Good job PFC. Get those pictures developed and get them to me ASAP. Be sure to properly mark everything. The brass is going to want this one done right."

"You got it sir. I'll have the evidence submitted and the pictures on your desk tonight."

"Good job Dinko."

Special Agent Athas identified himself to the head triage nurse and told her he needed to speak with Suk Kim. Given the extent of the injury, she informed him that Mrs. Kim was awaiting surgery.

"They should be coming down any minute to get her, so make it quick," she instructed the agent.

Athas entered the small cubicle, divided by yellow sliding curtains. "Hello Mrs. Kim. I'm Special Agent Athas from the United States Army Criminal Investigation Division. We can talk more after you get discharged, but can you tell me what happened tonight?"

Suk gently pulled up on the sling supporting her arm and looked at Athas. "I was just walking home like I do every night." Tears fell from her eyes. She gasped for air.

Athas stood at the foot of her bed with his open notebook in one hand and pen in the other. "Take your time."

Suk dabbed her eyes with the sheet from her bed. "Out of nowhere, he grabbed me from behind. He, he pulled my hair....and....and...he put his hand over my mouth. I couldn't breathe." Suk covered her head with her bed sheet and sobbed. "I'm not sure if I passed out or not, but he pulled me behind the school. I couldn't yell or anything. He tried to rape me, but I didn't let him."

Athas wrote as fast as he could. "Have you ever seen this person before?"

"No. I've never seen him, but I'll never forget his face. I thought he was going to kill me. He had this strange look."

Anxious to get all the details, Athas delved furthered into the suspect's description. "Can you describe him?"

"Yes." Suk looked down at her arm and through her tears she spoke. "He was a white man. I say man, but he really wasn't a man. He looked to be about 28. I couldn't tell how tall he was because he was on top of me, but I definitely remember he was wearing a black jacket and had a thin moustache and glasses."

"Ok folks, I'm sorry to interrupt, but it's time to go," the nurse said tugging the curtain open. Athas moved to the side while the nurse took hold of the metal bed rails and lifted them up.

Athas closed his notebook. "Can you give me a call when she gets out of surgery?" handing the nurse his business card.

"If it's ok with Mrs. Kim."

"Yes," Suk said, tightening her face from the pain.

Athas followed behind Suk being wheeled away. "Just one more thing. Do you think you could identify him?"

"Can you stop for a moment?" Suk asked. The nurse sensed the insistence in her voice.

She turned her head slowly to face Athas. "Special Agent, I saw the devil tonight, of course I can."

Athas stood in the middle of the hallway as the nurse wheeled Suk through the operating room electronic doors.

Given the severity of the circumstances, Athas knew he had to notify his Army CID commander immediately. He pulled out his cell phone and scrolled until he found the number and placed the call. "Lieutenant Lindner, I'm sorry to bother you at home sir, but it's Athas."

"Hey Lenny, no problem. What can I do for you?"

"Sir, we have a situation. A real bad one."

"Lenny is this one of your jokes? If it is, you're going to pay for this one."

"I wish it was Lieutenant. We have an attempted rape sir and I think it was by one of our soldiers assigned to the stockade."

There was silence on the phone. The twenty-five-year seasoned lieutenant cleared his throat. "A soldier from the stockade? How can you be sure?"

"We found a set of keys belonging to the cell block at the scene sir."

"Son of a bitch," the lieutenant shouted. "God damn it. Let me get dressed. I'll meet you at the office."

Chapter 2

Only a week since the suicide of Captain Abrams, Michaels still had not mentioned a word to Katie about her phone number being found just feet away from his dead body. Thoughts about her conspiring with Abrams to have the real killer murdered baffled him, yet he had not mustered the nerve to mention it. He struggled to put the final pieces of the puzzle together. The same thoughts continued to race through his mind. *How did she know who the killer was? How did her an Abrams connect?*

"Honey, can we talk for a minute?" Katie asked.

Michaels stepped from the kitchen into the living room holding a glass of red wine. "Sure Babe. What's up?"

"You might want to sit down for this," she said with a serious look.

Michaels wasn't sure what he was about to hear, nor if he wanted to, so he took a seat next to her. The thought of her confessing to being part of a conspiracy to kill the man who killed her mother raced through his mind.

Katie took ahold of Michaels' hand. "I have something to confess," she said with determination. Her eyes welled up.

Michaels took a deep breath and let out a huge sigh. "Ok," he said.

"You know the last thing I ever want to do is push you away from me. I love you Ronnie Michaels more than I have ever loved anyone." Tears rolled down her cheeks. "How can I say this, my daughter really likes you too, if that makes any sense? And she really enjoys Nicole when she's around."

Michaels smiled and chuckled. "Well I….," Michaels began saying.

"Shhh….just wait. It's taken me long enough to get the nerve up to say this." Katie drew a big breath and exhaled. "I've wanted to tell you this for days, but I just couldn't bring myself to. I'm afraid of losing you."

"Katie, just tell me Hun." There was a long pause.

Katie looked deep into Michaels' eyes. "How about we move in together? There you go. There I said it." There was silence. "The floor is all yours."

Chapter 3

At the Army CID office, Special Agent Athas sat at his desk working on his report. Photos of the keys, purse and handbag laid strewn across his desk. Athas was a respected career military police soldier for 10 years. Prior to being promoted to special agent six months earlier, he served as a military policeman, earning a reputation as a tenacious, straight forward cop who would go to every extreme to clear a soldier of a wrongful accusation or put cuffs on him if necessary. Prior to his last orders, he served one tour in Afghanistan where he received a Bronze Star for a fire fight, when he and his partner were ambushed. Though Athas made it through the conflict uninjured, his fellow soldier suffered a paralyzing wound to his spine from an RPG fragment. Athas was able to kill and minimize the multiple targets while keeping his sidekick from further injury. He was a true hero, but never accepted himself as one. Just a humble soldier doing his duty he always said.

Not someone you would call a fashion plate, Athas dressed every day in a partially wrinkled shirt and pants. He never mastered the art of tying his neck ties long enough, but it was the best he could do to look the part of a special agent. Regardless of his title, Athas was Army through and through.

The door to his office flew open. It was Lieutenant Lindner. Athas stood and snapped a crisp salute. "Good evening sir."

"Ok Athas, let's see what you got. This better not be some God damn wild goose chase, or I'll have your ass."

"Well sir," Athas said clearing his throat. "Here are the pictures of the keys found at the scene," he said handing them to him.

Lindner flipped slowly through each photo. "I'll be dipped in shit and hung out to dry. Whoever was issued these sure has some explaining to do." The lieutenant placed the pictures back on Athas' desk. "This is going to have to go all the way to the top. Athas, you are to discuss this with no one. That's an order. Do you understand soldier?"

"Yes sir Lieutenant."

Lindner walked to his office, slammed his door and picked up his phone. After an hour and several phone calls, the Garrison's general and the respective colonel and captain who oversee the stockade were all informed. Captain Stanley Weinman who commanded the stockade was ordered to determine which of his military police soldiers was issued keys 1095.

Chapter 4

Michaels wasn't prepared for what Katie had to say and was both surprised and relieved it wasn't an admission to taking part in a homicide. He scooted closer on the couch and wrapped both arms around her. "I think that's a great idea Dr.," he said with a Cheshire grin on his face. He kissed her gently on the lips. "Where should we move to?"

Katie held tightly onto Michaels' hands. "I can't live in my house. I keep waiting to see my mother in the kitchen or standing in the garden. It's so depressing."

"Would you and your daughter like to move in here? There's plenty of room."

The tearful Katie squeezed his hand. "But this is your space Ronnie."

"Yeah…and it will be ours Katie. Our house."

Tears filled Katie's brown eyes. "Are you sure? Let me talk to Kathryn, but I'm pretty sure she feels the same way."

"Yes, I'm positive. It's so funny you asked me this," Michaels said smiling.

"Why's that?"

"Because I was thinking the same thing, but was afraid you'd say no."

The two laughed. "Well since I spend almost every waking hour with you, I figured why not? Plus, I think you're an incredible guy, who I have tons of respect for, and Kathryn absolutely adores you and Nicole."

"I love you Katie."

"I love you Ronnie." Their arms enfolded around one another and their lips locked together. They exchanged kisses passionately until Michaels abruptly stood and clapped his hands loudly. "That's it. It's time to celebrate. Let's go somewhere and get two huge steaks. How about it, Dr.?"

"Sounds like a plan Detective or should I say Shithead?" The two laughed. "And by the way, I've never asked why they call you that."

Michaels chuckled. "It really came out of nowhere. My first day in homicide Tommy yelled out *Young Shithead* when he first saw me walk into the unit dressed in a suit and tie. I guess because I was the youngest in the unit. Other than that, there was no rhyme or reason for it. He just belched it out when he laid eyes on me and then through time, he shortened it to *Shithead.* And that's it. Now you know."

Chapter 5

Lieutenant Lindner walked from his office and into the area where the Army CID special agent's desks were located. "Captain Weinman is on his way, so stay put."

"Special Agent Athas here," he said answering his cell phone.

"This is Nurse Doreen from the Arundel Medical Center. We spoke earlier."

"Yes ma'am."

"Mrs. Kim is in recovery now. She should be back to her room in an hour."

"Great. How'd she do?"

"I didn't tell you this, but put it this way, several pieces of medical hardware later, she'll be able to use her arm again after a lot of therapy."

The phone call ended and Athas shared his thoughts with his lieutenant. "I got a feeling this is going to be a real shit storm....sir."

"You've been to the stockade Athas, does anyone over there strike you as someone who would do something like this? I mean....well....this is really some bad shit."

"There's a couple of strange ones over there, but hell sir this is the Army, everyone's a little strange," he chuckled.

"Athas, make sure you do everything by the book on this one. I want every T crossed and every I dotted. Are we clear?"

"Roger that sir. Don't worry. It will be."

Athas continued writing his report for the next hour when Captain Weinman stormed in.

"Good evening sir," Athas said, standing again to salute a commanding officer.

"If that's what you call it," Weinman said with a tone of disgust. He brushed off Athas and barged into the lieutenant's office.

Lindner fired a half ass salute to his longtime friend. "Boy this sure is something, huh Stanley?"

"He removed the keys from his pocket because he was playing basketball," the captain blurted out.

Lindner paused, trying to process what he had just heard. He couldn't believe his ears. Angrily, Lindner jumped from his chair. "What? Stanley, don't tell me you talked to our suspect already?"

"Suspect? We don't know he's a suspect. For God's sake Don, it was just a set of keys.

Christ, it's not like it was a bloody knife or something."

Infuriated, Lindner slammed his fist on his desk. "Just a set of keys? Do you hear yourself? It was an attempted rape Stanley. Jesus Christ," he shouted.

"Careful with your tone Lieutenant, remember your addressing a commanding officer."

Lindner's head snapped back, stunned by his arrogant comment. His longtime friend was pulling rank on him. Repulsed from Weinman's actions, he sat down slowly in his chair and tilted it backwards. "Ok, so that's how we are going to do this? Aye, Aye Captain," he said sarcastically. "Then as the commander of the Army Criminal Investigation Division, I will need the full name, rank and living quarters address of the soldier issued key set #1095. And I'll need that in one hour."

"His name is Schumaker. I'll have to get the rest of his personals tomorrow." Weinman turned to open the door when Lindner stood quickly from his chair causing it to bang into the wall behind him.

"No, I don't think so Captain. That won't suffice," Lindner said pointedly.

Weinman turned to face him. "Excuse me Lieutenant?"

"You heard me correctly….Captain. I will not wait for the suspect's personals until tomorrow. I have direct orders from Colonel Boilin that I am to get them from you tonight. If you are refusing to do so, I'll need to know so I can inform my colonel." Lindner sat back in his chair and scooted close to his desk. "Your choice Captain."

Rightfully challenged by a lower ranking officer, the anger showed in Weinman's glowing red face. He turned his back to Lindner and hesitated before opening the office door. "I'll have it sent over," and he swiftly walked from the barracks.

Hearing the door slam, Lindner shouted. "Fucking asshole," pounding both hands on his desk.

Athas could tell their conversation was heated but was unable to overhear the contents. He opened Lindner's office door. "Sir, is everything ok?"

"Come in Lenny. Have a seat." Athas took a seat across from his desk.

"How many years have we known each other?"

"My God sir, you were my sergeant at Fort Bragg, straight out of basic. Umm, several years later I served under you as my first sergeant in Afghanistan and now here as my lieutenant. That's darn near 10 years sir."

"And during all those years have you ever heard me bitch about a member of the upper command staff?"

"Negative sir. Not once."

"Well I'm about to for the first time, so what I'm about to tell you stays here."

"Roger that. What's seen here, said here, stays here sir."

"The illustrious Captain Weinman has already talked to his MP assigned those keys." Athas' eyes opened wide. The lieutenant broke the silence. "I'm sorry Lenny, but what he did is damn near dereliction of duty."

"What's his name Lieutenant?"

"Schumaker, that's all I know now, but he said he would send the rest of his information over tonight after I threatened him. Bastard."

"Sir, there's something coming across your fax machine," Athas informed him.

Lieutenant Lindner walked outside his doorway and ripped the paper from the machine. He read the handwritten information and handed it to Athas. "Here, he's all yours."

Athas eagerly grabbed the paper. "Let's see who we have here. He's Sergeant Wesley Schumaker, 25 years old, been in the Army now for six years. He's been assigned to the jail for the past year since he got his stripes. Hell, his living quarters are right down the street in Barrack 43."

Athas pulled his photograph up on his desktop from the confidential Garrison database.

"There he is. Based on the description the victim gave me, he sure looks like our guy."

"Let me see this joker," Lindner said pulling the color picture from the printer. "Playing basketball my ass you son of a bitch. Lenny, find out if your victim is willing to view a physical line-up. I don't want to use photographs. I want him standing right in front of her. That's what the brass is going to want if we plan on getting a court martial conviction."

"You're killing me Lieutenant. Ok, let me get to the hospital. My victim is in recovery."

"Let me know what she says, and I'll get on the horn and make some calls."

Athas grabbed his notepad. "Sir, I'll call you as soon as I know."

Before long Athas found himself in the Emergency Room. He could see the Kim family gathered around Suk in her cubicle. "Hi folks. I'm Special Agent Leonard Athas with the United States Army. I'm handling this case. Suk, this must be your husband and children?"

Adjusting her sling, Suk sat up. "Yes, this is my husband, Min, my son Ye, and our daughter, Seo-Yun."

"It's nice to meet everyone." Each acknowledged Athas with a smile and a slight bow of their heads. "How ya feeling Suk?"

"Ok, I guess. I'm still woozy from the anesthesia, but at least my arm is numb."

"Good evening everyone, I'm Dr. Debbie DiMartina. I'll need everyone to step out for a few minutes so I can take a look at this brave woman."

The Kim family and Athas stood outside the small cubicle. "Agent, do you think you will find who did this?" Mr. Kim asked.

"That depends on your wife sir. When the doctor is finished, I need a few minutes with Suk and then we can talk more."

"Mrs. Kim, I'm the doctor who repaired your arm. How are you feeling?"

Suk pulled the bedsheets to her chest. "It's numb, but it still hurts a little and I'm still groggy."

"Your arm was severely fractured so it's going to take a while to heal, and you'll need physical therapy to get everything back to normal. Get a good night's rest at home and keep ibuprofen in you. I've prescribed pain pills which you're going to need for at least the first week, if not longer, but that's up to you. Once the anesthesia wears off, it's going to be very sore. You had an acute compound fracture along with some detached muscles in your forearm. I was able to join the bones together with two plates and I've reattached your muscles. The healing process for an injury such as this takes at least six months. I'll need to see you for a follow up visit next week at my office to see how things are coming along. Do you have any questions for me?"

"No. Thank you, doctor."

"Nurse Doreen will go over the care and cleaning instructions for your arm and explain the medicines to your husband because most likely you won't remember a thing we discussed by tomorrow." Suk forced a smile. "When she's done, you can go home." Dr. DiMartina placed her hand on Suk's knee. "Mrs. Kim, you were a very strong woman this evening. Take care of yourself and call me if you need anything."

Suk's eyes welled up. "Thanks."

Once the doctor left, Athas walked in and pulled the curtain closed. "Mrs. Kim, I know you want to get out of here, so I won't be long. I have good news. I have a suspect in your case already, but I'm going to need something from you."

"What's that?"

"In order to get a positive I.D. and charge him, I'm going to need you to pick him out in a physical line-up."

"Is he going to see me?" she asked sheepishly.

"No, no ma'am. We have a special room with a two-way mirror. He won't be able to see you."

"But if he gets arrested, won't he see me in court? And know where I live?"

Hearing the trepidation in her voice, Athas tried to emphasize the importance of her cooperation. "Suk, what this man did to you was horrible. What he planned on doing is unimaginable and who knows if you would have even lived to tell about it." The tears poured from her eyes. She covered her face with her free hand and cried.

"If he did this to you, I'm afraid he'd do it again and the next person might not be as tough as you….you know, with what you did to him. He must answer for this Suk. We can't let him get away with it."

She continued to cry, reliving the attack like a movie in her mind. "I don't know agent. I don't know. Can I be left alone please? I just need my family right now," she asked.

"Yes ma'am of course. Just think about what I said, and I'll be in touch tomorrow." Athas slid the curtain open for her family to rejoin her. Each of them had tissues being used to dry their eyes. "Mr. Kim, can I speak to you for a moment?"

"Yes sir."

Athas walked to the end of the nurse's station, out of ear shot from Suk. "Sir, I need your help."

"Anything. What can I do?" he said in broken English.

"I need you to convince your wife to pick out the bastard who did this to her so I can arrest him and put him away. I think I know who did it. She's scared. I get that, but he's got to answer for his actions. And if he doesn't, who knows what he will do to his next victim."

Mr. Kim listened intensely with a look of sadness across his face. "Was she raped?"

This was a strange question to ask, Athas thought, "No sir, she wasn't."

Mr. Kim's shoulders dropped in relief. "Thank God." He looked down at the floor. "She's a very strong woman, but she also keeps a lot of things to herself. Is she willing to help you?"

"That's the problem sir, she wouldn't commit, and I have a good suspect. You see, I need her to do this tomorrow or the next day at the latest. The more time passes the more likely she may forget his face. We have to put this sick son of a bitch behind bars Mr. Kim. Help me, please."

"I can't promise anything, but I'll talk to her tomorrow," Mr. Kim said.

Athas handed him a business card and wrote his cell number on the back. "Take this. Call me as soon as you know something please. I don't care what time it is."

"Yes sir."

"Thank you so much. Go take care of her."

"Agent Athas, if she doesn't, you know, pick him out, will he get away with this?"

Athas looked at Mr. Kim. "I'm afraid so. And I'll tell you this, he will strike again." Mr. Kim bowed his head out of respect and walked away.

Athas walked to the hospital parking lot and dialed up Lieutenant Lindner on his cell phone. "Lieutenant, it's Athas."

"What do you have?" Lindner asked, sounding impatient.

"Nothing right now boss. My victim is reluctant to participate in a physical line-up with our suspect."

"Damn it," Lindner yelled.

"Her husband is going to try and talk to her in the morning and then call me."

"I got Colonel Bolin all over my ass. He wants to put this to bed right away. He couldn't believe what Captain Weinman did. I've never heard the man scream so loud."

Athas smiled, picturing the balding, round faced colonel shouting on the phone. "Roger that sir. The only thing we can do now is wait."

"Yeah, I guess if Schumaker isn't arrested tonight, he'll think he got away with it."

"Most likely sir. I believe so."

"Ok Athas. I'll see you in the morning."

"Yes sir Lieutenant."

Chapter 6

Tommy was already sitting at his desk drinking coffee when Michaels strolled in. "Good morning Shithead," he said with a big smile.

Michaels plopped down in the leather chair across from Tommy's desk. "Good morning Sergeant. What's so funny?"

"Well, it's finally happened. We're in for it now. The Chief's Office will never be the same. Renowned Detective Mark Howes is getting promoted. He's going to be a sergeant, and get this, he's going to be the adjutant to the Chief of Police."

Michaels laughed. "Dear God, help us all. Good for him, the little poodle headed bastard. Christ Tommy, like his arrogance isn't overbearing enough, now the department is going to put stripes on him. And in the Chief's Office to boot. We're all screwed." They both laughed.

"So, we will be getting a new guy to replace Mark."

"We're replacing him that fast?"

"Yup. He should be here anytime now. We're getting Jim Rzepkowski from Eastern District. He's in the Tactical Patrol Unit."

"Yeah I know Jim. He helped me on a few drug cases when I was in the Narcotics Section. It's funny, but we first met years ago when he worked as a Loss Prevention Officer at the Glen Burnie Mall."

"I think he's got five years on. I'm being told a lot of good things about him by Captain Fitz," said Tommy.

"He always seemed like he had his shit together. Good sense of humor too," Michaels added.

"Well that's good to hear, because he's your new partner," Tommy said, taking a sip of his coffee, waiting for Ronnie's reaction.

"What? New partner? Why me?"

"Because I said so Shithead. Besides, you've really impressed me, and I think you're ready for this."

"Thanks Tommy, but what about Dredge?"

"I'm putting the old big dick and Donald together."

"Lord have mercy on the Dredge. If he thinks I'm bad…now he's got Donald. When's his last day?" Michaels asked.

Tommy chuckled. "He's at the Chief's Office now. He's coming by later to pack up his shit. The Chief needed him right away. Apparently, there's a lot of transfers coming down."

Michaels lit up a cigarette. "Wow, this is going to be weird having a new person around here."

Lieutenant Tank filled Tommy's doorway with Rzepkowski standing close behind. "I found this guy wandering around the building," Tank said jokingly.

"Hey Jim, come on in," Tommy said, standing up to greet his newest detective.

Michaels eyed up his partner wearing a new suit and freshly starched shirt. "Damn Jim, a new suit and everything. I'm impressed."

"Well you know, going from JV to varsity, I figured I had to at least look the part."

"Good morning sir, I'm Officer Jim Rzepkowski," the new-be said shaking Tommy's hand. "Thanks for the opportunity sir."

"My pleasure. You need to relax son. And you're no longer Officer Rzepkowski. It's Detective," Tommy asserted.

"Come with me. I'll show you where your desk is," Michaels said.

Michaels and Rzepkowski went to the squad room where the desks for the homicide detectives were. Michaels pulled an empty notebook from his top drawer. "Do you have one of these?"

Rzepkowski reached into his top shirt pocket and pulled out a dollar store size notepad. "This is what I always use."

Michaels laughed. "You're in the big leagues now Jim. Here, you can have this one, but you'll need to get yourself some. You'll go through a lot of these. In this line of work your notes can make or break you."

Jim graciously took the notebook and advice. "I'll be sure to grab some tonight. Thanks."

Chapter 7

At 7:00 a.m. the next morning, Athas arrived at the CID Barracks expecting to be alone to work on his report. To his surprise, Lieutenant Lindner's government car was already parked in his reserved spot. "Good morning sir," Athas said to his boss pouring a cup of coffee from the freshly brewed pot.

"Are you ready to get this case wrapped up today?"

"I sure hope so sir. Now that it's light, I'm going to the scene and have a look around."

"I'd go with you but I'm waiting for Colonel Boilin to call. He wants an update."

Athas filled his tall stainless-steel cup full of coffee and chatted briefly with Lieutenant Lindner until Colonel Boilin called. As the lieutenant took the call, Athas threw on his jacket and climbed into his army issued Chevrolet Malibu. Only two miles from the CID, he pulled onto the vacant school lot. With light now casting on the grounds, Athas inspected the obviously disturbed grass in front of the school. He walked to the rear where the basketball court was located and the attack occurred. On the asphalt approximately ten feet from the basketball backboard post, he could see where the dirt, sand and pebbles had been brushed away. He scanned the paved area then walked to the opposite corner, looking carefully on the ground for any items left behind by the assailant. He hoped if his suspect was stalking his victim, he was smoking to calm his nerves and perhaps left a cigarette butt behind, but there was nothing.

Walking back through the attack location, Athas heard two crows squawking on the roof of the school. Casually, he glanced at the birds and back down in the direction he was walking. He quickly looked back up and stopped abruptly in his tracks. From his second look he made an alarming discovery. There was no rim on the rusty backboard. It was gone. *Schumaker couldn't have taken his keys from his pants to play basketball. You cannot shoot hoops without a rim, you dumb ass,* he thought to himself.

Using his phone, Athas took several pictures of the basketball backboard and the court. The sky was bright blue and the sun had eased up, shining brightly on the school's rooftop where the crows still sat sounding their calls.

With his business done at the school, he hurried back to the barracks where Colonel Boilin sat talking with Lieutenant Lindner. "Get in here Athas," Lindner shouted.

Colonel Boilin was dressed in his Class A uniform. The brass on his blouse was freshly polished, each in its proper place, according to army rules and regulations. Having served numerous tours in the middle east and a brief stent with the CIA, the left side of his uniform was stacked neatly with a plethora of medals, including the distinguished gold and bronze stars.

The spry agent moved quickly to the lieutenant's office doorway and snapped a salute to both commanding officers. They both returned the salute and Lindner instructed him to join them.

"Good morning Colonel."

"Good morning."

"Colonel. This is my ace, Special Agent Lenny Athas. He's assigned this case. He served with me at Fort Bragg and Afghanistan. He's got his shit together sir."

"That's good to hear. What's the status on the physical line-up?" the colonel asked.

"Her husband hasn't contacted me yet, but I did find something very interesting."

"What's that Athas?" Lindner questioned.

"Well you see sir, this morning I went over to the school and walked around. Just when I was about to leave, I saw something. Something that shot a big hole in our suspect's story."

"C'mon Athas spit it out," Lindner said impatiently.

"Remember the excuse Schumaker gave Captain Weinman about his keys?"

"Yeah…he said he had been playing basketball."

"Sir. You can't play basketball without a rim."

Lindner jumped from his chair. "What?" he yelled. "You're fucking kidding me?"

Athas grinned from ear to ear. "That's correct sir. The old rusty board is without a rim. It's highly unlikely he was bouncing a basketball off a backboard don't ya think boss?"

"God damn son. Great find. Outstanding work." The colonel stood from his chair and shook hands with Athas. "You're right Don. This soldier is an ace."

"Listen Athas, in no later than eight hours if you don't hear from your victim, I need you at her residence. We need to get her in here to identify Schumaker. Got it?" Lindner said firmly.

"Roger that sir. I'm on it. May I be excused sir?"

"Yes. But keep me informed as soon as you hear something," the colonel directed.

"Yes sir Colonel."

Athas sat at his desk and documented his observations in his notebook. He flipped back a few pages and found Mr. Kim's cell phone number. It was 8:30 a.m. He pulled up the number on his phone.

"Hello," Mr. Kim answered.

"Hello. This is Special Agent Athas. We spoke last night at the hospital."

"Ah yes Special Agent. I spent all morning talking to my wife. She's hesitant to come in. She's very scared…you understand?"

"Yes sir I do. But if he gets away with this, who knows what he will do next and to who? The next victim could be a small child Mr. Kim."

"I know this. I'll talk to her again and call you back."

"Ok. If you think it would be best for me to come over and talk with her, I can."

"No, that's not necessary. I'll call you back."

Discouraged and disappointed, Athas sat at his desk staring at his notebook opened in front of him.

Lieutenant Lindner noticed the scow on Athas' face. "Boy, who shit in your cereal?"

"It's my victim. She's not too eager to come in and do this physical line-up sir. Her husband is trying to convince her, and he's supposed to call back. Athas' cell phone sounded. He lifted his phone and squinted at the screen to see who was calling. "It's him. Special Agent Athas here."

"This is Mr. Kim. She's upstairs crying but she said she will do it."

"That's great Mr. Kim." Athas extended a thumbs up gesture to Lindner hovering over his desk.

"Where should I bring her? And what time?"

"Let's say 1:00 p.m. here at my office. Our address is 100 Officer's Lane. We're only 10 minutes from your house sir."

"Ok, we'll be there. He won't be able to see or talk to her, will he?"

"No sir, absolutely not. He'll be on the other side of a two-way mirror."

"Thank you. I'll tell her. Goodbye."

"Goodbye sir," Athas said hanging up the phone wearing a big smile.

"She's in boss," Athas announced.

"That's great. You notify the JAG Office and I'll get the order prepared to have Schumaker here," Lindner instructed.

Athas got up from his desk and walked toward the bookshelf full of three-ringed binders. "I'll search through the Garrison photo album and find seven more soldiers that have similar features to Schumaker and get them in here. Hell, that will be the easiest $50 they'll ever make in an hour."

Athas called the Judge Advocate General's Office, JAG for short, located within the compound of the Fort George G. Meade Army Base.

Comprised of 25 military attorneys, the JAG Office handles a wide assortment of duties to include discharge matters, traffic violations, Article 32 hearings and court martials. Like cases heard in state courts, members of the military charged with criminal violations have the option of having their case heard by a judge or a jury, both comprised of military personnel.

Lindner retreated to his office to notify Colonel Boilin of the latest development. Boilin would handle the official orders and notify Captain Weinman. It would be Weinman's responsibility to ensure Schumaker was at the CID barracks dressed in his fatigues.

At 12:30 p.m. JAG attorney, Major Dawn Sarro, arrived at the CID to receive her case briefing from Athas. As a prosecutor with over 20 years in the Army, Sarro would serve as counsel for the government representing the victim. At 5'8" tall, the slender, in shape counselor carried herself with a strong sense of command presence. Her curly red hair, with a hint of freckles, fit her feisty, confident personality. Among her peers she was a well respected litigator who knew the law and her way around the court room.

The line-up was scheduled for 1:00 p.m. Sarro sat at an empty desk across from Athas and diligently read the reports written by the responding Military Police Officers and the victim's statement documented in Athas' report. Flipping through the pages, she shook her head and made noises of disgust under her breath. From this point forward she would oversee every portion of the case, beginning with the first critical step, identifying the suspect.

"This poor lady. This is horrible," Major Sarro uttered.

"Ma'am, wait until you see how small she is. Unless Schumaker had stalked her for several days, he may have thought she was a child. Hell, she can't be any more than five foot tall, if that," Athas added.

Sarro read on, jotting notes on a legal pad in her near perfect cursive handwriting. "Agent Athas, can you tell me why Captain Weinman felt the need to speak to our suspect about this incident before you?"

Athas chuckled under his breath and looked around the room before he spoke. "With all due respect Major, in my opinion, I think he was out of line. Can I speak freely ma'am?"

"Absolutely you can agent. What's on your mind?" Sarro asked, lying her pen down.

Athas' face tightened. Sarro could tell he was pissed. "I think what Weinman did…I'm sorry, what Captain Weinman did, was criminal. He interfered with an official investigation. That's just my opinion ma'am."

"You're God damn right he did. I'm sitting here reading this wondering if I'm going to bring him up on charges. This is bullshit. He tipped him off. He allowed him to get his story and his alibi together." Sarro turned her attention back to the report and read on.

"I just hope she picks him out. It was awfully dark where this occurred," Athas said.

Surprised, Sarro lifted her head quickly. "What the hell. No rim? How can you play basketball with no rim?" she said with a perplexed look. "I love it. I want to see how he's going to explain that…pervert."

"I knew you'd get a kick out of that Major."

"Does Weinman know this?"

"Oh no ma'am. Just Colonel Boilin, Lieutenant Lindner and now you."

"Good. How are you coming along with finding soldiers to participate in this line-up?" she asked.

"All done ma'am. A soldier will do just about anything for $50 cash. I made about a dozen phone calls and was able to secure seven soldiers. They should be arriving by 12:45 p.m."

"Great. When they get here, put them in the conference room so I can look them over and give them instructions. We need to make sure they're all dressed the same and look similar to Schumaker, but not identical. You'll need to get some electrical tape to cover up the names embroidered on their uniforms."

Athas grinned and pulled open his desk drawer. "I still have this from the last line-up," he said holding up a black roll of tape.

"I see you have a photo of Schumaker in your file. What time is he supposed to be here?"

"12:45 also ma'am."

"Has he retained counsel?"

"I've not been told ma'am."

For the next several minutes, the soldiers Athas had recruited sporadically entered the CID building. Some wore a look of hesitation while others were happy to receive their money. Athas corralled the men into the conference room, while Sarro positioned herself at the doorway eyeing them over to ensure their uniforms and physical features were similar. The last thing she wanted was the line-up to be thrown out of court because of a minor discrepancy. Once seated, Sarro addressed the group in her firm tone. She provided specific direction regarding their conduct and what to expect during the exercise. While she talked with the soldiers and answered their questions, Athas placed electrical tape over the names on their shirts.

Noticeably a few minutes late, Captain Weinman walked into the CID with Sergeant Wesley Schumaker trailing close behind. Both appeared to be sporting bad attitudes on their faces.

"Have a seat and don't talk to anyone," Weinman ordered Schumaker, acting as if he was his defense counsel.

"Good morning Captain," Athas said, saluting Weinman from across the room.

Weinman shot Athas a cocky glance and walked uninvited into the lieutenant's office, interrupting a private conversation between Lindner and Sarro.

"Schumaker's here," he uttered in an arrogant tone.

With her back to the door, Sarro turned to face Weinman. "Excuse me Captain, but we're in a private meeting. Do you mind?"

Unprepared to see a ranking officer, Weinman was caught off guard. "Umm, umm, sorry, I'm sorry Major. I didn't realize," he stuttered, saluting her.

"Yeah...close the door and wait in the lobby. Make sure your soldier goes nowhere. Understood?" she ordered. Lieutenant Lindner smiled from ear to ear.

Freshly bitch slapped, Weinman gently closed Lindner's office door and took a seat in the small waiting area. By now the two agents working the evening shift had arrived and were seated at their desks, just in time to witness the fireworks.

"What's happening sir?" Schumaker awkwardly asked his captain.

"Shut the fuck up Wes. Ok? I don't want you to say a God damn word. Not to me. Not to nobody. Are we clear?"

Schumaker lowered his head. "Yes Captain," he mumbled.

Sitting at his desk, Lindner was incapable of holding back his shit eating grin. "With all due respect Major, that was outstanding. He needed that. He walks around this base like his shit doesn't stink, expecting everyone to kiss his ring."

Stoned face, she responded. "I see he still hasn't gotten over the fact he was skipped for promotion to major. No wonder. Lieutenant, go tell Weinman he and Schumaker need to wait in the interview room down the hall so our victim doesn't see him."

"Yes ma'am. Done," Lindner said scurrying from his office to pass the message on to the disgruntled men.

By 1:00 p.m. the line-up volunteers were waiting to be called into the staging area. Athas sat at his desk anxiously waiting for Suk to arrive. With each minute that passed, he worried more. It was now 1:15 p.m. when Weinman walked from the interview room and knocked on Lieutenant Lindner's door. Lindner waved him in.

"My soldier was ordered to be here by 1:00 p.m. for a physical line-up and it's now 1:15 p.m. How much longer does he need to stay?" Weinman asked.

Sarro dropped her pad on the edge of Lindner's desk and squared off to the captain. "You have some nerve. Listen Weinman, I don't give a fuck if your soldier is scheduled to get married, is going to have surgery, has diarrhea or is about to cure cancer. The order stands. He is not leaving these barracks. I suggest you march back into that room, hold his hand, wipe his eyes and tell him to hold onto his ass. Now I don't want to hear from you again. Shut the door on your way out," she said, swiveling in the chair, turning her back to him.

Again, Weinman closed the door and with his face beet red, he walked shamelessly back to the room where Schumaker awaited.

Athas called Mr. Kim's cell phone repeatedly. There was no answer. To make matters worse, by 1:30 p.m., some soldiers let it be known they had to leave by 1:45 p.m. because they were scheduled for the late shift. Lindner called for Athas to join them in his office.

"Any luck?" Sarro asked.

"No ma'am. I've tried calling her husband's phone several times and there is no answer."

"If she doesn't show, he's going to get away with this. We'd never convict him with just a set of keys and no rim. Never," Lindner stated.

Sarro took a seat at the table across from the lieutenant's desk. "I'm sure she's petrified after what he did to her. I'd hate to see him walk."

Athas looked over as he saw another member of the CID, Special Agent Ed Horn, walking toward Lindner's office. "Lenny, Lenny," Horn called out.

Athas walked out to see what was so important when he noticed Suk standing in the waiting area crying on her husband's chest. Lindner and Sarro were pleasantly surprised.

"We're back in business," Sarro whispered to Lindner.

Athas joined them. "Hi Suk. Thank you so much for coming. How ya feeling?"

Suk lifted her head. Tears poured down her face, ridden with fear. Her eyes were puffy from crying and lack of sleep. Her lower lip was purple and swollen, as was the entire left side of her face. Her arm was stabilized in a cast, supported by a light blue colored sling.

"Is he here? Is he going to see me?" she asked while sobbing.

Athas' heart ached for her. "He's not going to see you, Suk. I promise. Not today."

"Agent Athas, how about you bring these nice folks into the lieutenant's office so we can talk in private," Sarro suggested.

"Yes ma'am Major. Follow me Mr. and Mrs. Kim. We can talk in my boss' office."

Suk and her husband sat at the round table in Lindner's office. Sarro sat next to Suk and handed her a wad of tissues. "Suk, I'm Major Dawn Sarro. I'm the attorney prosecuting this case. I'm on your side," she assured her. Suk sat in the chair holding her husband's hand. Tears steadily trickled down her face. Sarro scooted her chair close to Suk. "I must say as a woman, I appreciate you having the courage to come today. I read what happened and what was done to you was outrageous, and what you did was so brave. The animal that did this must be held accountable and without you we can't do that. So, I need you to stay strong." Dawn squeezed her hand. "In a few minutes, you, Special Agent Athas and I will go into a room, and I'm going to ask you to look at eight men. Remember, they cannot see you. I want you to take your time and tell me if you see the person who attacked you last evening. Can you do that for me?" Suk raised her head slowly and nodded affirmatively.

"Each man will be holding a card with a number. The only thing you need to do is look at each person and if you see the man from last night, tell me which number he is holding. Once that is done, your husband can take you home."

Lindner stood from behind his desk. His swift movement caught Sarro's attention. "Now what does he want?" Lindner said, starting toward the door.

"I'll take care of this Lieutenant," Sarro said firmly.

Major Sarro stormed from the lieutenant's office and confronted the captain outside the door. "Captain Weinman I hope you have an emergency to bring to my attention, otherwise I must say you are really pushing things."

"Major, this is getting ridiculous. Do you have any idea how much longer we will be? I have things to do," Weinman said in a curt tone.

"Let me make this real clear Captain. You are now on very thin ice. Unless you want me to charge you with interfering with an official government investigation, I suggest, no correct that, I'm ordering you to take your ass back to the interview room and babysit your soldier until I say so. Don't try me again."

With everyone gathered back in the lieutenant's office, Lindner was keen to get things rolling. "If we're ready, you all can take Suk into the observation room and Athas can put Schumaker with the others."

"Sounds good Lieutenant. Mr. Kim, you can have a seat in the waiting room and Suk can come with me," Sarro said.

"Excuse me Major, what should I tell the Captain?" Athas inquired.

Sarro smiled. "Tell him I said to leave the building."

"Roger that ma'am." Athas walked to the interview room where Weinman and Schumaker were seated. When he opened the door, Weinman was leaning unusually close to Schumaker, whispering in his ear when he was startled by Athas. The look on Weinman's face was odd, Athas thought, given his rank, like he had been caught doing something inappropriate. Athas paused for a moment, "Sergeant Schumaker, you need to follow me."

Captain Weinman stood abruptly. "I'll be going with him."

"Negative sir. Major Sarro said for you to leave the building now…sir."

Weinman's forehead clenched together. He shot a nasty look at Athas. "Schumaker, I want you in my office as soon as you are done."

"Yes Captain," Schumaker uttered.

Weinman stormed from the room, brushing forcefully into Athas standing in the doorway.

Athas escorted Schumaker to the conference room where the volunteers awaited. He handed each a square piece of cardboard with a black colored 10-inch high number on the front and had them line-up in sequence. Schumaker held #3 in his hand.

"When I open the door, I'll need you all to walk in. When number eight gets to the end of the platform, you are all to turn to your right and hold your card chest high. If there are no questions, follow me."

Sarro and Suk took a seat at the small table in the observation room. Sarro held Suk's trembling hand. "It's ok Suk. You can do this."

The door to the line-up room opened and the men slumbered in. Sarro watched Suk's eyes dart back and forth examining each of their profiles. In unison, they turned and faced her. Suk's eyes locked on Schumaker. Her body quivered like she was freezing cold. Schumaker looked at the floor in his lame attempt to hide his face. Suk burst into tears.

Sarro placed her hand on top of Suk's tightly sweating grip. "Suk, do you see the man who attacked you last night?" she said softly. She sobbed uncontrollably while she nodded her head up and down. "Which number is he holding?" she continued in her soft voice.

"That's him. Number three." She turned in her seat, putting her back to the glass. Schumaker's face sent chills through her body. Now with her blood pressure rising, her arm throbbed in pain.

Sarro pressed the speaker button on the wall. "Thank you gentlemen, that will be all. You are free to leave. Number three, remain in the room, Special Agent Athas will need to speak with you." Sarro stood and placed her arm around Suk's shoulders. "That was a big step Suk. Good job. I'll walk you out to your husband." Sarro glanced back at Athas. "Don't start with him yet. I want to talk to you first."

Athas watched Schumaker pace back and forth, looking toward the one-sided glass. Athas studied him closely, wondering what evil thoughts were going through his mind.

Sarro returned to the room smiling. "How's our boy doing?" she said barely able to contain her happiness.

"He's pacing so fast he's about to wear a hole in the rug. He reminds me of a caged tiger in a zoo," Athas said.

"I'm going to my office and start the paperwork to have him charged. We need a witness to his statement with you. Do you have someone who can sit in your interview with him?"

"Yeah, Special Agent Horn's here. He can sit in with me."

Chapter 8

Tommy walked from his office holding a piece of paper. "Well, that honeymoon didn't last long." Michaels looked up from the report he was writing. "We got a double boys. You fellas start over to Glen Burnie Guns and Ammo. Michaels this one is yours. Jim, you go with him." Excited, Jim stood from his desk and grabbed his jacket.

"Jesus Christ Jim, we're not going to a fire." Michaels laughed.

"Teach him something Shithead. I'll see you guys over there."

"Yes sir. Come on Jim, let's go lock someone up," Michaels said to the eagerly awaiting detective.

"You know where it is, don't you Shithead?" Tommy hollered from his office.

"Yeah, it's on B & A Boulevard in Glen Burnie. I've been in there several times buying ammo."

"I've already called the Evidence Collection Unit. Jeff and your dad will meet you there," Tommy added.

Michaels put on his suitcoat. "What about the on-call medical examiner?"

"I'll call Doc Jones now," Tommy said.

"Thanks. Come on partner lets go see some dead bodies," Michaels said without a hint of emotion.

Chapter 9

Athas was still watching Schumaker from the other side of the two-way glass, when Special Agent Horn notified him that Lindner wanted to see him in his office. "Ok. Ed, it's probably best if you read my report before we start our interview. It's on my desk in the folder marked Kim."

"Will do. I'll take care of that right now," Horn said walking with Athas back to their office.

"Get in here Lenny," Lindner said, waving Athas into his office. "Here you go." Lindner handed Athas an official U.S. Army envelope with the name *Sergeant Wesley Schumaker* and CONFIDENTIAL stamped on the front. "These are orders forbidding Schumaker to leave the base without permission from Captain Weinman."

Athas took the envelope. "That's a shame his commanding officer is Weinman. Respectfully sir, that's a big frigging joke."

Understanding his frustration Lindner chimed in. "I know Lenny, but that was the best I could do from the colonel, who by the way said, *good job*."

"Thank you sir, but first I need to see if I can get him to confess, or at least put himself further under the bus."

"You and Horn get in there and see what you can do. If Major Sarro gets the charging documents here in the meantime, I will let you know. Is Horn with him now in the interview room?"

"Negative sir. He's reading my report first. Shit. I left him in the line-up room." Athas jumped from his chair and raced down the hallway.

Sitting at his desk, Horn noticed the commotion. "What's going on?"

"I left Schumaker in the room," he yelled, running toward the steps. Horn shot from his chair and ran behind him. When they got to the line-up room the door was open. Schumaker was gone.

"Fuck," Athas shouted. Horn opened the emergency exit door and Athas followed behind. Both ran outside searching for their suspect. Cars were traveling on the road adjacent to the CID barracks. People, some in uniform, were walking casually on the sidewalk. Schumaker was nowhere in sight.

Chapter 10

The two new partners set out for Jim's first case. "Hop in partner. I'll drive," Michaels said.

"Sounds good."

"Now look, you need to start writing everything down in your notebook. The time you got notified, the weather, what time we arrive, everything. Note everything inside the scene as if no cameras exist. Remember you'll be writing your report from your notes and then you'll be testifying a year or more later, depending on appeals. So, your notes have to be dead on," Michaels laughed. "Dead on. Get it?" The two laughed.

When they pulled up, there were marked patrol cars and two Evidence Collection vans parked out front. Uniformed cops were milling around on the sidewalk, waiting for their arrival. The sporting goods store was an old, eggshell colored cement building with one inch welded steel bars covering the windows and door. The extra security was in place to keep criminals from entering after hours, not during the middle of the day. One thing Michaels had learned since being in the unit, was that death followed no clock, nor did it care who or how old the next victim was. The business had been a staple in the community for years. Store inventory included a wide assortment of revolvers, semi-automatic handguns, shotguns, rifles and a stockpile of ammunition.

"Good afternoon gentlemen," Michaels said to the uniformed sergeant and police officer standing near the business entrance.

"Oh my God, look who it is," the sergeant said, smiling at Detective Rzepkowski.

Focusing on his notes, Rzepkowski raised his head. "Hey Sarge," he said to the tall, lanky, balding old-timer.

"You're one of the golden boys now huh?"

Rzepkowski grinned while he shook his hand. "I don't know about golden, but I'm here sir."

"Hell son, I remember when your little pimpled faced rookie ass came to my shift straight out of the academy. You didn't know shit back then and now look at ya. I'm proud of ya boy."

"Thanks, Sarge."

"I got Officer Carini waiting at Northern District for you guys," the sergeant said. "I didn't want him around here, especially if the press shows up."

Confused, Michaels spoke up. "What do you mean sir? What's Carini got to do with this?"

"Carini's Dad owns this place. Today some asshole came in, probably all whacked out, and shot his father. Thank God Carini killed him," the sergeant said bluntly.

"Sergeant Suit didn't tell us that. Speak of the devil, here he is now," Michaels said, noticing

Tommy's unmarked black Crown Victoria pulling up with cigarette smoke pouring from his window.

"The illustrious Sergeant Tom Suit. What a character," the patrol sergeant said. "The evidence techs are already inside, and my officer here will sign you in when you're ready."

"Thank you sir," Michaels said, turning toward Tommy's car.

Tommy rolled down the window of his cruiser with his phone to his ear. Michaels and Rzepkowski waited while he spoke to the on-duty patrol lieutenant at the Northern District Station.

Tommy waived his men over. "I guess you know by now this is a police shooting."

"Yeah, the sergeant just said Officer Carini is at the station. Apparently, Carini's father owns the store, and someone killed him, and Carini killed the suspect. That's all I know so far. Who's going to interview him?"

"You are Ronnie." Tommy got out of his car, flicked his burnt cigarette to the ground and lit up a fresh one. "Jim can stay here with the evidence guys. I want you to talk to Carini."

"You got it man. Tommy, just so you know, I'm not reading him his rights. No way. The man just lost his Dad. I'm not going to make him feel like a criminal," Michaels said adamantly.

"I'm good with that. You two go inside. I got some phone calls to make. Once you get a look at the scene, then get to Northern and talk to him. I don't want him waiting any longer than he has to."

"I'm on it. C'mon let's go in Jim." Michaels and Rzepkowski walked inside slowly like they were entering a haunted house. They didn't know what to expect. The business consisted of two rooms. The front was rectangularly shaped, with a long L shaped glass display case which began by the entrance and extended toward the back of the showroom. At the end of the case was a small opening designated for employees to enter, giving them access to the weapons from behind the lengthy counter.

"Shithead," Jeff Cover belted out.

"Jeff Cover, Jeff Cover, Jeff Cover. Long time no see brother," Michaels answered the seasoned evidence technician.

Jeff lowered the camera from his face. "I know…we've had a nice dry spell for a while."

"Hi Ron," Ray said, stopping briefly from taking measurements of the room.

"Hi Dad. Guys, let me introduce you to my new partner, Jim Rzepkowski."

"Yeah we know Jim. You're from the Eastern District, right?" Ray asked.

"Yes sir. You helped me on that B & E ring I worked last summer. Remember Ray, you lifted the fingerprints from the window my suspect used to get into a house in Green Haven. He got five years because of that print. I'll never forget that."

"Welcome to homicide Jim," Ray said.

"Oh no, don't tell me Shithead's your partner?" Jeff asked.

Jim glanced over at Michaels. "Uh yeah, is there something I should know?"

Jeff and Ray both laughed as they returned back to what they were doing. Jeff spoke while he steadied the camera in front of his face. "You'll see Jim. That's all I can say. You'll see." With a confused look, Jim focused his attention on his notebook.

Barely inside the front door, broken glass from the display case lie on the floor and inside on several pistols. Michaels peered behind the shattered counter. Lying on his side, with his head submerged inside the display case was a deceased white male in his thirties, wearing a black tee shirt, dirty faded blue jeans and untied work boots. A trail of blood drained from a wound near his left eye socket and onto a tag tied to a nickel-plated pistol next to his head. A rusty double barreled sawed off 12-gauge shotgun laid on the floor next to the dead man's right hand. Two spent shotgun shell casings were visible nearby on the tile.

It was obvious the piece of shit had fired at least two rounds before he fell victim to an unforgiving piece of lead. "Let me guess, the gun enthusiast over here taking a dirt nap must be our suspect," Michaels asked sarcastically.

"Yup that would be him," Jeff answered. "If you look close enough, you'll see it was a ricochet that killed him. The projectile actually went into his skull backwards."

"I'll have to walk around the counter to get a better look," Michaels said looking over at Jim. "You ok partner? You ain't gonna blow chunks on your first scene are ya? Because this ain't shit."

"No, no I'm good. This is fascinating," Jim added writing busily in his notebook.

"Great, come with me so we can get around to the other side of this display case and see what Jeff's talking about." Michaels stopped and turned to Jim. "Whatever you do, listen to what Jeff says. He's a fountain of knowledge. Trust me. The dude is good, and I mean really good."

Rzepkowski nodded and looked in Jeff's direction. "Will do."

The two detectives walked toward the cash register near the employee access. Only employees were allowed through the small entrance way, which led to the armory room where guns were repaired and excess ammo and gun inventory was stored.

"Watch your step over there," Ray said to his son and Jim.

Passing through the isle closest to the register, both detectives looked down on the tan tile floor. A large puddle of clear fluid, mixed with dull red blood, hair and bright red brain matter led the way to the next corpse, draining from a gaping hole out of the sixty something year old man's forehead. The massive projectile entered the upper portion of the victim's forehead near his hairline ripping open an oblong hole the size of an egg. Portions of his brain and skull fragments filled the wound.

"Jesus fucking Christ. He was shot with a shotgun slug...never had a chance," Michaels said, repulsed over the senseless death. Michaels and Jim stood next to the pooling skull juices. The man was lying on his stomach with his left eye open. Both detectives filled page after page with notes and their own crude crime scene drawings.

Pissed off, Michaels let out a big sigh. "Who would ever think something as small as a head could hold so much fluid, so much blood? I mean really," he said so matter-of-factly. "This is so sad. Fucking piece of shit. This is the kind of shit that fucking lights me on fire. There is no reason for this," he said raising his voice. "None. Here, this poor guy, probably invested his entire life's savings to run this business, and it all comes to an end in seconds when some asshole, most likely stoned out of his fucking mind, decides to come in and start shooting. And to think his own son had to see his father like this." His voice lowered. "The only good thing is Carini got to end his life. Thank fucking God. Trash like this shouldn't walk this earth."

Jim stood in awe looking at Mr. Carini's glazed over eye. "At least our suspect got an early death sentence," Jim said shaking his head.

They carefully held onto the countertop, while they stepped over the body and into the back room where Carini and his father had been working on guns before all hell broke loose. In the middle of the room was a large high-top table with four chairs, one of which was laying on the ground. On top of the table were two disassembled revolvers, a can of gun lube, some tools and two rags. Michaels and Jim scratched out more notes, then proceeded back to the front to inspect the killer's body.

Walking through the broken glass surrounding the body, Michaels and Jim squatted to get a closer look of the deadening wound. "Damn Jeff, I see what you mean. The bullet mushroomed, then planted itself nicely into his temple backwards. You mean to tell me this is what killed him?" the surprised Michaels asked.

"That's all I could see," Jeff answered, now taking photographs of Mr. Carini.

Jim leaned closer, "Shit, it's barely in his head."

"Yeah, but it did its job. His existence has ended. I hope he burns in hell," Michaels uttered. "Alright, I've seen enough. I'm going up to Northern District and talk to Carini. You stay here, ask questions and assist Jeff and my dad with whatever they need."

"Ok. Did you need me to sit in on the interview with you?" Jim asked.

"No, you heard Tommy, he wants you here. Plus, I don't want Officer Carini to feel like he's being interrogated or tagged teamed. He's been through enough. The way I see it, this is just a glorified witness statement and whoever doesn't like it can go fuck themselves."

Shocked by the behavior of his cold and callused partner, Jim followed him from behind the counter. "I'll be back," Michaels shoved his hand against the front door to open it and walked into the bright sun.

"Shithead," Tommy said leaning against his car talking with Captain Donoho.

"Captain, Sergeant," Michaels said formally.

"You headed to the station?" Tommy asked.

"Yeah. It's just fucking uncalled for. That's all I got to say."

"Ok son, hurry back," Tommy said.

Chapter 11

Athas yelled to Lindner sitting at his desk. "Lieutenant, lieutenant he's gone. Schumaker's gone."

"God damn it. What do you mean he's gone Lenny? Colonel Boilin is going to be on fire," he yelled. "You better get on the phone and notify Major Sarro. She's not going to be happy with this either."

Athas bowed his head in embarrassment. "I know. Sorry sir."

"What are you standing there for? Just find his ass…go, go."

"I'll notify the dispatcher to alert the MP's," Horn said.

"Hold off on that. Let me talk with Major Sarro first and see if we have any charges on him yet, otherwise he's only failing to obey a direct order at this point," Athas said. He took a seat at his desk and snatched the phone from the cradle. On the first ring she answered, "Major Sarro."

"Major, this is Athas, sorry to bother you but I have some bad news."

She sounded unfazed by his words. "What is it Agent Athas?"

"It's Schumaker ma'am. I left him alone for a brief minute and he walked out." Athas could hear her breathing heavily.

"Has his commanding officer been notified?"

"Lieutenant Lindner is notifying Colonel Boilin and Captain Weinman now Major. Do we have charges on him yet ma'am?"

"Yes, as a matter of fact I do. My secretary just handed them to me. The United States Army vs. Sergeant Wesley Schumaker is hereby charged with one count of Attempted Rape, one count of 1st Degree Assault and one count of 2nd Degree Assault. I'll charge him later for failing to obey a direct order once you get your hands on him. Now go find him. Get on this. I want him found…now, and I'd suggest you call your victim ASAP." She slammed down the phone.

"Horn, have Dispatch broadcast a lookout for Schumaker. He's facing two felony charges and one misdemeanor. That fax coming through now has all the specifics. I need to brief the LT."

"Roger that," Horn said walking briskly toward the line of papers streaming from the ancient facsimile machine.

Athas stood in the doorway of Lindner's office, while he listened to his irritated boss on the phone. "Lenny, your cell phone's ringing on your desk," Horn shouted.

By the time Athas made it to his desk the phone had stopped. He looked at the caller ID. It was Mr. Kim. "Fuck," he said anxiously pushing the redial button.

Mr. Kim answered. "Hello, Agent Athas?" he asked, sounding worried.

"Yes sir. What can I do for you? How's Suk doing?"

"He was just here." Athas' eyes bugged out.

"Who, who was there?" Athas stuttered.

"The man who attacked my wife. He was just outside our back door." Athas could feel his heart sink. "Are you sure it was him? What was he wearing?"

"My wife was standing at the kitchen sink doing dishes, when she looked up he was standing in front of the window two feet from her face. She screamed so loud, I thought he was in the house. What are we supposed to do? She's scared to death. I thought he was with you. Why did you let him go?"

"I'm on my way. If you see him again, call 911. I'll be there in 3 minutes. Lock the doors."

Lindner and Horn were paying close attention to Athas' conversation. "Get your radio and your gun. Let's go," he said to Horn. The two agents rushed from the building into Athas' car. With his lights and siren activated, they sped to

Pioneer City where the Kim's resided. "Check around back," Athas instructed Horn.

Watching Athas arrive from the front window, Mr. Kim opened the door with a concerned look. "Come in agent. We haven't seen him anymore."

Athas walked inside the aging townhome. Mr. and Mrs. Kim's son stood in the middle of the living room floor. On the couch sat their daughter hugging Suk, crying uncontrollably.

"Honey, Agent Athas is here."

The door swung open, startling everyone. "Nobody's out back Lenny," Agent Horn announced.

Athas knelt next to the couch. "Suk." Her head was buried in her daughter's chest. Both were clutching tightly to one another. "Suk. Can you tell me what the man you saw was wearing?"

Suk slowly raised her head. Her hands were shaking like the evening she was accosted. Tears gushed down her withered face. On the verge of hyperventilating, she attempted to speak. "He, he, had on, on, on a green tee shirt and those, those army pants." Suk turned and let her face fall into her hands. "I can't do this agent. I can't. I can't," she repeated through her palms.

"Suk, I need to know what type of army pants. Were they just green? Or were they camouflage?"

Suk nodded her head, still covered by her hands. "Camouflage."

Athas looked at Horn and the others standing around him. He knew he had to ask the next question. "Are you sure it was the man you picked out today? One hundred percent."

Suk jumped from the couch, ran to the nearby bathroom and slammed the door. The sounds of her vomiting was heard by everyone. The sheer thought of that horrifying night and the reminder of the evil look on the man's face terrified her.

"What are we supposed to do? He knows where we live," said Mr. Kim.

"Well, I can tell you the entire base is looking for him right now. When we do find him, he will be arrested and hopefully held in jail until trial," Athas said, trying to offer some hope.

Suk came out of the bathroom, dabbing her eyes with a wad of toilet paper. "Are you ok Mom?" her daughter asked.

"Yes honey," she said taking a seat again on the couch.

"We're going to leave now to coordinate a search. Remember, if you see him anywhere, I don't care where you are, call 911. Whatever you do Suk, don't travel alone," Athas said.

As Athas and Horn left the Kim home, they could hear the deadbolt being latched behind them.

"We gotta catch this bastard Eddie and fast," Athas said as the two got into Athas' car.

"I agree," Horn said just as something caught his attention. "Hey Lenny. Did you see the green SUV that just went down Pioneer Drive?"

"No, I was looking at my phone. The lieutenant wants us back at the barrack ASAP. Why?"

"I could have sworn it was Captain Weinman driving with someone in the passenger seat. I might be wrong, but it sure did look like Schumaker."

"What? Are you serious?"

"I'm pretty sure. The passenger looked over this way, then turned his head quickly. See if you can catch up to them."

Athas stomped on the gas and maneuvered his way from Arwell Court onto Pioneer Drive. "Are you talking about that SUV at the traffic light?" Athas asked.

"Yep, that's the one."

"The light's red, so I'll follow him and see where he goes." Athas leaned forward in his seat not believing his eyes. "What the fuck is he doing? He's running the light, Jesus Christ."

"Go after him," Horn yelled.

"I can't Eddie. We got no jurisdiction. You know that. We're not on base."

"I know that was him. He's got no business over here. I'll bet that was Schumaker. I know it was. Son of a bitch," Horn said striking his fist on the dash.

"Fuck it. I'm going after him," Athas said, racing around the line of cars. "Turn on my lights and siren Eddie. Let's get this asshole," Athas said while he swerved through the traffic.

"There he is, up ahead. He made a sharp left onto Lucky Lane. He's flying," Horn pointed out.

"Yeah, I see him. He's trying to hide from someone, no fucking doubt. If these slow ass people would move, I could catch him. Move!" he hollered over the yelping siren.

Athas weaved in and out of traffic until he made it to Lucky Lane. "He's gone," he said hammering both hands on the steering wheel. "God damn it. Let's get back. The lieutenant said he needed us ASAP."

Back at the CID, the parking lot was full. Standing near one of the marked MP jeeps was Colonel Boilin, Major Sarro, Lieutenant Lindner and four military policemen. "Shit, they've been waiting for us. Here comes my ass chewing," Athas said.

Athas parked his car. "Sorry everyone. We got tied up at my victim's house."

Colonel Boilin was noticeably pissed. He stepped toward Athas. "Was it him? Was he at your victim's house?"

"Yes sir. No question about it."

"We're coordinating an all-out search for him because of you Athas. Your lieutenant has asked the county police to keep checks on the Kim residence and broadcast a lookout also. I want you guys to go to the stockade and his barracks and talk to every God damn soldier he lives with, works with, drinks with, or wipes his ass with, and find out where he might be. Do you understand me son?" the colonel ordered.

"Yes sir Colonel, immediately sir."

Before Athas could walk away, Major Sarro chimed in. "When you do get your hands on him, I want to be notified right away. Get my cell number from your lieutenant," she said turning quickly to leave. "Yes ma'am were on it. Umm, ma'am." Major Sarro turned around. "What is it?"

"Ma'am, this may be nothing, but Special Agent Horn thinks he saw Captain Weinman in the same community where my victim lives just as we were leaving."

Sarro's lips tightened. "What?" She looked at Colonel Boilin, then turned to Horn. "Tell me what you saw Agent?"

Nervous, Horn struggled to swallow. "Well yes Major, when we were about to pull off from the victim's house, I saw a green SUV, like one of ours, you know Army issued, driving out of Pioneer City with someone who looked like Schumaker in the front passenger seat. Whoever it was, looked in our direction and then ran the red-light ma'am. Seemed awfully strange."

Sarro was listening carefully. "Which way did he go?"

Horn looked over at Athas. "Why are you looking at him? I said, where did he go Agent?" she said raising her voice.

Athas lowered his head. "Umm, without justification Colonel and Major, I activated my emergency equipment while off base and attempted to follow him. I'll take whatever punishment..."

Still upset, Colonel Boilin interrupted. "Son, I don't give a fuck about that. I just wish you would have caught the son of a bitch. Didn't the Army teach you how to drive?"

Sarro called over to Lindner. "Don, you know Weinman pretty well, what type of government vehicle does he have?"

"A green SUV."

"God damn it. If I find evidence that arrogant bastard had Schumaker in his truck, I'm going to fry his ginger ass," Sarro said fuming with anger.

"Lieutenant Lindner, call Captain Weinman's barracks and tell him I want to see him in my office immediately. If he's not there, call his cell phone," Sarro ordered.

Lindner pulled out his cell phone and called the Stockade Command Center. "Captain Weinman's office, can I help you?" his secretary answered.

"This is Lieutenant Lindner at the CID, is your captain available?"

"Ah, no sir. He had to rush out. He said he had an urgent personal matter to take care of."

"Mmm, Ok. I'll try him on his cell. If he does return before I reach him, tell him Major Sarro needs him in her office immediately."

"Yes Lieutenant. Will do sir."

Lindner hung up and called Weinman's cell. The phone rang once, then switched to voicemail. He held the phone out and pressed the redial button. This time the phone didn't bother to ring, instead it went straight to voicemail. "Captain. This is Lieutenant Lindner. Major Sarro needs you in her office immediately." He ended the message and by now Sarro was standing next to him. She was livid.

"He turned off his damn phone, didn't he?" Sarro asked.

Lindner looked at the furious major. "It sure does look like it ma'am."

"I'll be at the office. I want to know as soon as you get him no matter what time it is." Sarro hopped in her car and sped from the lot.

"Athas, you and Horn get busy on that assignment Colonel Boilin has given you," Lindner ordered.

"Yes sir, headed there now sir," Athas replied.

Chapter 12

Michaels walked into the Northern District police station where he was greeted by longtime friend Lieutenant Steve Finck. "Steve-o, what's happening buddy?" reaching out to shake his hand.

"Hey Ron, good to see you. How are things going for ya? Did you ever get remarried?"

Michaels smiled. "No, but I've met a wonderful person. You'll have to meet her someday."

"Good for you. I'm glad to hear that. I guess you're here for Officer Carini? That's a damn shame. I guess the guy was all doped up?"

"Yeah, shit like this really pisses me off. I'll have to wait for the tox report to come back, but I'm sure he was whacked out on greens or something. Fucking asshole. Where's Carini and how is he doing?"

"He's been sitting in my office talking with me. I just came out to get him a cup of coffee. You know, surprisingly he's doing pretty good."

"Would it be ok if I used your office to interview him?"

"Sure, help yourself. Here, take his coffee. I'll make sure no one bothers you. Good seeing you."

"You too buddy. Thanks."

Michaels had been acquaintances with Officer Raymond Carini over the past five years. He knew Carini was a good cop with a strong reputation of being a good worker. He was generally a quiet person, someone who didn't get caught up in the department politics or rumor mill drama. He was sitting comfortably in a straight back vinyl chair across from the lieutenant's outdated metal desk.

"Here you go brother, one cup of black coffee as ordered, sorry it's not something stronger."

"Hey Ronnie, thanks."

"Listen Bud, I'm really sorry about your dad. I feel so bad for you. I am so glad you got to kill that piece of shit."

"Thanks Ronnie. Is my Dad still at the store?" he asked wiping the tears from his eyes.

"Yeah. I just left there. They were waiting for Doc Jones to arrive. Once he shows up…well you know, he has to go to the Medical Examiner's Office in Baltimore." Michaels sat behind the desk and laid his notepad in front of him. "I want you to know this is a justified shooting. No question about it. Are you ok with talking to me? I'm not reading you your Miranda rights or none of that bullshit. I'm not doing that to you. You've been through enough."

"Yeah...sure...no problem. I appreciate that. I can't believe how fast everything happened. One minute we're in the back, fixing guns, laughing and joking, and before you know it, he's dead. It all seems surreal, like I'm dreaming or something." Carini looked at the floor and began to get upset. "I'm sorry."

"No, no, don't be sorry. Shit you're holding up better than I would. Damn," Michaels told him.

Over the next 45 minutes Officer Carini provided Michaels with a detailed account of the tragic events that played out in less than one minute. Chills rushed through Michaels' body when Carini described vividly how he heard the loud thud of his dad's body falling to the floor, following the deafening sound of the shotgun blasts.

Throughout the interview, Carini tried desperately to keep his composure. It was almost as if he felt embarrassed to cry. Michaels could tell one part of their conversation in particular stuck with Carini and enraged Michaels. Carini leaned back in his chair and stared at the ceiling with tears rolling off the sides of his face. He took a deep breath. "The part that I'll never forget." Carini paused, struggling to keep himself together to talk. "Was, was..." Carini cried harder, still focusing on the light above him. "...hearing the guy laugh when my dad hit the floor. He sounded like the joker in a Batman movie. Like it was fucking funny or something."

Michaels eyes filled with tears. He moved from behind the desk and sat in the chair next to his friend. "I'm so sorry brother," Michaels uttered softly.

"He wasn't just my dad, he was my best friend. Christ, we fished, we hunted, we worked together in the store…the man taught me everything." The two cops hugged tightly. Carini couldn't hold his emotions back any longer. He cried on Michaels' shoulder for the next several minutes. It would be a moment neither would ever forget.

"Would you like me to drive you home?" Michaels asked Carini, now drying his own eyes with tissues.

"My car is at the store, if you could drop me off there. I'll give you the key to the door and the alarm code if you wouldn't mind locking up when you're done. I'll have to hire someone to clean everything, I guess. How much longer do you think you'll be?"

"We're done here brother. I'm ready when you are."

After a short drive, Michaels was back at the scene. Parked out front was Doc Jones' car and the van from the Medical Examiner's Office. Carini hurried to his car parked in the rear of the store.

Michaels watched as he drove off, then walked back into the store.

"If it isn't Shithead," Doc Jones blurted out with his camera draped around his neck.

"Oh my God Doc," Michaels said with a serious look. "Is that a new camera? What happened, did Moses want his Polaroid One-Step back?"

Everyone in the room laughed. "Funny Shithead. I'll have you know my son got this for my birthday. And yes, smart ass, they still make film for One-Step cameras, so don't say a word."

Michaels greeted everyone. "What's left to be done partner?" he asked Jim.

"We just got Mr. Carini into the van, now it's time for the dirtbag," Jim said.

"Shithead can you and Jim assist this fella from the ME's Office. We need to get the body from behind the counter to the middle of the store so he can put him on the gurney," Jeff said.

"Sure. I'd love to." Michaels reached out and shook the hand of the young man from the Medical Examiner's Office. "We've never met before. My name is Ronnie Michaels with the homicide unit. Who are you?"

"Hi sir. I'm Steven. I'm new. This is only my second day as a driver."

Michaels eyed up the 22-year-old, geeky looking white male dressed in his outdated grey pants, and a Mr. Rogers hand me down sweater. "It's nice to meet you. So Steven, what do you suggest we do?"

"I guess we could slide him on a blanket and pull him all the way around to the front," the young man offered.

"A blanket? Are you fucking kidding me? Steven, did you know this worthless piece of shit killed the man that's already in your van, who just happens to be a cop's father?" The newcomer was caught off-guard by Michaels' aggressiveness. "So I say, fuck that. Let's take a short cut and the three of us can lift him up onto the counter." The room got quiet. Everyone in the room looked at Michaels like he was crazy.

"Well, I guess we could," the young man replied.

Michaels clapped his hands together loudly and grinned like he would often do when he was excited. "That's it. Great idea. Let's move this motherfucker. I got shit to do."

Jim and Steven began walking toward the employee entrance leading behind the counter. Michaels looked over at the body and swung his legs up and over the countertop putting him on the other side next to the dead body. "This was probably exactly what this asshole did," Michaels said to anyone listening. "You got all your pictures and measurements Dad and Jeff?"

"Yup. We're all done. I had to remove the projectile from his head because it looked like it was about to fall out," Jeff said.

"Good." Michaels bent down and removed the dead man's wallet. He pulled out the driver's license, stuck it in his shirt pocket and threw the billfold to Jeff. He then rifled through his pockets, but there was nothing.

"There's nothing else on this asshole." Michaels grabbed onto the dead man's ankles and yanked the body from the gun case. "Come on out ass nuts. You're about to take your last ride."

Jim and Steven made their way around to Michaels, watching him like he had gone mad. "You guys grab under his arms and I'll get his legs," Michaels ordered.

The three men grunted as they hoisted the body to the top of the counter. Steven made it a point to ease the man's head on top the glass case.

"I'll pull the gurney up and we can slide him on it," Steven said like he had just thought of a good idea. Jim and Steven turned and began walking around to the front of the case, thinking Michaels was behind them, when they heard the distinct hollow thud on the hard tile. They quickly turned. The noise was the dead man's head bouncing on the floor. "Oops, he fell. I guess we can call that a transport injury. Poor bastard," Michaels said laughing.

The men stared in amazement at Michaels who had just shoved the body from the display case. Michaels scaled over the counter once more landing him next to the body now lying face down. As if what he had just done wasn't morbid enough, he straddled over the midsection of the dead man, grabbed a chunk of his hair and jerked up his stiffening head. "Hey Doc, take a picture."

Doc Jones and the rest of the men in the room watched Michaels, not believing their eyes. Not a word was spoken. "C'mon Doc, take a picture with your new camera. I want one."

"Ronnie, are you serious?"

"Fuck yeah, take the thing."

Bewildered, Doc Jones lifted his camera and snapped off a shot. The picture ejected from the front port and he handed it to Michaels, not bothering to wait for it to develop. Michaels dropped the head. "Ok, well that's enough fun for me. Come on Jim let's get something to eat. Welcome to homicide."

Chapter 13

Schumaker's housing unit was a short 15 minute drive from the CID barracks. Each Army housing unit accommodated twenty soldiers comfortably, each having to occupy a small room, just big enough to fit two single beds, two nightstands, two dressers and a closet for each. One bathroom was situated between two rooms, causing four soldiers to share a bathroom equipped with a double vanity sink and one shower.

As they arrived, three soldiers were seen sitting on the front steps enjoying a smoke. "Good afternoon gentleman," Athas said displaying his open wallet with his Army credentials displayed. "I'm Special Agent Athas and this is Special Agent Horn from the Army CID."

"Ut oh, somebody must have screwed up," one of the soldiers said, hotboxing his filter less Camel.

Neither agent reacted to his comment. "So, when's the last time any of you seen Sergeant Schumaker?" Athas asked. The Latino and two white soldiers looked aimlessly at one another and said nothing.

"Oh, were going to play this game huh?" Athas felt his face getting red. "Just so we are all clear. I'm giving you a direct order to answer my questions. And if you don't, Major Sarro from the

JAG's Office will be court martialing everyone who refuses to cooperate. The three soldiers began squirming on the steps, coughing, and clearing the unexpected phlegm in their throats.

"Um sir, I saw him this morning leaving the building. He looked like he was in a hurry," one of the soldiers offered.

"Yeah, I saw him too. He normally doesn't lay his head here though. He stays at his girlfriend's a lot," the young Latino soldier said in broken English.

"Do you know his girlfriend's name, or where she lives?" Horn asked.

"I ain't never met her, but I've heard him talk. I think her name is Venessa and she lives in the condos next to the food store down the street, just off base."

"What about you, soldier?" Horn asked the third man sitting silently. The soldier blew the smoke from his mouth and threw his finished cigarette in the dirt filled coffee can next to the steps.

"I ain't no snitch, but is he in some kind of shit?"

"Look we don't have all day. Tell us what you know, or I'll just call Major Sarro now."

"No, no man, chill. I just thought it was weird last night when I saw him. My roomy and I share the same bathroom with him and another dude. Like he said, Schumaker ain't here much, but he came in the bathroom when I was washing my hands. He was all out of breath and shit. He looked like he'd been in a fight or some shit. His pants were all dirty. What was weird was he said if anyone asked, say that him and I were in the TV room most of the night. I said that's cool, but I ain't taking no court martial over no one…nope…fuck that."

"What time was this?" Horn inquired.

"I know exactly what time it was. It was 1900 hours sharp. Jeopardy was about to come on," the soldier said smiling.

"How many others are inside now?" Horn asked the men.

"We're it. The others are in training. We worked the midnight shift at the Logistics Center," the private stated.

"Give Special Agent Horn each of your names and duty assignments while I make a phone call." Athas walked into the parking lot and telephoned Major Sarro.

"This is Major Sarro."

"Major, it's Athas."

"What do you have for me?" she asked sternly.

"One of the soldiers who shares a bathroom with Schumaker ran into him last night at 7 p.m. He said he looked like he'd been fighting. He...."

"Sorry to interrupt you Athas. But you'll never guess who is standing in my doorway."

"Who ma'am?"

"It's Captain Weinman and Sergeant Schumaker. Get over here ASAP," and she hung up the phone.

"I see you found your soldier Captain," Sarro said leaning back in her chair. "So, where did you decide to walk off to Sergeant?"

"He came to my office," Weinman said.

"Bullshit. I didn't ask you Captain. I asked your sergeant who disobeyed a direct order."

Schumaker looked at Weinman like a lost puppy. "Major he was following orders. I..."

Major Sarro raised her voice. "I don't care to hear from you Captain. I asked your sergeant a question."

"Don't answer that soldier," sounded a deep voice behind Schumaker and Weinman. "Excuse me gentlemen," Major Joshua Barnes said walking between the two men and into Sarro's office. "Good afternoon Dawn," Major Barnes said in his normal arrogant tone.

"Joshua."

"It's my understanding there are charges pending on Sergeant Schumaker. Is that true?"

Sarro picked up a manila folder from her desk. "Yes, it is. And as soon as Special Agent Athas arrives, he'll be taking him over to the CID to process him and take his fingerprints and photograph."

The tall uniformed major approached Sarro's desk. "May I see what my client is being charged with?"

Sarro handed him the folder. She looked at Weinman sporting a cocky look on his face. "We called your office a little while ago and your secretary said you abruptly left. Where did you go?" Sarro asked.

The captain looked around and started getting fidgety. Major Sarro enjoyed watching his nervousness take control. "Yeah I had an urgent personal matter to take care of."

Major Sarro shot him a look of disbelief. "You're not needed here anymore Captain. Leave. I see Special Agent Athas has arrived."

"But…." Captain Weinman said.

"Captain…leave. That is an order." She watched him turn and storm down the hallway.

Sarro turned her attention to Athas and Horn now standing next to Schumaker. "He's all yours agents."

Athas reached to the back of his waistband and pulled out his shiny Peerless handcuffs. "Put your hands behind your back Sergeant. You're under arrest."

"Agent Athas, I'm Major Barnes, Sergeant Schumaker's defense counsel. I trust you won't be talking to my client unless I'm present?"

"No need to worry. My agents will only be booking him and taking him before the judge for his bail review," Sarro informed him.

Agitated, Athas got eye contact with Major Sarro. "Major, could you order Sergeant Schumaker to stay away from the victim in this case and her residence?" Major Sarro looked at Athas with a puzzled look on her face. She could sense something was amiss.

Arrogantly, Major Barnes spoke before she could utter a word. "That won't be necessary. My client won't be going anywhere near the victim in this ridiculous matter. Now let's get this done so we can dispose of these false allegations. Don't you all have better things to do with your time?"

Barnes' words infuriated Sarro. "Major, an attempted rape is far from ridiculous. And yes, I can do that for you Special Agent. In the presence of your counsel, Sergeant Wesley Schumaker you are hereby ordered to stay away from the victim in this case, Mrs. Suk Kim, for which you have been charged with Attempted Rape and Assault in the 1st and 2nd Degree. This includes her residence or place of employment. Furthermore, you are forbidden to contact her or anyone in her family by any such means for an indefinite period. Do you understand this direct order from a superior officer?" Sarro stared at Schumaker from behind her desk.

Schumaker looked pathetically at his attorney. "Pursuant to Army regulations, you must acknowledge me Sergeant," Major Sarro insisted.

"Yes Major, I understand," he said meekly.

Barnes walked over to Schumaker with his wrists bound in cuffs. "I'll see you in a few at the bail review Sergeant. Remember, don't say a word."

Athas and Horn escorted their arrestee from the building and drove him to the CID where Lieutenant Lindner awaited their arrival in the prisoner sally port.

"Look who decided to come back and visit us," Horn said sarcastically to his lieutenant.

"I'm going to start my paperwork Eddie while you process him," Athas said.

"He'll be in lock-up by the time you're done. I'll wait for you, and we can both take him to the courthouse."

"You got it Eddie. I'll be right down," Athas said while he and Lindner headed up the stairs to his office.

Nearly two hours had passed when Athas and Horn transported Schumaker to the Army Judiciary Center where the military court was located. Inside, they unshackled the prisoner who took a seat at the defense table next to Major Barnes.

In the military court system, a ranking commissioned officer, no less than the rank of Major or Colonel presides over initial appearance hearings. He or she must determine if the accused is released with or without posting money for bail or incarcerated until the court martial hearing.

At the prosecution table Athas and Major Sarro sat side by side discussing the likelihood of their prisoner being held without bond until the hearing date. Lieutenant Lindner and Agent Horn sat on the wooden bench directly behind them. The door leading from the judge's chambers opened. Expecting to hear the clerk announce the judge, the prosecution team was flabbergasted to see Captain Weinman talking and laughing jovially to someone behind the door where the judge's office was located. Athas and Sarro looked at one another. They were dumbfounded.

Captain Weinman walked in the direction of the counsel's table avoiding eye contact at all expense with Sarro and Athas. If it were possible, Sarro's eyes would have burned holes in the back of Weinman's head while he strutted by like a fanned out turkey. Weinman smiled and winked at Barnes and Schumaker who were huddled talking.

The same door that Weinman had just waltzed through, opened, and out came the court clerk. "All rise." Dressed in his full Class A uniform, the Colonel presiding over the hearing took a seat in the high back, black leather chair behind the judge's bench.

The few gathered in the courtroom stood while the clerk introduced the Honorable Colonel Blevins. Sarro turned and shot Weinman a nasty look.

"You may be seated," the colonel directed. "This is the bail review hearing for Sergeant Wesley Schumaker of the United States Army. The government has levied the following charges on Sergeant Schumaker. Count 1: Attempted Rape in the 1st Degree." Sarro drew her attention to the defense table and peered at Schumaker, standing with his head down. The colonel continued reading from the paper in front of him. "Count 2: Assault in the 1st Degree and Count 3: Assault in the 2nd Degree." Colonel Blevins looked up and scanned the courtroom, then addressed the attorneys. "As you know, the purpose of this session is for me to determine if the accused will appear in this court to answer for these charges." The colonel eased back in his chair and folded his arms. "Counselors, instead of dragging this out, I've reviewed these allegations and the unblemished record of the accused provided to me by Captain Weinman."

Major Sarro sprung from her chair. "Your honor."

"Have a seat Major Sarro. I'll hear from you when I'm ready." Sarro dropped in her seat and looked at Athas in amazement. "Major Barnes, it's my understanding that Captain Weinman is Sergeant Schumaker's commanding officer, is that correct?"

Major Barnes stood. "Yes sir Colonel, that's correct." Furious, Sarro stared at Barnes who wouldn't dare look in her direction. "Colonel, as you are aware Captain Weinman is a highly decorated, respected member of the United States Army with nearly 20 years of distinguished service..."

Colonel Blevins interrupted Barnes and unfolded his arms. "Yes, I am well aware of his service record Major. He and I served together during Desert Storm. We've been in the trenches more than once."

Sarro let out a big breath of air and slammed her folder closed. She knew it was worthless to speak. It was the good ole boy military system playing out before her.

Barnes continued, "I have spoken with Captain Weinman who has assured me in no uncertain terms that Sergeant Schumaker will attend any and all hearings regarding these..." Barnes looked over at Sarro and Athas with a smug look. "...frankly outrageously ridiculous allegations sir."

Sarro stood. "Colonel..."

Colonel Blevins interrupted, "Major Sarro, I've looked over the sparse information in this file and I'm just not seeing enough evidence to hold

Sergeant Schumaker until trial. Frankly, there's just nothing here."

"But..," Sarro interjected.

"Major Sarro be seated," Colonel Blevins instructed. Sarro was boiling mad. "I've known Captain Weinman for years and I have all the trust, respect and confidence in him. He's a man of honor. So, when I'm told he has assured this court that a member of his command will appear at any and all future court dates, then I believe that to be fact. Let's not prolong this any longer than necessary." Colonel Blevins began writing on a piece of paper in front of him. "In the matter of the United States Army vs. Sergeant Wesley Schumaker, this court hereby releases the accused on his own recognizance. Trial will commence two weeks from today. Major Sarro, you'll need to get all reports, notes, statements, photographs and anything else you may have up your sleeve to defense counsel within 24 hours for discovery. Am I clear?" the colonel questioned.

Sarro sat and stared at her case folder.

Colonel Blevins raised his voice. "Major, am I clear?"

"Yeah Colonel. I got it," she said in a disrespectful tone.

Colonel Blevins frowned at her. "This court is now adjourned." The colonel struck the gavel extra hard on the wooden pad and stood from his chair.

Appalled, both Athas and Sarro whisked their folders from the table and started toward the door. At the defense table, Weinman, Barnes and Schumaker stood smiling and shaking hands.

"Have a nice day Major," Captain Weinman said to Sarro.

Not about to look at the gloating men, she instinctively extended her arm in Weinman's direction, raised her middle finger, and presented him with a trophy *fuck you,* just inches from his face.

Chapter 14

Steven lowered the gurney to the ground while Jeff and Ray lifted the corpse into the awaiting body bag. Michaels stood by Steven and the dead man. "Come over here partner," Michaels said to Jim. Jim turned his notebook to a clean page, thinking he was going to need to document more information. "You won't need that. Put that fucking thing in your pocket," Michaels said. Jim closed his notebook and walked closer to Michaels, unsure what to expect. "Let this be the first maggot you get to zipper up." Michaels stepped back. "Don't forget to say *bye bye motherfucker*." Everyone stood and watched while Jim slowly pulled the zipper up from the bottom.

"Bye, bye," Jim uttered quietly.

"No, no, no. You have to say it like you mean it. Remember, he's a fucking worthless bag of shit," Michaels shouted. "Fuck him. Now take two."

Jim looked at the upper torso and head still exposed. "Bye, bye you disgrace of a human being." And he zipped the rest of the bag up.

Michaels smiled. "That's better. You did good partner. Now let's get out of here."

Rzepkowski followed Michaels outside, mesmerized over what he had just experienced. *Is this what this job is going to do to me?* he thought to himself. Outside Sergeant Suit was sitting in his car smoking, talking on his cell phone. He ended the call and tore a piece of paper from his notebook when a car came to an abrupt stop next to the marked patrol car parked out front. A 50 something year old lady exited the car in a frantic state.

The uniformed officer jumped from his car, as did Tommy. Michaels and Jim stood and watched. "Ma'am can I help you?" the patrolman asked.

"Yes, yes that's my son's car," the lady said pointing to the old blue Nova parked near the front door of the crime scene. "Is he ok? Did he get in trouble?"

Before the officer could answer, Tommy walked over to the distraught woman. "I'm Sergeant Suit with the county police. I was just sending Detective Michaels over to your house to speak with you." Tommy motioned Michaels to join him. "When's the last time you saw your son?" Tommy asked.

"About two hours ago. He lives in my basement. Earlier today he was talking out of his head like he was on something. He kept mumbling something about *he was going to shut some people up for good*. He was acting crazy, and he sped off in his car. I've been driving around looking for him. I'm worried sick."

"You should have been ma'am, because that no good piece of shit son of yours, umm let me see what his name is…"

"Ronnie," Tommy shouted.

Michaels ignored Tommy, reached into his shirt pocket and pulled out the killer's driver's license. "Your precious Scott killed a police officer's father in cold blood. Thankfully the police officer put a bullet in your son's head. So, there you have it. Your son is dead. Come on Jim." Michaels stormed toward his car and Jim followed. *What a first day,* Jim thought.

By now the lady was shocked, surprised and upset from the news she just forcefully ingested. "Dear God, no, no," the woman cried. "Where is he? I want to see him," she shouted with tears gushing down her face.

The front door opened and out came Ray and Jeff controlling the front of the gurney with Steven at the rear. They began guiding the cart down the cement steps. "Oh my God is that my Scotty," she screamed running toward the door. Tommy and the officer held onto the woman, keeping her from getting closer. Michaels and Jim took a brief look before they got into Michaels' cruiser.

"Ma'am. You can't see him right now. He must go to the Medical Examiner's office first. I'm sorry." The crying woman laid her head on Tommy's chest mumbling her son's name over and over. Tommy put his arms around her to console the broken woman. That was the last vision Jim and Michaels would see of that scene.

During the drive back to the CID, Michaels and Jim barely spoke. They could hear Michaels' cell phone ringing in his jacket pocket. It was Tommy.

"Yo," Michaels answered.

"What the fuck was that all about?" Tommy said, incensed over Michaels' actions. Afterall, she wasn't the one who had done wrong. Most likely, she had her own stories of years of mental anguish brought about by her child now situated inside a plastic bag in the back of a van.

Michaels knew exactly why he was angry. He paused for a moment. From the passenger's seat, Jim could hear the tone of Tommy's voice. Though he had never done a death notification, he knew from the training he received, this one was flat out wrong.

"Yeah I fucked up. Sorry. I was just so pissed off after interviewing Officer Carini and seeing him cry. Sorry man."

"Don't say you're sorry to me Ronnie. That doesn't fucking matter. That poor woman just lost her son. That was her kid. Her own flesh and blood. Face it. You fucked up and you need to go see her and apologize. You're better than that Ronnie. You hear me?"

Michaels knew Tommy wasn't asking, he was telling. "You're right. I'll take care of it."

"Good. I don't know when the last time you seen our friend, but I suggest you go pay her a visit."

Michaels paused. He still hadn't told Tommy of his growing personal relationship with Dr. Katie Esterling. Knowing he couldn't speak freely with Jim in the car, he cut the conversation short. "Yeah, no problem."

"Great. Drop Jim off and go the fuck home. I'll see you guys tomorrow," Tommy said ending the call.

"Ouch, he sounded pissed," Jim said.

"He's right though. That was bad. Don't do what I did. Don't let your emotions lead you around like a dog on a leash. Jim, you'll see. This job will eat you up and spit you out. Few cops know what it's like to be a homicide detective. It's a well-kept secret." Jim watched and listened carefully to Michaels. For a split second, he wondered if this was really the job for him.

Michaels pulled next to Jim's car in the parking lot of the CID building in Crownsville. "Good first day Jim. See ya in the morning."

"Ok Ronnie. Thanks."

"As soon as Michaels started home his phone sounded. It was Katie. "Good afternoon Dr.."

She laughed. "How is my favorite detective?"

Michaels giggled. "I'll bet you say that to all your patients."

"My lord," she laughed again. "How many times must I tell you? You're not my patient."

"I'm just messing with ya Babe. How was your day?"

"Well since my daughter is with her father tonight, I wanted to see if you'd like to go out to dinner and we can find out about each other's day then."

"I think I've just been asked out on a date," he said jokingly.

"Yes knucklehead, I'm officially asking you out. And if it's ok with you I'd still like to have a date night even after I move in."

"It's a deal."

"You're a dork. I'll be by to pick you up at six Ronnie. Is that ok?"

"Perfect. See ya soon."

"In case I haven't told you lately. I love you Ronald Michaels."

Michaels sported a huge smile. "Welllllll, now that you mention it…."

"Funny boy. Goodbye," Katie said, also wearing a beaming grin.

Chapter 15

Major Sarro felt like her head was about to burst by the time she and Athas made their way back to her building. Once there, they passed several people in the hallway. Neither dared to acknowledge anyone. They were about to explode.

Sarro slammed her door shut and threw her case folder across her desk. "That pompous son of a bitch," she yelled. "Fourteen days? Fourteen fucking days for an attempted rape case and Barnes didn't even object? What the fuck. Something's up. I think it all has to do with that slimy bastard Weinman." Sarro fell into the leather chair behind her desk and expelled a long sigh of frustration.

Athas had never been in Major Sarro's office. The aging military mahogany furniture had all the signs of an overworked attorney. Case files were piled high on her desk, surrounded by no less than 10 phone messages left by her secretary. File drawers were open with folders pulled halfway out. Besides the organized chaotic clutter, what caught his eye were the trophies on the credenza near the window.

"Major, are these yours?" he asked pointing to the six tall trophies, some with medals hanging from them. Catching her completely off guard, Sarro spun in her chair, snickered and smiled. "Yeah they're mine. Shit, I was the first female ever on the Fort Meade Sniper Team a few years ago.

These are only a few of my awards. The rest are boxed up." She swiveled her chair back facing her desk.

"Do you mind if I take a look?" Athas asked.

"Sure, go ahead" she muttered modestly.

Athas scooted around her desk and picked them up one by one and read the plates. The tallest were for first place and only one for scoring second. While he read and admired the display, he looked out the large window overlooking part of the base.

Sarro stood from her chair and looked out the window. "That's asshole Weinman's office there," said Sarro.

Athas pointed off in the distance across Mapes Road. "About three blocks away is Schumaker's barracks where he stays sometimes. Which reminds me, I need to tell you about my interview with a couple of the soldiers who spoke with him the night of the attempted rape."

Sarro sat down in her chair. "I'm sure what you have is good, but can we do this another time? I'm guessing what you're going to tell me is only going to piss me off even more."

Athas sat in the chair across from her. "I've never seen anything like this," he said. "Schumaker's got to be related to someone in the know. This is all too strange. I'm going to poke around a little if it's ok ma'am."

She managed to temper her irritation enough to offer him sound advice. "He's a commanding officer to you, remember that. So the less I know, the better." Sarro flashed a wink at Athas.

"Yes ma'am. Roger that. Loud and clear." He smiled. He knew exactly what that meant.

"By tomorrow I need two clean copies of all your notes, photos, statements and reports. I'll fax a subpoena over to the hospital for the medical records. I'm not losing this case. That sick little fuck ball is going to pay for this if it's the last thing I do as an attorney. Go on, get out of here, I'll talk to you later."

Chapter 16

At 6 p.m. promptly the doorbell rang, and Michaels was greeted by Katie, wearing a short grey skirt, a silky white sheer blouse, red heels and a smile highlighted with a hint of red lip gloss. Her wavy long brunette hair covered her shoulders and laid perfectly on her chest. She was stunning. Michaels was pleasantly surprised. "Hi Detective. I'm here to take you out on a date. Are you ready?" she asked, wrapping her arms around his neck, laying a wet smooch on his lips.

Michaels couldn't hold back his ear to ear smile. "Oh my God Katie. You belong on the cover of a magazine. You're drop dead gorgeous." The two exchanged a passionate kiss and were off for an enjoyable evening of Italian cuisine and good wine at their favorite restaurant, Bella Napoli.

Katie and Michaels sat at a table for two in the dimly lit remote corner of the restaurant. As usual, Michaels kept their conversation focused mainly on Katie, asking about her daughter and what new and interesting clients she had, without revealing their names of course. Katie was sure not to break her code of ethics when it came to her job. She was a professional, at least when it came to her office work.

"Enough about me. Tell me about your day Detective Michaels. Weren't you supposed to get a new partner?"

"Yes, I did. His name is Jim. He seems like a good cop. I think he can handle it." He took a sip of his red wine then watched as he swirled it in his glass. "At least he did today."

"Why? What did you have today?"

In between bites of his hefty portion of chicken parmigiana, Michaels told Katie about the day's events. Like always, she was intrigued by his work, asking probing questions about the suspect and Officer Carini. Having lost her own mother to a vicious killer, she could relate all too well to the emotional pain Officer Carini felt. Still unsure as to the extent of her involvement with her mother's killer, Michaels listened closely to Katie's inquiries and comments. He could see her face change when he talked of the suspect. Conversely, she was noticeably glad when she learned the details surrounding the killer's demise.

"Did you have Jim do the death notification?"

Michaels took the wine glass back in his hand and took another sip. Also, an expert in reading people, Katie saw Michaels' expression morph into disappointment. "What happened? Did he mess it up?" Michaels looked into his glass for help and grunted. "What happened Ronnie? Talk to me."

"I should have let Jim do the notification. God knows he would've done better than me."

Katie could see his disparaging look of disgrace. She reached across the table and held his hand. "Tell me about it."

Michaels hung his head. "I was a total asshole to the suspect's mother, who didn't deserve my wrath."

Katie squeezed his hand. "Go on."

"I was so fucking mad at the shooter for what he did, I took it out on his mother."

Being a true professional listener, Katie showed no reaction. "Tell me what you did Hun."

Michaels eyes welled up. "I blamed her and said her son was fucking dead. It was horrible and right in front of the new guy and Tommy, who is on fire. I can't blame him. He wants me to apologize to her." Michaels took a gulp from his glass and scanned the restaurant to see if anyone was watching.

Katie pulled Michaels' hand toward her. "Listen to me." Michaels drew his attention to her warm brown eyes. "The good thing is you realize your actions were wrong. If you didn't, then we'd have to deal with that, but we don't. You just got caught up with your emotions, probably more so because a friend, another cop, lost his father. You may have transposed yourself into his shoes and thought of someone killing your own father, which would magnify your feelings."

Michaels quickly brushed the tear trickling from his eye. Like a typical cop he attempted to mask his true feelings with a joke. "Hey, I thought I wasn't your patient anymore Doc?"

Katie ignored him. "Do you feel like you should apologize to the lady?"

"Oh, most definitely."

Katie released his hand, took ahold of her own wine glass and held it close to her mouth. "Then do it. Do it first thing tomorrow. And when you talk to her tell her why you acted the way you did. I'm sure she'll understand. Remember, the brave and fearless Detective Ronnie Michaels is still a person who can't always be perfect. When you are done with her, be sure to talk to Jim, and tell him how inappropriate your actions were."

Michaels filled his glass with the remaining nectar in the bottle. "Excuse me sir," he said to the nearby server. "We're going to need another one of these," he said waving the empty bottle. Returning his attention to Katie, he attempted once more to deliver a lighthearted comment. "Hell, Dr. Esterling, thank you for this session tonight. I guess I should pay for dinner now." They both laughed.

"You just hush it Detective. In our own strange ways, we've always been there for one another. Now let's eat. I love you." They both raised their crystal wine glasses and tapped them together.

"I love you," Michaels said, feeling comforted once more by Katie's words.

"If it's ok Ronnie, I have a friend willing to move into my home and start renting it as early as next week. Is that too soon for me and Kathryn to begin moving our things in your house?"

"You mean our house? And yes, that's great news."

Katie smiled and paused. "Yes, our house."

Early the next morning, Michaels set out to begin his barrage of apologies. First, he needed to throw himself on the sword with Tommy who had cooled down substantially over night. Michaels joined Tommy in his office. "You still pissed at me?" Michaels asked.

"Just disappointed," he said.

"I know. I fucked up. I'm going to pay the lady a visit this morning and try to fix things. My girlfriend has given me some good advice as to what to say. It's something she's very good at. Speaking of my girlfriend, I've been meaning to tell you a little secret."

Tommy lit up. "Yeah, what's that?"

"Remember our friend? The one you had me go see? The one whose mother was killed?" asked Michaels.

"Yes, the good Dr., sure I do."

"Well...we're seeing each other."

"Get the fuck out of here," Tommy said jokingly.

"Yeah man. It's the happiest I've ever been. Hell, she and her daughter just moved in."

"Stop it…you're killing me," Tommy said in a happy tone. "Good maybe she can straighten your ass out. Get out of here and go do whatever she said to do."

"Got it. I'm out of here," Michaels said leaving Tommy's office feeling relieved in more ways than one.

Next, he gutted himself like a pig to Jim, telling him to never let his emotions, no matter how jacked up he was, get dumped on an innocent family member. Being an intuitive seasoned cop, Jim understood what led Michaels down such a dark path. "It's ok brother. I understand," Jim assured him. "Listening to the officer yesterday tell his story wasn't easy for you to hear. I get it."

Michaels liked Jim's response. He gave him a hard slap on his arm. "I think you and I are going to be a good team."

Jim grinned. "Thanks Ronnie. I'll try my hardest."

"Now I need to take a ride over to the lady's house an eat a big shit sandwich. Why don't you start writing up yesterday's crime scene while I'm out filling up on turds, and I'll see you here later.

Maybe I'll still be hungry enough to buy you lunch."

"That sounds like a plan." Jim pulled the notepad from his jacket pocket and flipped to the first page.

For the next hour and a half Michaels sat with yesterday's suspect's mother who he surprised at her home. She had been sitting at her kitchen table drinking a cup of tea crying profusely. Still wearing the same clothes, it appeared she had been up all evening. The detective's cruelness displayed less than 24 hours ago was replaced with sincere compassion. Michaels redeemed himself over their 90 minute, in prompt to, conversation.

Following his heartfelt apology and explanation, he held the weeping mother's hand and heard the life story of her child who was once a sweet boy who loved taking anything electronic apart since he was a small child and putting it back together. As he became an adult, he apprenticed with an electrical company and eventually became a talented electrician and an assistant manager at a business he was soon to run. As the story would go, like so many have experienced, all that would turn into a spiraling shit storm when the addiction to oxycodone dictated his every move. That's when her son changed and her sleepless nights began. Before leaving her home, they hugged and she graciously thanked him for stopping by.

Chapter 17

Over the next nine days the entire homicide unit investigated one case. Now partners, Dredge and Donald were deep into a brutal murder involving a suspected drug informant. The poor bastard, who according to the narcotics detectives wasn't even working with them as a confidential informant, had both hands severed from his body while alive, then decapitated with a shovel that was conveniently left behind.

The unit worked continuously interviewing witnesses and several members of a large scale cocaine organization. In need of some good news, Donald put his best good luck tool in place…he removed his pants. Now sporting plaid boxer shorts, a dress shirt, necktie, black socks and cordovan loafers, Donald made himself comfortable at his desk, enjoying a cup of coffee, while he worked on his report.

In a few short hours, Donald's good luck disrobing ritual paid off. Michaels' knowledge from being a former undercover narc proved valuable in identifying some of the main players, guiding them to one of the known muscles of the group, Alandro Perez. Luckily, Perez didn't receive his degree in street smarts or intelligence, when he purchased the shovel on camera at the nearby hardware store. Thanks to the bloody bar code on the weapon and the partial fingerprint on the handle, the 1st Degree Murder and Maiming charges kept Perez held with no bond. All in all, the newly organized unit got the chance to work together, laugh a lot, pound down a few cocktails after work and form the bond Tommy wanted. Once again, the eccentric, cocky Sergeant had sculpted an unstoppable team.

Chapter 18

Five days before the Court Martial hearing, Major Sarro and Special Agent Lenny Athas met with the military police units who first responded to the scene on the night of the attack. Together Sarro and Athas choreographed the order of witnesses, presentation of evidence and discussed in detail Athas' testimony. As for their victim, understandably so, Suk was still frightened and apprehensive to be in the same room as Schumaker. Considering everything would go as planned, arrangements were made for Suk to remain in Sarro's office under guard with Special Agent Horn on the day of the hearing until she was needed. With their first round of witness and evidence preparation complete, only three days remained. Given Sarro's determination to win this case, it wouldn't be surprising if she held one or more pre-trial prep meetings with Athas and the other witnesses.

Chapter 19

Shortly after 10 p.m., the Kim family were enjoying each other's company in their living room, sharing their happenings of the day like they did each night. Suk sat on the couch with her daughter, Seo-Yun, who was snuggled next to her eating a bowl of ice cream. Her son, Ye, sat on the floor leaning against the couch playing on his phone. Tired from a long day at work, Mr. Kim retired upstairs for the evening. Full of smiles, Seo-Yun was telling Suk about a new boy she had met at school. Being a typical brother, Ye teased her about her new friend.

What started as a relaxing evening turned to disaster. Simultaneously the three screamed at the top of their lungs. Glass from the front facing window shattered, followed by an explosion, sending shards of glass and gasoline into Suk's hair, face and clothes. A large fireball burst into their home, engulfing the curtains and the recliner where Mr. Kim had been sitting seconds before. Seo-Yun raced to the kitchen where the phone was mounted on the wall to call 911. She grabbed the receiver and pressed the numbers in an organized panic. Before the female call taker from the dispatch center was able to speak, she heard a shot ring out and the phone clatter to the floor. Bright red blood gushed from Seo-Yun's mouth and the left side of her upper arm. Her eyes rolled while she struggled to stand. The projectile shot through the window of the back door ripped through her soft skin, piercing its way through both lungs, her beating heart, only to stop in her opposite arm. Barely coherent, she stumbled to the living room where she collapsed on the couch in front of her family. This would be their last evening together.

Chapter 20

Michaels answered his desk phone. Just shy of 10:20 p.m., it was the Dispatch Center.

"Homicide, this is Detective Michaels."

"Hi Detective, this is Rose Marie from Dispatch."

"Hi Rose Marie. Now I know you're not just calling to say hello, are you? No one ever calls us to say hello," he said sarcastically.

She laughed. "Well, not really. We have a fire and a shooting in Pioneer City at 710 Arwell Court. The Fire Department is on scene, Sergeant Suit is responding, and the Evidence Collection Unit has been notified."

"Is this a homicide or just a shooting for now?" Michaels asked.

"That I don't know. The victim was transported by ambo to the hospital."

"Ok, we're on our way from the CID." Hearing half the conversation, Jim anxiously stood next to Michaels' desk. "Grab your shit partner, we got a shooting in Pioneer City. Take separate cars in case we have to split up."

When Michaels and Jim arrived, the street was lit up like a Christmas tree. Lights from the two fire trucks and numerous police cars reflected off the windows in the low rent townhouse community. Like vultures, people gathered to watch the fire personnel extinguish the blaze, still smoldering on the front of the residence. The detectives got out of their cars and cringed as they saw several fireman traipsing on the grass outside the front window, some dousing the second floor rafters with a large hose, while others used pry tools to expose the hidden floor beams. Both knew what, if any, evidence left on the ground would most likely be destroyed by the men just doing their job. Michaels lit up a cigarette. He knew this was going to be a long night.

Both walked to the front of the scene where they were greeted by longtime friend and academy buddy, Officer Kevin Falls. "Hey Ronnie, what's going on man?"

"Same old shit Kevin. What've you been up too?" Michaels said, shaking his hand. "Do you know Jim? He used to be assigned to the Eastern District, now he's in homicide with me."

"Yeah I've seen him around in court before. Nice to see you Jim. You're with a good man here," Kevin said smiling at Michaels.

"Thanks brother, so, what do we have here Kev?" Michaels asked.

Kevin looked in the direction where Suk stood crying in front of his patrol car holding her son. "See that lady wearing the sling, standing next to that kid?"

Michaels easily picked them out in the crowd. "Yeah."

"Supposedly, they were sitting in their living room along with the lady's daughter, when there was an explosion at the front of their house." Kevin pointed to a lady wearing a blue uniform kneeling next to a row of small bushes in front of the home. "That Fire Marshall over there said based on the glass fragments and smell of accelerant, someone threw a Molotov Cocktail at their window."

"Damn. I haven't heard of one of those things in a long time. I was told this was a shooting," Michaels said.

"It is. The 15-year-old ran into the kitchen to call 911 when someone shot her. The father jumped in the ambo with her, but what I've been told, she didn't make it."

"Any suspects?" Jim asked.

"I'm not really sure. I asked the son if his sister had anybody after her or if she was in a gang, but he said *no*. He said his sister never talked about anyone bothering her, but the mother…" Kevin looked down at his clipboard, "her name is Suk Kim, did say something you might want to look into. I don't know how true it is, but she said something about having a case coming up with some dude in the Army."

"Really?" Jim uttered, looking a Michaels.

"Yeah. She was crying so much I couldn't understand her. It was an attempted rape, I think. It may have just been an assault. I couldn't tell ya."

"Hey Sarge. Hey guys," Jim said noticing Tommy, Jeff and Ray walking through the crowd.

"What's going on here?" Tommy said with a concerned look. "Officer Falls, do me a favor and get these God damn people away from this lawn. This is a crime scene for Christ sake. Tie crime scene tape to the neighbors outside light and around some of these cars." Tommy's actions were typical. He was not only a former respected homicide detective, but one hell of a leader. He got shit done. Period.

"Ok people listen up," Kevin shouted to the crowd. "I need everyone in front of this address to move off the grass and the sidewalk." Many still mesmerized by the hoopla began moving a touch too slow for the officer. "C'mon people, let's go unless you plan on getting locked up tonight." The onlookers stepped up the pace while Jim and Michaels assisted him in cordoning off the area with bright yellow crime scene tape.

Tommy walked to where Michaels and Jim were tying the last end of the tape to a rainspout at the corner of the residence. "I got a call from the Dispatch Center. Doc Jones is at the hospital. Your victim was D.O.A." Tommy paused and looked at both detectives. This one is yours Ronnie. We need this solved."

"Don't worry brother. We're all over this like a cheap suit." Michaels turned his attention from Tommy and addressed Kevin once more. "Hey Kev, has anyone searched around back?"

"I don't think so. I was the first uniform to get here, and I've been busy dealing with all this shit. You want me to go look?"

"I got it Ronnie," Jim interjected.

"Thanks. I'm going inside," Michaels said.

"Oh Ronnie, I have a name of a girl who said she saw some white guy wearing a long dark dress coat. She said he was acting weird and walking in front of this place just before she heard the explosion." Officer Falls pulled out his notebook and tore out a page and handed it to Michaels. "Here's her name and number Ronnie if you want to talk with her. She lives on this block."

Michaels took the paper from Kevin and shoved it into his pants pocket. "Thanks man. Now let me get my ass inside and see what's going on."

Jim retrieved the flashlight from his car and walked toward the back of the townhome. The address where the mayhem occurred was an end unit. With only a few porch lights on, the backside of the townhouse was adjacent to a large overgrown field. The thick clouds and sliver of a moon presented the ideal cover for a lurking killer. Unsure if the gun wielding shooter was still nearby, Jim was careful to shine his light selectively with his hand close to his Sig Sauer. When he turned the corner, he could see the light from the kitchen of the crime scene. First, he inspected the six window panes on the door with his flashlight. The glass portion was covered with a cream colored curtain making it difficult to see inside. Looking closer he could see it. It was a single bullet hole. Jim slowly scanned through the uncut grass in close proximity of the door. Illuminating the hard packed dirt and matted down grass with his light he searched for shoe prints, cigarette butts or anything left behind by the killer. But nothing unique stood out. He continued his meticulous inspection of the ground and there it was, barely visible, wedged among a clump of dead grass. It was a spent 9mm shell casing. It was the brass that held the projectile which found its way into Seo-Yun's body, ending her life before it had hardly begun. He pulled out his phone to notify his partner.

Michaels answered his phone. "Let me guess, you chased the suspect down, made an apprehension and he confessed."

"No but I did find an empty shell casing along with a bullet hole in the glass on the back door. I'm going to need Jeff or Ray to measure, photograph and collect this. I don't want frost or anything to contaminate it."

"You go partner. Good find Jim. You are the fucking man," Michaels exclaimed, ecstatic to hear his discovery. "Ok buddy I'll send one of them your way."

Ray was shown the vital piece of evidence. After taking the necessary measurements and photographs, he carefully collected the casing using a pair of tweezers so not to damage any potential fingerprints. Inspecting the bottom, Jim noted the impression of the firing pin and the writing on the base which read *9mm Luger.* Secured in the clear evidence bag, Ray took a number of photographs of the bullet hole, along with the limited view of the kitchen from outside.

"This had to be a random shooting," Ray offered. "Jim, come over and stand right here." The inquisitive detective stood next to Ray. "Call Ronnie and tell him to stand where the phone is." Jim dialed up Michaels and instructed him to stand by the phone. He did so and Jim could barely make out his own partner.

"Shit you're right. Maybe it was some type of gang initiation or something. I mean, fuck, a Molotov Cocktail and a blind shot through a curtain? That doesn't make any sense," Jim said perplexed.

Inside, the scene consisted of no evidence except for the blood-soaked couch cushion where Seo-Yun sat until she was rushed out by paramedics. The fireman finished up and soon the bright flashing lights diminished to just the few streetlights that still worked. Outside, a few nosey people hung around, but most wandered back to wherever they came from. With the outside of the townhouse now processed, Jim and Ray joined Michaels and Jeff inside.

"What do you need me to do Ronnie?" Jim asked.

"How about you stay here until the crime scene is done and I'll take Mrs. Kim and her son to the office and take their statements."

"What's on your mind Jim? You're staring at the front of the house like you see a ghost," Michaels inquired.

"This might be a longshot, but before we leave, I want to collect as much of the glass used for this Molotov Cocktail as we can. Who knows, it may provide something," Jim said.

"Look at you Jim. Great idea. Have Ray and Jeff help you. We'll hook up in a few hours. See ya buddy."

"Sounds good," Jim said as he walked toward the charred overhang.

Chapter 21

Outside the living quarters where Sergeant Schumaker seldomly resided, fifteen soldiers milled around in civilian attire after their fire alarm bell sounded. Oddly referred to as a GI Party, this evening was set aside for a thorough cleaning of the barracks by the residing soldiers, regardless if they lived their part time or not. It was the military's way of naming something that couldn't be anything further than the truth. Unsure of who or why the alarm was pulled, several of the men walked to the adjacent parking lot, while others stood in the grass. It was an unorganized evacuation to say the least and all the men knew it was bullshit. While they awaited the arrival of the Fort Meade Fire Department, Sergeant Schumaker appeared among the crowd sweating and panting heavily. Schumaker mingled among the crowd, making short meaningless conversations with some of the soldiers.

At the Army CID office, Special Agent Athas sat across from Lieutenant Lindner's desk talking about the much-anticipated court martial.

"Have you supplied Major Sarro everything she needs for trial Lenny?"

"Yes sir, two copies of everything. One for defense counsel and one for her. This should only last a day or two at most. There's not many witnesses to testify," Athas pointed out.

Lindner looked at his watch and picked up an envelope from his desk. "Lenny it's getting close to quitting time. Can you drop this off to Captain Weinman's office on your way home? I'm sure he's not there this late, but if you could slide it under his door that would be great."

"You got it boss. Let me take care of a few things here first and I'll get it right over."

"Thanks Lenny. It's been a long day. I'm out of here."

"Yes sir. Good night Lieutenant."

Still in her office working late, Major Sarro could see the red flashing fire truck speeding toward Schumaker's barracks. She stood from her chair and watched.

After the all clear was announced, the men reluctantly filed into their building like ants using both the front and back doors. Cognizant of the disorder taking place, Schumaker left his car on the lot, walked toward the roadway and out of sight. He knew he had been seen by several soldiers.

Chapter 22

Already aware of Seo-Yun's death from her husband, Michaels drove Suk and Ye to the police department's CID. Together, they sat in the back of Michaels' car crying and clutching on to one another.

"I'm really sorry about your loss Mrs. Kim. When we get to my office, I want to talk with both of you so we can determine who would do such a thing. Start thinking of who Seo-Yun's enemies were, who she may have upset recently," Michaels suggested. "Unless this was a random shooting, somebody wanted her dead."

"Or me," Suk said softly while she sobbed.

Michaels re-adjusted the rear-view mirror to see Suk's face. "What do you mean?"

"That soldier. The one who did this to me," she said lifting up her broken arm.

Michaels jerked the steering wheel to the right and his car skidded to a stop on the gravel shoulder. He turned and faced Suk. "What soldier?" Suk put her head down and tried to hold back her tears. "Tell me. This is very important," Michaels urged.

"A soldier tried to rape me a little over a week ago. He broke my arm during the attack, and I've seen him behind my house since then."

Michaels threw the car into drive and sped to his office only a few minutes away. Inside the CID, Suk couldn't withhold her tears as she cried and yelled her daughter's name. An hour after arriving, Suk settled in and told Michaels of the horrifying evening she was nearly raped. Everything was now clear to Michaels. Tears poured from her eyes as she relived the evening once more telling the story over again. The feelings of guilt took hold of her mind and body, causing her nearly to faint. Feeling her daughter's death could have been averted had she not pursued the matter with the military police, overcame her. Michaels walked to the Rape Squad and checked with good friend, Detective Bonnie Lowe, about Suk's attempted rape, but she was unaware of any such case. Michaels was confused and worried Suk had never reported the incident. Frustrated, he walked to his office where Suk sat.

Michaels took a seat behind his desk. "Suk, did you report this attempted rape you just told me about?" Michaels handed her more tissues and sat back in his chair. Suk couldn't control her emotions.

She continued looking down. "Yes, Agent Athas is handling it."

Michaels was confused when she said the word agent. "Suk, is the military handling this case? Did you report this to them?"

She wiped the tears from her face and opened her purse. She pulled out her wallet and handed Agent Athas' business card to Michaels.

"Special Agent Leonard Athas, United States Army, Fort George G. Meade, Criminal Investigation Division." He flipped the card over and saw a handwritten cell number. "If you'd excuse me Suk." Astounded with the news, Michaels dashed to Sergeant Suit's office to make a phone call to Special Agent Athas. Michaels sat behind Suit's desk and with a clean piece of paper from his notebook ready, he placed the call.

"Hello, this is Agent Athas."

"Hi Agent Athas. My name is Detective Michaels with the Anne Arundel County Police Homicide Unit."

"Homicide? Well, good evening Detective, what can I do for you?"

"We had a murder this evening…"

Athas swiftly interrupted. With a large lump in his throat, he struggled to speak. "Oh my God, don't tell me it was Suk Kim?"

Michaels was caught off guard from his response. "No Agent. It was her daughter. What do you know?"

"Damn." There was silence. "I'm sorry Detective, but I was afraid something like this would happen. FUCK," he yelled.

"We need to meet. What's your first name?" Michaels asked.

"It's Lenny. Lenny Athas."

"Ok Lenny. My name is Ronnie Michaels. Where can we meet after I'm done interviewing Suk?"

"How about my office? Do you know where the Army CID building is?"

"I haven't been there in years. Is it still at the same place?"

Athas snickered. "Hell yes, we'll never move from this dump."

"I hear ya. I'll meet you there in about an hour when I get done with Suk and her son."

"Roger that."

Michaels returned to his desk when he noticed Dredge and Donald strolling in. "Hey guys. Suk, Ye, let me introduce you to Detectives Dave Hart and Donald Hauf. They are homicide detectives and they will be working on this case with me."

In his low somber voice Dredge offered his assistance. "Tommy told us to come by and see what you need."

"Suk, excuse us, we'll be right back. Let's go into Tommy's office and I'll fill you in." The three men stood in front of their sergeant's desk. Dredge closed the door and lit a cigarette. Michaels laid out the limited details he knew of the murder and the attempted rape. "If you guys wouldn't mind taking statements from both Suk and her son while I go over to the Army CID building, that would be great."

"Sure son. Were they both in the house when it occurred?" Dredge asked.

"Yeah. Be sure to have Suk lay out the attack on her and everything she did with the Army to get this soldier charged."

Dredge took a big draw on his Merit cigarette and looked toward the ceiling. "He wasn't held until court for this?"

"Fuck no. Sounds like our court system huh?" Michaels commented.

The man of few words grunted and snuffed his cigarette out in the ashtray on Tommy's desk. Within minutes, Michaels rushed to meet Special Agent Athas while Dredge and Donald began the tedious task of typing detailed statements from both witnesses.

Michaels parked in the reserved parking spot near the front door listed for the Army *CID Commander*. Inside he and Athas introduced themselves then talked like they had known each other for years. In the law enforcement world, regardless of where you worked, whether you were a fed, in the military or a local cop, you were part of a brotherhood and could speak to each other like family and that's exactly what they did. Now the motive which triggered the tragic events that unfolded just hours before was clear.

Athas sat at his desk while Michaels made himself comfortable at Agent Horn's desk. Both had similar notebooks in their hands writing feverishly on the fresh pages.

Athas laid his notebook down and leaned back in the chair. "What I don't get is, why did he kill her daughter? That doesn't make sense."

"Because he couldn't tell it was her, plain and simple. The curtain on the back door had light enough fabric where you could make out a person, but not enough to identify someone."

"Would he have known if it were a male or female?" Athas asked.

"Oh, fuck yeah," Michaels snapped.

"Well that makes sense then, because they are both short and have the same build and hair style," Athas added.

Athas searched through his cell phone and called a number. After five rings a sleepy sounding voice answered. "Hello."

"Major Sarro, this is Agent Athas. Sorry to call so late, but I thought you'd want to know this."

Freshly divorced, Major Sarro was alone in her quaint two-bedroom home, courtesy of the United States Army. She flicked on the lamp and propped herself up. Next to her on the nightstand was a half full glass of white wine and a pad of paper and pen she used frequently to jot down notes, even at the oddest hours.

"What is it?" she said trying to clear her head.

"Our victim, Suk Kim…her daughter is dead."

Sarro sat up. Her eyes blinked rapidly. She reached over and guzzled down the last of the wine. "What? Oh no. Are you serious? That poor family. What happened?" she asked, not prepared for what she was about to hear.

"He killed her ma'am…Schumaker. It had to be him."

Her mouth dropped. Anger rained over her. "That son of a bitch. He killed her daughter? Why? Why for Christ sake? Is he trying to scare her from testifying? Jesus fucking Christ."

"I'm at the office with the detective from the county homicide unit and we're trying to figure that out ourselves. The detective said she was shot from the outside, through a glass pane in the backdoor that had a curtain. He said it was hard to see through. The shooter may not have known who he was shooting."

"Stay put Lenny. Let me get dressed. I'll be right over."

"Yes ma'am."

Athas swung his chair around. Michaels was already facing him listening to his conversation. "That was the Major from the JAG office who's prosecuting our case. She's on her way."

"JAG Office?"

"Yeah. It stands for Judge Advocate General. That's what the military legal office is called. It's similar to your States Attorney and Public Defender's Offices."

"So, where can I find this Schumaker guy?" Michaels asked.

"He has assigned living quarters on base, but because he's a sergeant he's permitted to reside off base as well. I learned he frequently stays at his girlfriend's condo. I dug up her address. He's required to keep that on file."

Athas searched through the accordion folder on his desk, stuffed with reports and photographs. He burrowed through and produced a piece of thin teletype paper. "Here's the information on his car. Do you want it?"

Michaels flipped to a new page in his notebook. "Yeah, go with it."

"He drives a 1995 Honda Civic, with Georgia plates N52585, listed to an address of 1017 Jazzman Place." Athas pulled out a second piece of paper. "Here we go. His girlfriend's name is Venessa Kinley. Her address is 22595 Laurel Way, condo 24." Michaels scribbled the information in his notebook when he was startled by the opening of the office front door. In stormed Major Sarro dressed in street clothes.

Athas stood from his chair and saluted the Major. Sarro returned the salute and immediately walked toward Michaels to introduced herself.

"Hi Detective. I'm Dawn Sarro with the JAG Office." The two shook hands and she pulled up a chair across from Michaels.

"It's nice to meet you. My name is Ronnie Michaels. I'm with the county Homicide Unit."

"How can we help your case?" she asked. "I want to put this smug son of a bitch away forever. Oh, sorry for my language," she said.

"No apology needed. I'm old school police. I don't like sick fucks like him."

"Good." Sarro smiled and drew her attention to Athas. "Lenny, you have my permission to share everything we have with Detective Michaels. Give him our reports, statements, whatever we have."

"Roger that Major. Will do."

"As you all know, in cases like these, we work from the inside out. Obviously, Schumaker is the most likely one to have motive to kill in this case, whether it was accidental or for intimidation purposes. When is his military hearing anyway?"

Sarro let out a sarcastic laugh. "It's in five days. Five fucking days and he does this?"

Michaels closed his notebook and stood from his chair. "Can you all take me to his residence on base?"

"His barracks? Sure, do you want to take my car?" Athas offered.

"No, I'll follow, in case I get my hands on him," Michaels said.

"Here's an extra mugshot and copies of our reports and statements for your file," Athas said handing him a 5x7 black and white picture of Schumaker stapled to the outside of a Manilla folder.

Michaels studied the picture while Athas and Sarro watched. "The face of a rapist and a killer. They come in all shapes, sizes and colors, but one thing they all have in common is that cold look in their eyes. Let's go find him."

The three made their way to the parking lot, when Sarro stopped short before opening the passenger door to Athas' car. "Detective Michaels, I failed to tell you something. Fuck." About to get in his car, Michaels stopped and looked inquisitively at Sarro. "He's already retained counsel."

Michaels snickered. "Maybe he has in your case, but not mine. Fuck him. Let's go."

Sarro turned to Athas, "I like him."

On the way to Schumaker's barracks, Athas and Sarro both found it odd when they noticed the light on in Captain Weinman's office, and his SUV parked out front.

"That's awfully strange. Why is that asshole in his office so late?" Sarro pointed out.

"I couldn't tell you ma'am, but that sure doesn't make any sense."

A few minutes later, they arrived at Schumaker's barracks. By now it was midnight and the lights were out. Athas scanned the parking lot. Schumaker's car was nowhere to be found.

"I don't see his car," Athas said quietly.

"Fuck it. Let's wake everyone up. I need to look for myself," Sarro said.

With Athas leading the way, the three barged through the front door of the barracks and switched on the main overhead light. Most of the soldiers sat up in their bunks. Some bitched and complained, while others buried their heads beneath their pillows.

"Listen up everyone. For those of you who don't know me, I'm Special Agent Athas from the Army CID. If you don't know what that is, it stands for the Criminal Investigation Division. I need Sergeant Schumaker out of his bunk, front and center, now…," he shouted. "Sergeant Wesley Schumaker, are you here?" Athas questioned loudly.

One of the soldiers from the middle of the barrack spoke. "He's not here sir. Now can you turn the lights out?"

Athas was determined. "Which rack is his?"

Someone else chimed in. "Number 5. He's never here. Please kill the lights sir, I need to get up in two hours."

Athas turned to Major Sarro and Detective Michaels. "Are we good?"

"I don't see him," Sarro said.

"Let's go." Athas slapped the light switch to the off position and the three walked to the parking lot.

"Now where? His girlfriend's place?" Michaels asked. I know right where her condo is. It's not too far from here. Follow me," Michaels said.

"Wait Detective. Technically, that's out of my jurisdiction and I'm not permitted to assist another agency outside of a military installation without a whole bunch of red tape," Athas reluctantly said.

"Get in the car Lenny. Screw Army policy. We need to find this sick bastard," Sarro asserted.

"Yes ma'am," Athas sneered.

Michaels sped to the Laurel condo complex, located 15 minutes from the Ft. Meade base. They parked in the two handicap spots in front of the building and got out of their cars. The three scanned the lot in search of Schumaker's Civic. It was nowhere in sight.

"I don't see it," Michaels said.

"Me either," Athas added.

"Fuck it. You got your gun?" Michaels asked.

"Well, umm…yes sir," Athas answered, looking at Sarro for direction.

"Lenny the way I see this, we have a rouge soldier on our hands. I'm sure there is something on the books that says we can assist outside jurisdictions in cases like these, so let's go." The three hurried into the building and scaled the steps to the second level.

"Number 24?" Michaels asked.

"Yes," whispered Athas. Michaels looked at the dimly lit peephole, then placed his ear close to the door.

"Do you hear anybody inside?" Sarro asked.

Michaels carefully rested his head against the door and listened. "Nope. Nothing." He pounded on the door three times with his fist. He looked once more at the peephole, waiting for it to darken, but there was nothing. He knocked harder, but still no response.

"He's gone dark on us," Sarro said.

"Major, isn't Schumaker supposed to be under the care and control of Captain Weinman at all times?" Athas asked.

"Who is Captain Weinman?" questioned Michaels.

Sarro rolled her eyes. "That's his captain extraordinaire. The most arrogant asshole you'll ever meet. But that's a good point Lenny. Technically he is."

"Well, if he's supposed to be under his care, why not call him now?" Michaels suggested.

Sarro and Athas looked at one another. "That would be up to Major Sarro," Athas offered.

Sarro searched through her phone and called Captain Weinman's cell. Michaels and Athas stood silently in the hallway and watched. After two rings the phone went to voicemail.

"That fuck ball declined my call. How dare he. The nerve of that bastard. I'm calling him again." This time it went straight to voicemail. Captain Weinman had turned off his phone.

"Ok, let's get out of here. I need to head to the office. I'll give you guys a shout in the morning. If you hear anything, call me. I don't care what time it is," Michaels told them.

"Sounds good. We'll talk in the morning," Athas said.

Sarro reached out and shook Michaels' hand. Her strong grip got his attention. "Remember, whatever you need, just ask. I want to see him go down."

"Thank you Major. I appreciate all your help. I'll reach out in the morning unless I hear from you sooner."

Back at the county CID building, Michaels joined Jim, Donald and Dredge in Tommy's smoked filled office.

Tommy lowered his coffee cup from his mouth. "Shithead," he yelled.

"Boys, boys," Michaels said, lighting up a Marlboro. "Jim, I didn't know you smoked."

Jim pulled the Black & Mild plastic tipped cigar from his mouth and forced out a puff of smoke. He laughed while he looked at his burning stogie. "I figured if you can't beat 'em, join 'em."

"What do ya got Ronnie?" Tommy asked.

"We got a sergeant in the Army on the run who is about to be tried for an attempted rape in five days… who either killed the wrong person or is one desperate fuck trying to keep Suk from testifying against him."

"What makes you think he's on the run?" Jim asked.

"Put it this way. He ain't at his living quarters, nor is he at his girlfriend's."

Sitting comfortably in the leather chair across from Tommy's desk, Dredge spoke up. "Donald and I canvassed the entire neighborhood, and no one saw shit. Hell, most people wouldn't even open their doors for us. I put both witness statements on your desk."

"Thanks guys," Michaels said.

Looking at his burning cigar, Jim told of his latest discovery. "I identified your Molotov Cocktail." Jim now had everyone's attention. "Remember I told you I wanted to gather the glass from the container used?"

Michaels was all ears. "Yeah."

"Well, me, your Dad and Jeff filled up several evidence bags with glass, which I'm sure some belonged to the front window, but I did find a partially burnt label." Jim flipped several pages back in his notebook. "Here it is. The purple label had orange writing written on it, *Orange Raspberry*. It's a 64 ounce bottle made by *Tropicana Twister.*"

"Sixty-four ounces? Damn Ronnie, that would hold a shit ton of gas," Donald blurted out.

"Jeff has the glass fragments. He said he would submit them to the FBI to re-construct the bottle from the pieces we found."

"Damn partner, good find again," Michaels boasted. "Guys, thanks for all your help. Tommy if it's ok with you, Jim and I will get in early tomorrow so we can track down our suspect."

"Sure Ronnie. What else do you need?" Tommy asked.

Michaels took a long drag from his cigarette. "Either a real good witness or some luck. I'll take either one right now. Dredge, did Suk tell you where they would be staying tonight?"

"Yes, at a relative's house close to Suk's work. I'll leave the address and phone number on your desk."

"Great buddy. Thanks."

Tommy snuffed out his cigarette. "Alright guys, overall this was a very successful evening. Good work everyone. Dredge, you and Donald work evenings tomorrow in case something comes in. Ronnie, I'll see you and Jim in the morning." After a few minutes the men herded from the building and made their way home.

Michaels parked in front of his townhome next to Katie's shiny black Mercedes Benz. With several things still left to bring over, this would be the first evening she and Kathryn would begin living in their new home. Michaels shut off his car and paused before he stepped out. How nice he thought it was going to be to finally have someone he cared for by his side each night. The smile on his face grew bigger when he saw the door to his home open. Katie filled the doorway in a silk nightgown holding two glasses of wine in her hand. She had been waiting and watching for Michaels to arrive.

"Well look at this surprise. Oh my God Katie, you didn't have to wait up for me baby. You look amazing."

Katie handed him his glass of Merlot and kissed him softly on his lips. Michaels walked inside and she closed the door behind him. She sat her glass on the table next to the door and wrapped her arms around his shoulders and looked deep into his eyes. "I wanted to make our first night special. Michaels started to speak but Katie put her finger to his lips. "Shhh. Thanks for having us. Kathryn is sleeping, but she's been in her room all night decorating. It's the first I've seen her this happy in weeks. So, I just wanted to say thank you. Thank you for being there for me when I was supposed to be there for you. I love you. Now come in Detective and tell me all about your evening. Since I didn't hear from you, I assumed something happened. Did you get a case?"

The two sat in the living room for the next two hours and talked of Michaels' evening. They polished off the large bottle of wine, while Katie listened intently. She was intrigued and touched by the meaningless death of Seo-Yun, almost the same age as Kathryn. Sitting side by side on the couch holding hands, their conversation soon turned from work to the newest step in their relationship. A touch tipsy from the potent wine, they embraced on the couch and clawed at one another's clothes while their lips explored each other's face and neck. Without a word they continued to kiss and disrobe one another down the hallway like two newlyweds.

A trail of pants, shirts and underwear followed them into the bedroom they now shared. It would be a night of passionate ecstasy.

Chapter 23

Early the next morning Tommy, Jim and Ronnie formulated a game plan over coffee, cigarettes and a Black & Mild cigar. Tommy paced the center aisle of the squad room, listening to his men, then guiding them to the best possible tactic. Michaels propped open the back door and the cold air swirled the smoke about the room.

Using his desk phone, he placed a call to Agent Athas' office. "I wonder what time these guys get in?" Michaels asked.

"Army CID, Special Agent Athas."

"Hey Lenny, it's Ronnie Michaels from county homicide."

"Good morning Ronnie. I had a feeling you guys might be in early today, so I made sure I was too. What can I do for you?"

"Has anyone heard or seen our boy, Schumaker?"

Athas laughed. "Nope, not a peep. I drove through the parking lot of his barracks this morning and didn't see his car. Have you been over to his girlfriend's yet?"

"No, not yet. Can I get that Captain's name and telephone number, the one that's supposed to be babysitting him?" Michaels asked.

"Absolutely." Athas pulled the Garrison directory from his desk drawer and gave him Captain Stanley Weinman's office number. "Let me know if you need us to do something on our end."

"Ok thanks. Hey, what time does this Captain roll in?"

Athas looked at his watch. "Probably by 0900."

"Great. Thanks Lenny, I'll keep you posted."

Tommy stood in the doorway by the rear office stairwell looking out to the woods bordering the old CID building. He lit another cigarette. "No word from our guy?"

"Nope. They haven't heard shit. And he's not at his barracks either. I'm calling his captain to see if he has a clue where he is."

Michaels pressed the numbers firmly on his phone while Jim and Tommy watched. The phone rang five times and just as Michaels was about to hang up a voice came over the phone.

"Good morning, Captain Weinman's office."

"Yes hi, my name is Detective Michaels with the Anne Arundel County Police Homicide Unit. Is Captain Weinman in?"

"No he's not, but he should be in soon. Shall I have him call you Detective?"

"Yes ma'am that would be great. I'll give you my cell number."

Michaels gave the secretary his number and hung up. By now Tommy and Jim were standing in front of Michaels' desk. "Ronnie, while you're waiting for him to call, why don't you and Jim take a drive to his girlfriend's house," Tommy said.

"I sure would like to know where this asshole is," Jim exclaimed.

"That makes two of us. Let me grab a coffee for the road and we can get out of here partner."

Jim and Michaels freshened their cups, put their overcoats on and made their way to Michaels' car. Fifteen minutes into the half hour trip, Michaels' cell phone rang. It was the same number he had called earlier to Weinman's office. "Michaels."

"Yeah, this is Captain Stanley Weinman with the United States Army. Whom am I speaking with?" sounded the stern voice.

Michaels put his phone on speaker and nudged Jim's arm. "This is Detective Ronald Michaels with the Anne Arundel County Police Homicide Unit. How are you this fine morning?" Michaels said sarcastically. Jim and Michaels both smiled.

"I'm busy, that's how I am. What is it that you need?" he asked in a curt tone.

Michaels jerked his head back, stunned by the man's shitty demeanor. "What I need is to speak with Wesley Schumaker, sir."

"I don't know how you civilians act, but he's a sergeant. I prefer my men to be addressed accordingly, God knows we deserve it."

Michaels and Jim were astonished with what they were hearing. Fearful to damage his chances of speaking with his suspect, Michaels patronized the captain. "Sorry sir. My apologies, yes of course." Michaels paused. "I need to speak with Sergeant Schumaker."

"He's been on leave for a few days, but I'll have my secretary leave this for him when he returns."

"Well thank you so much sir and when do you expect...." Before Michaels could finish his question, the phone went dead. "That motherfucker hung up on me. Can you believe that arrogant asshole?"

"What a dick. He sounded like Jack Nicholson in that movie, *A Few Good Men*," Jim said.

"Yeah, you're right. I guess I should have yelled *You can't handle the truth*!" They both laughed. "Hey Jim, it's still early, before we see if this girl is home, let's check the local stores around the area of our crime scene to see if any carry the big bottle of Orange Raspberry you found. Off the top of my head, I can't think of any more than ten to fifteen stores."

"Fuck, why not? We can knock that out in no time the way you drive," Jim said sarcastically.

"Christ, now you're starting to sound like Dredge. There's nothing wrong with my driving. I just don't like fucking around. I wanna get where I'm going so I can do what I gotta do and go. It's that fucking simple."

Jim added his two cents. "Yeah, but every time I get into this car, I feel like I'm on a scary ride at the carnival. I'm waiting for some man to reach over and buckle me into a five-point harness." Michaels laughed. "Really, there should be a recording that says... *place your head firmly on the seat rest, be sure your safety strap is secure and hold the fuck on. You're about to go for the ride of your life...good luck you poor bastard.*" By now both were nearly pissing their pants while they belly laughed the entire way to the first store.

"You get the first one," Michaels said, barely able to speak. "I can't stop laughing." Jim dried his eyes and walked into the small local store that carried the basic essential groceries, breakfast foods, snacks, and a wide assortment of drinks. Still hardly able to contain his laughter, Jim perused the shelves, but there were no Tropicana Fruit drinks of any sizes.

Over the next hour, Michaels and Jim scoured every store that sold drinks in a 25-mile radius of the homicide scene. None of them carried the item they were searching for, but oddly enough, all the stores were the mom and pop types, none were large grocery stores, except one.

"Isn't there a Giant Food store close to Venessa's condo?" Jim asked.

"Yeah Jim. I forgot about that one. Hell, it's only about a football field away from her condo too."

Michaels double parked his new grey unmarked car in the fire lane of the Giant Food store. "Come on partner, let's both check this one out," Michaels said with a glimmer of enthusiasm in his voice.

From the look on his face, Jim was noticeably excited. "I have a good feeling about this one." The two walked into the store and as luck would have it, the drink isle was directly in front of them.

"That's a good sign," Jim said. Their pace quickened as they simultaneously locked in on the large glass drinks on the bottom shelf.

"That looks like the one brother. Same color label," Jim said, bending down taking hold of the bottle like it was a bar of gold. They both eyed up the container. "Yup, 64 ounces. That's definitely the same label as the one at the scene. No doubt. That can hold an awful lot of gas," Jim exclaimed.

"No wonder the fire was so big. They're lucky they all didn't burn to death," Michaels said.

Jim nodded. "I was thinking the same thing the night we were there."

"Come on, I'm going to buy this son of a bitch," Michaels said.

Now in possession of a duplicate of their shattered explosive device, the men made their way to the parking lot where Venessa lived.

"I don't see his car," Jim said scouring the lot.

"Fuck it. Let's knock on the door anyway," Michaels asserted.

Inside the building, Michaels could hear sounds from inside. "I can hear a TV. It sounds like it's coming from the living room." Michaels tapped three times on the door using the brushed nickel door knocker. He backed up and watched the peephole. Impatiently, he took hold of the knocker and tapped harder. "This is bullshit. I'll pound on this door all fucking day until someone answers." Michaels prepared to pound on the door with his fist when he heard movement inside. The light from the peephole darkened.

"Who is it?" a female mumbled.

"County police," Michaels said holding up his badge in his wallet.

The door opened and there stood an attractive white female, with shoulder length blonde hair wearing colorful cotton pajamas. From the looks of her eyes and disheveled hair, it was obvious she'd been sleeping. She rubbed her eyes and attempted to focus on the two men.

"Are you Venessa?" Michaels asked.

"Yes. What happened?" she asked with a concerned look.

"I'm Detective Ronnie Michaels and this is Detective Jim Rzepkowski." Michaels and Jim made their way into the foyer uninvited. Venessa backed up. "Is Wesley Schumaker here?" Michaels asked bluntly.

"No, no he's not. But I've been out of town for a few days. I just flew in late last night. What's wrong?"

"Can we sit down and talk?" Michaels and Jim made their way further into her home.

"Ok, yes come in. Would you please tell me what's wrong?"

Both detectives took seats in the living room. Venessa slid the blanket to the side on the couch where she had been sleeping and sat down.

"Venessa, when's the last time you talked to Wesley?" Michaels inquired.

She scooted to the edge of the couch. "Is Wes hurt? Tell me. Is he ok?"

Jim had his notebook open and looked at Michaels. "Yes, he's fine, but we need to ask you a few things. Are you aware of the military charges he's facing?" Michaels asked.

Venessa relaxed and leaned back. "Yes, that whole thing is just crazy. Like Wes said, it's your typical case of mistaken identity. I mean she is Asian. He's not worried about it at all, but what's that have to do with you guys? You did say you're with the county police, right?"

"We're just investigating a firebombing at the person's house who accused Wesley. We don't believe Wes is involved, but we have to clear him." Since Michaels hadn't said he was a homicide detective, he purposefully left out the fact they were investigating a murder. Michaels loved the fact he was lying his ass off to Venessa, but he didn't care. Just like his old undercover days, he lied to get information. This time it was all about learning everything he could to help his case.

Her shoulders lowered and the wrinkles on her face disappeared. "Well sure. What can I do for you?"

Michaels knew he had her just where he wanted. "We have a lot of things at our scene. Frankly, it was a real junk heap." Michaels was setting her up and she had no idea what she was about to walk into. Michaels pulled his notebook from his inside suitcoat pocket and opened it to a blank page. He may just as well have been pulling out a fishing line and putting a big juicy worm on a hook, meant just for Venessa. "Ok Venessa, we have a lot of burned cigarette butts at our scene. What brand does Wesley smoke?"

"Oh, Wes doesn't smoke." She leaned back in her seat. Michaels could tell she was untroubled and now comfortable talking. Michaels acted as if he was making notations in his notebook from her answers, but he wasn't. It was all an act.

"Let's see here. How about fast food? The person who lit this fire may have been munching out on some fast food before he lit this place up. Does Wesley have a favorite joint he loves?"

Venessa smiled and chuckled. "Oh yeah. That's a thing between us. Every time we go out for fast food, we must go to Burger King for him and Arby's for me, and then we park somewhere and eat together. That's just our thing."

Michaels looked at Jim. "Well partner I guess we can throw away the Hardees' bags we have."

"Yes, we sure can," Jim said, playing along.

Michaels laughed as he made out once again to be writing in his notebook, knowing he was about to cast the baited hook in front of her. Jim sat quietly across from Michaels with his own notebook open in his hand. Michaels looked at Venessa and smiled with a look of relief on his face. "Boy I'll tell you what, you sure are helping us clear a lot of junk out of our evidence room, thanks."

"Oh, no problem."

Michaels looked down and flipped the page. He raised both eyebrows and made a look of astonishment, like he had just read something of surprise in his notebook. "Oh, I almost forgot. What about fruit drinks? Does Wes have any particular fruit drink he likes?" Michaels raised his head and looked nonchalantly at her.

Venessa smiled. "Now there is something that Wes and I both agree on. We have a favorite drink we both love. Darn, what's it called?" she asked herself out loud. She ran her fingers through her hair while she racked her brain.

Michaels' eyes darted over to Jim who was enjoying the show. The two looked at each other briefly then drew their attention back to Venessa. Michaels sat anxiously in his seat, repeating the flavor Orange Raspberry, Orange Raspberry, Orange Raspberry to himself, thinking subliminally it would transfer to her.

She finally spoke. "Orange Raspberry. That's it. Orange Raspberry, that's what it is."

Michaels and Jim glanced at each other quickly so not to draw attention to her response. It was all either could do to hold back their smiles. It was an exact match of the flavor listed on the partial label from the Molotov cocktail.

Venessa stood from the couch and walked toward the kitchen. "Here, take a look." Michaels followed close behind like a puppy dog, curious to what he was about to see. "I can show you. We bought two bottles before I left town. We drank one of them. It may be in the trash, unless Wes emptied it. Venessa looked inside the kitchen trash can, moved a few things to the side. "Nope, he didn't empty the trash." With that, she pulled out the gem. An empty 64-ounce bottle of Orange Raspberry, by Tropicana Twister. It was a replica of the one used the night of the murder.

"Do you mind if I take that with me? I'll just throw it away when I'm done, if that's ok with you?" Venessa handed him the bottle. Michaels gripped it tightly. He knew once it was in his hands, he wasn't about to give it back. *This is mine now,* he thought to himself.

"Yeah, that's fine. I don't want it back. Let's see...the other one should be in the fridge. She opened the refrigerator. "Hmmmm....it's gone." Michaels stood beside her. He could plainly see the barren refrigerator was void of the second bottle. An awkward silence came over the room while she stared at the empty shelves.

"That's strange. He couldn't have drunk that whole thing that fast."

Michaels hid the smirk on his face. He and Jim both knew where the missing bottle was...in about 100 pieces, scorched from flames and tainted with fuel in evidence bags at headquarters.

The three returned to the living room and sat down. The look on Venessa's face had changed from calm to uneasiness. "Should I be giving that to you?" she questioned Michaels.

Michaels ignored her. Tension blanketed the room. He knew there was no way he was giving the bottle back. Never. Quickly he changed the topic. "When was the last time you saw Wes?"

She paused. "Just before I went to New York for my job."

Michaels continued with his questioning. "Do you know where he is now? We just need to clarify a few things with him so we can put this to rest."

Michaels and Jim watched Venessa struggled to answer the question. "Umm, he said he was going away for a few days to visit his parents."

Michaels could hear the reluctance in her voice to answer his question. He knew it was time to turn up the heat. "Christ Venessa, I feel like I'm at the damn dentist office. Why do I feel like I'm pulling teeth here? I'm just asking you a few basic questions. Are you covering for him or something?" he said raising his voice.

Her eyes welled with tears. "No, no. I'm not covering up anything….I"

Michaels interrupted and kept his stern tone. "Well, I sure fucking hope not. I wouldn't want to see you get wrapped up into something you didn't do. So…where does Wesley's parents live?"

She looked at the floor and spoke softly. "They live in Georgia. I don't know exactly where."

"Do you know when he'll be back?" Michaels asked forcefully.

"Huh?" she said under her breath.

Michaels moved to the edge of his seat and leaned in her direction. He was pissed. "When the fuck will he be back Venessa?"

Tears dropped from her eyes onto the carpet. She began shaking her head. "I don't know. I don't know. I'm sorry but he didn't tell me."

"Ok, we're leaving now. When you see Wesley have him call me." Michaels tossed his business card on the couch next to her. "My cell number is on the back and thanks for the bottle." Jim stood up and couldn't hold back the smile on his face when he heard Michaels' parting comment. The two detectives walked to Michaels' car without a word. Once seated inside, they both laughed and shouted with excitement.

"Holy shit, did you see her face when she opened that fucking empty refrigerator?" Michaels said.

"I know. You were standing so close to her you practically had your head on her shoulder. It's a good thing she didn't see you. You had the biggest smile I've ever seen on your face," Jim said while slapping Michaels a high five. "Good job brother. You couldn't have set her up any better. That was fun to watch."

"Thanks to her, we now have enough to get a search warrant for her place. Hopefully, we'll find the gun or ammo matching the one you found at the crime scene."

"When we get back to the office, I'm going to contact Tropicana Twister and see if they can tell us any other stores in the area that carry that size and brand of fruit drink," Jim said.

"Good idea. While you're doing that, I'll fill in Major Sarro and Athas, then start on the Search Warrant. They're gonna love this."

By early evening Jim and Michaels did what they had set out to do. They were armed with one Search and Seizure Warrant and had received another bit of damaging information from a Tropicana Twister rep. The Giant Food store, located a short distance from Venessa's home, was the only store in the nearby area that kept their inventory stocked with Tropicana Orange-Raspberry, 64-ounce bottles. The excellent detective work sparked by Jim added yet another piece to the puzzle, implicating Wesley Schumaker as their killer.

By now Dredge and Donald had made their way into the CID building. With his entire squad together, Tommy emerged from his office to address his troops. "I want everyone in here tomorrow afternoon. We're going to execute a Search Warrant on their suspect's condo. Jim and Shithead did a good job." Like a proud father, Tommy leaned over and gave both Michaels and

Jim a stinging high five. "That's what I'm fucking talking about." Tommy had a unique way of keeping everyone charged up, regardless of the time of day, or how long anyone had been awake, and this case was no different than the others.

By 2:30 p.m. the next day everyone was gathered back in the office along with Jeff Cover. Smoking a cigarette and drinking his coffee in the middle of the squad room, Tommy walked the center aisle slowly talking to everyone. "Shithead, you and Jim drive with me. Dredge, you and Donald can drive in one car in case something comes in, and Jeff you can follow us. The S.W.A.T. Team is meeting us at the Giant Food store near her house. Ronnie, once we get there you can drive with the S.W.A.T Team Sergeant and show him where the residence is. You boys ready?"

"I am. Let's do this," Michaels said. "I'd love to find that fucking gun."

The men made their way to their cars and began their caravan to the grocery store. Not much was said in Tommy's car on the drive over. Everyone was pre-occupied thinking about what they were going to discover.

Corralled in the same lot where Michaels and Jim were the day before, the men looked over the physical layout of the dwelling and discussed their assignments.

"Sergeant Suit, who's taking me for a drive-bye," Sergeant Cain of the S.W.A.T. Team asked.

"Detective Michaels will show you where we're going." Tommy hollered over to Michaels who was describing the actual layout of the residence to a member of the entry team. "Ronnie, use my car and take Sergeant Cain to the target building."

"Yes sir." Tommy threw his keys to Michaels and in minutes he and the S.W.A.T. Team supervisor pulled from the half full lot.

After a quick look, Michaels and the sergeant returned. "Let's saddle up. It's time to go to work," Sergeant Cain instructed his team. The five heavily armed men climbed into the back of the Armor Personnel Carrier, or APC for short, along with their sergeant. The sixth S.W.A.T. Team member hopped into the driver's seat and they were on their way.

"I love hearing a ram slamming into someone's door. It's such a pleasant sound," Michaels said jokingly.

"Yeah, and so is an AR-15 laser sight dancing across the center of your chest," Jim added. The three men laughed as they watched the entry team stealthfully dismount the APC and rush in a synchronized fashion into the building. One member, carrying the flat black colored 50 pound battering ram, otherwise known as the *key*, was joined by a second team member. He took hold of the ram's second grip and together, like they had done countless times before, forcefully introduced the *key* square onto the doorknob. The door's latch and deadbolt were no match for the immense power of the hardened steel. With the door breached, they dropped the *key* to the floor, making a loud thud and drew their semi-automatic pistols from their tactical holsters.

In less than 45 seconds, Sergeant Cain called Tommy on his cell. "Sergeant Suit here."

"Hey Tommy, it's Jerry. You guys can come in. There's one female here. She was in the shower when we entered. She's very quiet, almost like she was expecting us."

"We're on our way. You guys can leave. Tell the boys I said thanks."

"Ok Tommy, just give me a call when you need us again. We love this shit."

Tommy chuckled. "I know you do Jerry. I know you do." Tommy put the phone in his pocket and he and the rest of the unit walked inside, being sure to step over the mangled hardware on the floor. Venessa was sitting on the couch with her hands behind her back secured in ziptie cuffs.

"You can take those off," Michaels said to the S.W.A.T. Team officer guarding the weeping Venessa. "Hi Venessa, we're here to do a search of your place pursuant to a Search & Seizure Warrant signed by Judge Williams of the Circuit Court. This copy is for you and anything we take will be noted on an inventory sheet that you'll get a copy of."

Venessa took the warrant and laid it face down next to her. She wiped her eyes and looked at Michaels. "But why am I under arrest? I didn't do anything. And why are you searching my house?"

"You're not under arrest. Those men only put cuffs on you for their own safety. It's what they do all the time." Michaels bent down on one knee facing Venessa. "Listen to me. At this time, I believe you didn't do anything wrong. But we both know there should have been a large bottle of Orange-Raspberry drink in your refrigerator yesterday, and it wasn't. You'll read in the warrant the one in your trash can you gave me matches the one used in a homicide we're handling."

"Homicide? What homicide? Do you think Wes killed someone? No way. No way on earth would he do something like that."

"Look, I'm not here to argue with you. I suggest you read the warrant. In the meantime, these men and I will systematically go through your home searching for evidence. This man here," Michaels said pointing to Tommy, "is Sergeant Tom Suit. He's my supervisor. He'll stay with you while we do our search."

"Dredge, you and Donald can leave. Ronnie and Jim can knock this out in no time," Tommy said.

"You sure boss?" Donald asked.

"Yeah, they can handle this. Get out of here."

Chapter 24

With the Court Martial hearing just one day away, and Athas' victim's daughter murdered, this case meant more to Sarro. She was hell bent on not losing, which caused her to re-visit everyone's testimony, and rehash the precise order in which she would present her evidence. Agent Athas sat across from Major Sarro in her office among her organized clutter. Together they went over the testimony of each witness, covering everything from the observations made by the initial responding MP's and ambo personnel to the attending doctor at the hospital. The doctor's job would be to describe, in detail, the incredible amount of force it would take to inflict a fracture so severe to Suk's arm. Not only would she have to explain in layman's terms what it took to repair her arm, but she would have to explain the other injuries and paint a graphic picture of Suk's battered body.

Following Athas' testimony would be a segment in the trial Sarro desired the most, putting Captain Weinman on the stand. Since the captain had taken it upon himself to tell Schumaker about the keys left by the attacker, then let him tell the jury why he revealed the single most important piece of evidence to the suspect, before any investigator had a chance to speak with Schumaker, along with his reason for the keys being there.

Sarro made no attempt to hide the sneer on her face. "I hope this really pisses him off. Lenny, the only way I can get his ass on the stand and compel him to testify is to subpoena him. When you leave here today, I want you to find him and personally serve him…not his secretary…not one of his flunkies…but him and only him." Athas too wore a similar look on his face as she handed him an official Army envelope with the vengeful subpoena inside.

"I fucking love it ma'am. I mean, excuse my French Major…"

"Lenny, you need to lighten up. It's ok. I like you and we are going to put this worthless disgrace of a human being away. Not only will he do time for this offense, but he'll have to answer for his murder charge. Fuck him. What worries me is Suk. She's our weakest link. Will she show up now that her daughter's been killed? And if she does, will she be able to convince the jury she picked the right man in the lineup? The bottom line is everything is going to rest on her."

Chapter 25

Like he had done so many times before as an undercover narc, Michaels began his search of the small one-bedroom condo. Also having done several warrants prior to his new assignment, Jim's job was to assist by staying close to Michaels, keeping track of any items seized while Jeff was tasked with photographing and packaging anything taken.

"Let's start in the kitchen and work our way from there," Michaels told Jim.

"Sounds good to me. Let me guess…the trashcan first?" Jim asked.

"How'd you guess?" Michaels slid the medium size plastic can near the sink. With his rubber gloves on, he began removing items and placing them in the sink. Halfway through, Michaels found a telling piece of evidence. "Fucking bingo," he said elated over his find.

"What's that brother?" Jim asked, watching a small piece of paper dangle from Michaels' hand.

"It's a fucking receipt from the Giant Food store. Holy shit I can't believe this. It shows they purchased two bottles of the same size and flavor fruit drinks just 2 days before our homicide."

Jeff took possession of the receipt, photographed it and placed it in an evidence bag. "Good find Shithead."

Michaels was happy. "I love it when a plan comes together."

"Now we need to find the long overcoat that witness saw the guy wearing just before the explosion," said Jim.

"Yeah Jim, I forgot all about that. Let me find a 9 millimeter handgun, and it will be all over with."

"That would be sweet Jesus," Jim responded.

"Ronnie, I checked the living room. There's nothing in here. The only thing left out here is the hallway coat closet," Tommy said.

"Have at it Tommy, if you want. The sooner we're done the sooner we'll be out of here." Michaels continued to meticulously search the master bedroom, hall linen closet and bathroom to no avail. There was no weapon and no long coat anywhere to be found.

"Ronnie, come here," Tommy hollered. Michaels and Jim scurried toward the foyer where Tommy stood in front of the coat closet looking at the top shelf. Venessa's body peacocked, drawing her attention to the area where the men stood. It was obvious from her posture and change of expression, something of interest was among the coats.

"What is it Tommy? Please tell me it's a gun," Michaels said.

"No, but it's the right caliber ammunition," Tommy exclaimed.

"Fucking A. Jeff, photograph that box of ammo please before we take it out." Jeff snapped off a few photographs before Michaels pulled the box down for inspection being sure to carefully handle it with his rubber gloves. When he opened it, he noticed several bullets missing. He removed one to see the base of the casing. "Fuck."

"What's wrong Shithead?" Tommy asked.

Michaels leaned over and whispered in Tommy's ear. "It doesn't have the same markings as the one found at the scene."

Michaels walked the box to the couch where Venessa sat. "So Venessa, are these yours?"

Venessa seemed genuinely shocked to see ammunition in her home. "Were they in my closet?"

"Sure were. Are you saying these don't belong to you?" Michaels pressed.

"I've never seen them before."

Michaels looked at her cell phone vibrating on the coffee table. From the caller ID he could see it was Schumaker. "Answer that Venessa. I want to talk to him."

"Wes, the police are here. They're searching my apartment. What the hell. Hold on, one of them wants to talk to you."

"Wesley, hi, Detective Michaels here. How's it going?"

"Um, ok," Schumaker answered.

Aware Miranda rights didn't apply when talking on a phone, Michaels fired away. "Quick question for ya bud. We found a box of 9 millimeter bullets in Venessa's coat closet. Are they yours?"

Michaels could hear Schumaker clear his throat. His voice crack as he tried to speak. "Um…ah, ah, oh yeah, they're as old as I am," he stuttered.

"They're as old as you are huh? Ok, where's the gun?"

"Gun? Gun? I, I don't own a gun," he said.

"Oh, that's funny…they're bullets missing from this box. I figured you must have shot them since Venessa didn't have a clue they were in there."

Schumaker cleared his throat once more and forced a cough. "I, I don't remember. It's been so long. Can u, um…just tell Venessa to call me…I gotta go," he said, ending the call.

At the conclusion of the search, Jim handed Venessa a copy of the inventory sheet. Michaels left her a second business card with his number handwritten on the back. "Here's my card again. You better be careful who you decide to protect." The men made their way to the parking lot.

"Jeff, before we leave do me a favor. Give me the lot number from the inside flap of that box of bullets please."

"Sure Shithead what are you going to do with that?" Jeff asked.

"I have an idea. I'll let you know if it pans out."

"Alright guys, we've had enough fun for the day, let's get the fuck out of here," Tommy said.

Jeff put the evidence bags on the front passenger seat of his truck and removed the box of ammunition. Careful not to damage any prints, Jeff opened the lid where he could plainly see the lot number stamped in black ink. "Ronnie, the number is RAC-29082."

"Got it brother, thanks."

Chapter 26

Finishing up the evening with Major Sarro, Agent Athas made his way back to his office with the subpoena for Captain Weinman.

"Lenny are you sure you don't want me to go with you on that subpoena service?" his lieutenant asked.

"No sir. I got this. No problem whatsoever."

"Well, it's getting late. You might want to leave soon. I don't know how long he stays in his office. Have you heard from the county guys today?"

"No. I'm sure they're busy. I'll give them a call tomorrow first thing."

"Ok. Good night. I'll see you at 0730 hours."

"Good night Lieutenant."

Athas got into his Army issued vehicle and drove to Captain Weinman's office. With January ending, the skies were quick to darken. Athas noticed a faint light inside of the small aging structure. Seeing a light on without any vehicles on the lot was peculiar. He turned his headlights off and slowly entered the lot. Athas stepped from his car, being careful to close his door with minimal noise. Peering around the building he could see Weinman's green SUV parked in an unusual spot. This was strange given the fact Weinman had his own reserved space. Athas caught a glimpse of two shadows on a wall in the captain's office. He walked softly up the steps. His gut told him something wasn't right. When he reached the top stair, he was shocked. He could see the profile of Captain Stanley Weinman standing upright, leaning against his desk. Kneeling in front of him was what appeared to be another man servicing him with a blowjob. Shocked, Athas attempted to move to the side of the staircase to conceal his silhouette. The aging wood creaked, revealing his presence to the captain and willing companion. Startled, the captain and his lover looked in the direction of the sound, only to see Athas. The man kneeling got up and walked out of sight. Athas couldn't believe what he had just witnessed. The man he saw giving pleasure to Weinman resembled Schumaker. Knowing full well he had been seen, he knocked on the wooden door. Weinman frantically tucked his shirt in and fastened his belt.

"I'll be right there," he yelled. Athas stood in awe as he watched the captain's lame attempt to straighten his attire. He unlocked the door and swung it open. "Jesus Christ, what is it son? Apparently, you don't know how to follow the God Damn chain of command. What the hell do you want?"

Dumbfounded from his observation, Athas stood speechless looking at Weinman. He couldn't believe what he had just seen, knowing all too well, this alone, if reported, would not only end Weinman's career, but lead to serious and embarrassing sanctions.

"Well speak up boy. I'm busy," he said, looking down on him in a condescending fashion. "Well?" he grumbled.

"Sir, I've been directed by Major Sarro to serve you with this official Army JAG Office subpoena." Athas looked down at Weinman's pants. "Sir, it directs you to appear as a government witness in the United States Army versus Sergeant Wesley Schumaker." Athas pulled the papers from the envelope and handed it to him.

"A witness for the Army? What kind of cock-a-mammy bullshit is this? You're going to pay for this, so help me God," he shouted.

Athas loved watching the captain stir. "Sir I'll need you to sign the bottom copy for me. Do you need a pen sir?"

"I got my own God Damn pen." Frustrated, Weinman leaned the subpoena against the open door and searched for the space in which to sign his name in the pale light.

"It's down the bottom sir," Athas said calmly.

"I know where the fuck it is, you green horn." Weinman scribbled his name on the document and threw it at Athas causing it to fall on the steps. Athas watched as the paper came to rest but then looked back at Weinman who fumbled to close the door.

"Sir, sir, there is one more thing." Furious, Weinman looked at Athas with the door clutched tight in his hands.

"Now what?"

"Umm, your pants are unzipped...sir." Weinman slammed the door shut. Athas picked up the paper and walked to his car like his ass was on fire. Adrenaline pumped through his veins. He lifted his phone and was about to make a call when he looked back, only to see Weinman standing in front of his office window facing the lot. Athas dropped the phone in his lap and drove off.

Athas knew he had to tell someone what he just observed. Though not 100% positive, he knew it was Schumaker with Weinman. "Son of a bitch," he shouted. After a short 20 minute drive, Athas pulled into the driveway of the modest split foyer home where he and a fellow soldier roommate lived. *I got to tell somebody*, he thought to himself. He continued to ponder over what to do as he changed clothes and prepared to go out for a few beers. His nerves had the best of him, and he desperately needed to calm himself. Now in street clothes, he sat on his bed wrestling with thoughts of his next step. He knew a false or unfounded claim against a commanding officer could destroy his own career, reputation, and any possible chance for promotion. The thoughts of his own court martial laid heavy on his mind.

Athas climbed into his Acura parked in his driveway. Before driving off, he pulled out his cell phone and held it in front of him. He wasn't sure what to do, but he felt he had to tell someone, so he placed a call to Major Sarro. The phone rang once, then twice before he hung up. Second guessing himself, he put the car in drive and started down the road toward a popular bar just off base when his phone rang. It was Sarro.

"Hello, this is Agent Athas.'

"Lenny, it's Dawn. Did you just call me?"

He hesitated for a moment, contemplating if he should tell her the truth or say it was an accident. "Ah, yes ma'am…I did."

"Sorry, I went out for a drink after work and my phone was in my purse and I couldn't hear it. What did you need?"

He took a big sigh. His trepidation overcame him. "Um, well ma'am."

Sensing his hesitation, Sarro interrupted. "Lenny, are you ok? Did you serve that asshole tonight?" He took another deep breath which she could plainly hear. "Listen to me. Where are you right now?"

"Well ma'am," he paused. "I was headed out for a drink myself." He took another deep breath. "Ma'am I saw something tonight.

Something you're not going to believe, and it involves Captain Weinman and Sergeant Schumaker."

Sarro could sense the apprehension in his voice. "Ok, that's enough with the ma'am stuff. Look, would you care to join me for a drink? It sounds like we both need one and we can talk. Oh, and hey, call me Dawn."

Athas smiled. "Yes, yes ma'am, I mean yes Dawn, ma'am," he said. They both laughed.

"Great, do you know where the Driftwood Inn is, just off the base?"

"Yes ma'am....I mean, Dawn. I'm about 5 minutes away."

Sarro laughed. "I'll see you when you get here. What will you be drinking? Whatever it is, I'll have a cold one waiting for you."

"A Miller Light and a shot of Jack Daniels. You'll want a shot too after you hear what I saw."

"Now that sounds like a plan"

The anxiety Athas was feeling eased. He felt comfort in telling someone like her. Someone who not only didn't care for Weinman, but someone who could advise and protect him legally.

"Did you give him the subpoena?"

"Oh, I sure did."

"Wait, don't say anymore. We'll talk when you get here."

Athas was relieved. The thought of having drinks, socially, with Major Dawn Sarro, made him feel peculiar in a good kind of way. Besides respecting her professionally, he always thought she was attractive and liked how tough she was. Driving at a good pace he noticed in his rearview mirror a car flashing it's high beams. The car got uncomfortably close to the back of his, while the blinding lights continued to flash. He eased his car to the shoulder to find out what was wrong. Looking a short distance down the road, he could see the glow of the neon signs from the Driftwood Inn reflecting off the parked cars.

Chapter 27

At the office, the detectives sat at their desk and shot the shit for a bit about the Kim case. Michaels fired up his computer and before long had a telephone number to the Remington Arms Corporation Security Division. He placed a call.

"Security may I help you?" the female answered.

"Hi, my name is Detective Michaels. I'm with the Anne Arundel County Police Department's Homicide Unit in Maryland. How are you today?"

"Hi Detective. I'm just fine. How can I help you?"

"I'm investigating a murder which occurred a few days ago here in Maryland. We just finished doing a search warrant and I recovered a box of your ammunition. I have the lot number stamped on the inside of the box and I was wondering if you could tell me when these were manufactured and where they would've been delivered to?"

"Well yes and no Detective. I'll be able to tell you the month and year they were made, but only the area of the state they were delivered, not a specific store."

"That would be just fine, thank you."

"Ok, go ahead with the number."

"It's RAC-29082."

"Got it. What's a good contact number for you?"

"301-222-3460. I really appreciate your help."

"Hey, no problem. We always take care of law enforcement. Our system is down right now, so I'll have to do a hand search tomorrow for ya," she explained.

"Oh, that sucks."

"I'll call you in the morning if that's ok sir?"

"Yes, thanks again. Goodbye."

"Goodbye."

Tommy entered the homicide squad room with a freshly lit cigarette. You could tell he had something important on his mind. He had this way about him. He would just look at you and not say a word. "You boys hungry? Feel like breaking some bread?" Everyone agreed and they made their way to the CID parking lot.

"Should we take separate cars?" Donald asked.

"Fuck no. We can all pile in my car. Get in," Tommy ordered.

Being the senior member of the unit, Dredge helped himself to the front passenger seat of Tommy's new black Ford Crown Vic, while the rest piled in the back. "This has a lot of room in it," Jim said, flanked by Donald and Ronnie.

"Take notice everybody. It still has that new car smell. That won't last long. It'll smell like an ashtray by this time next week," Michaels said laughing.

"Fuck you Shithead," Tommy shot back.

Once at their local hangout, Kaufmann's Restaurant, the manager informed them there would be a short wait before the next available table. Like good sheep, the team followed their leader to the bar for a cocktail before dinner.

With beverages in hand, Tommy made a toast. "To locking up the next dirtball and solving another case. Good job Shithead and Jim. Like I've always said about you guys, it's not a matter of IF we solve a case, it's WHEN."

The five tapped their drinks and each took a sip when Donald sprayed a stream of Budweiser from his mouth. Barely able to contain himself he choked while the others watched him, trying to figure out what was so funny.

Laughing, Donald pointed at Michaels. "What the hell's so funny?" Michaels asked. Michaels looked down, only to his chagrin, to see his zipper down with his starched white shirt protruding out. By now, not only was the entire squad laughing, but so were the two couples sitting at the nearby table. Embarrassed, Michaels turned toward the bar and made the adjustment to his pants. With the entire unit in tears, Michaels couldn't help but join them. "I wonder how fucking long I've been walking around like that? Christ, I hope I wasn't talking to Venessa with my shit hanging out."

"Shithead, I was having a flashback from the Annapolis Mall when you were walking around with that big hole in your pants. That was funny, but this one ranks right up there," Donald said still chuckling.

Michaels took a gulp of his Miller Lite bottle when Tommy's cell phone sounded. He pulled his phone from his jacket and looked at the number. "It's Dispatch." He pressed the button to receive the call. "Sergeant Suit."

"Hi Sergeant Suit, this is Leo from Channel 5."

"What's up Leo?"

"We got a homicide in Western District, on Route 170 near the old Westinghouse Building. I've notified an Evidence Collection Unit and Doc Jones from the Medical Examiner's Office."

"What can you tell me about it?"

"The only thing I've been told is a body was found in a vehicle by someone walking bye."

"Ok. You don't need to call anyone from the unit, they're all with me. Put us enroute." Tommy stuffed his phone into his jacket pocket. "Come on boys. We got a body." Tommy finished the last of his Stolis and slammed the ice filled glass onto the bar. The rest of the men gulped down their beverages and just as they came in, they left following close behind Tommy.

As the crew grew near, they could see the police cars and medical units blocking a full lane of traffic. One officer directed the cluster fuck of cars, while a few other cops milled around a car parked on the shoulder. Tommy activated his grill lights and siren and maneuvered his way through the rubber necking onlookers.

Chapter 28

Inside the Driftwood Inn, the flashing lights from the emergency vehicles caught everyone's attention. Dawn sat at the bar waiting patiently for Lenny, anxious to hear what he had to tell her. Working on her third cosmopolitan, her mind raced wondering what was so important. People made their way into the bar and talk spread among the patrons like old ladies in a hair parlor.

A man entered the bar, peeled off his jacket and took a seat on the stool next to Dawn. "What's going on out there? Is there an accident or something?" she asked the stranger.

"No. I don't think so. One of the paramedics told me someone was found dead."

Dawn nursed her drink for several more minutes. The bar was buzzing with talk about the happenings outside. "Can you hold my spot please?" she asked the bartender. "I'm going outside and see if I can find my friend."

The bartender flipped a small blue plastic cup upside down next to her glass. "You got it ma'am. It's all yours," the young male bartender assured her.

Dawn worked her way through the crowd standing behind the yellow police caution tape. She watched the uniformed police officer direct the cars past the scene, looking for Lenny.

Tommy's car came to a quick stop. "Who's up for the next case?"

"I think it's me," Dredge said in his low gravelly sounding voice.

Tommy and his four detectives advanced toward the car on the shoulder. Looking beyond the crime scene tape, they could see Jeff and Ray taking photographs. They were permitted into the scene by the rookie manning the crime scene log. As they neared the car, they could see the open driver's door. Dredge led the way with his notebook open, with Donald standing next to him. Michaels went to the opposite side of the car and looked through the windows. The back seat was empty as was the front passenger area.

"Hey Ronnie, do you want me to open the door for you?" Jeff asked with his camera hanging from his neck, dawning a pair of blue elastic gloves.

"Yeah, if you don't mind. What do we have here Jeff?" Michaels asked.

"It looks like a thirty something year old white male shot in his chest, neck, face and forehead. Somebody wanted this guy dead, that's for sure. He's peppered with bullet holes."

"Are there any shell casings on the ground?" Michaels asked.

Jeff lowered the camera from his face. "No, we couldn't find any. It must have been a revolver used. It looks like he was getting out of his car when he was shot, because the driver's door was open, the window is all intact, and his left foot is on the pavement."

Michaels stood outside the passenger door while he waited for Jeff to finish with his photographs. Finally, Jeff opened the door. It would be another body forever etched in his mind, but this one more so than the others. It was Athas. Chills rushed through Michaels' body. The hairs on the back of his neck and arms stood. He bent down again to look at the blood-stained head laying on the console armrest. The man, the soldier, the cop, who he had come to respect, who shared his same zeal to catch a criminal, laid still in his blood soaked shirt, with bright red blood oozing from the bullet holes. Michaels eyes welled with tears. The cold unexpecting wrath of death appeared once more, but this time it was someone he knew. He stood outside the car. His notebook fell to the ground. He was oblivious to the noise of the traffic and people talking around him. His entire body felt numb. Everything seemed to be moving in slow motion.

Jeff stopped what he was doing. "Ronnie, Ronnie," he called. "Are you ok?"

Michaels regained his composure. He looked down and retrieved his notebook. "That's Special Agent Lenny Athas from the United States Army. We've been working the Kim case together." From the sound of his voice and the look on his face, Jeff could feel his friend's grief. From a distance Michaels could hear his name being called. "Detective Michaels. Detective Michaels," sounded a female. He looked at the woman standing next to the crime scene tape among the crowd, waving to him. Still overcome by his emotions he focused on the lady, surprised to see Major Sarro.

"Excuse me Jeff, I have to go do a death notification." Jeff watched Michaels walk past with a blank stare. Jim looked up and saw his partner walking toward the crowd. He looked at Jeff who was also watching Michaels. Jim drew his attention to the group of people gathered behind the tape. Among the bystanders he noticed the smiling attractive female looking at Michaels. The distraught detective continued toward Sarro. As he got closer, his head, arms and shoulders dropped. The smile disappeared from Sarro's face, but she still had not put everything together. Then it hit her. Her eyes opened wide in disbelief while a bolt of shock ran through her. With only the bright yellow tape between them, Michaels lifted his head. "It's Lenny. Somebody killed Lenny."

Dawn burst into tears. Michaels put his arms around her while she sobbed. She jolted her head up. With both hands she grabbed onto each side of Michaels' arms, looking at him with her tear filled eyes. "It was him. Oh my God, it was him," she blurted, as if she had been overcome with an epiphany.

Puzzled Michaels asked, "What do you mean Dawn?" Who?"

"Weinman. Weinman had to be the one. Weinman killed Lenny," she insisted. The crowd drew their attention to Sarro. Those standing close, gave her space while she cried and paced in circles.

Still not putting the pieces together, Michaels pressed Sarro for answers. He didn't give a fuck who watched or listened. "Wait, wait, are you saying that? What do you know?"

"He was on his way here?"

"Who?" Michaels interrupted.

Frustrated, Sarro squeezed Michaels' hand and looked in his eyes. "Lenny was. Lenny was on his way here to meet me. I sent him over to Weinman's office to serve him with a subpoena. Afterwards he called and said he had something important to tell me, something involving Weinman and Schumaker."

Michaels lifted the crime scene tape up and pulled Sarro to the other side. "Stay right here," Michaels said, making sure she couldn't see Athas. Michaels walked in the direction of Dredge, now standing with Tommy, Donald and Jim near the rear of the car. "Dredge, I need to talk to you." He looked at Michaels and noticed the distressed look on his face.

"What's up son?" he asked.

"Come with me." The two walked to the driver's side of the car and looked in at Athas. From this angle they could clearly see the damaged inflicted by the bullets. At least one round tore through his shirt and into his sternum. Another grazed the side of his neck and lodged into the seat after ripping through the skin, exposing flesh and muscles. The third had struck the side of his nose, penetrating his skull, and the last was a perfect round circle, the size of a 9mm projectile directly above his left eyebrow. Blood and clear brain matter had drained from the wounds and now began to dry on his face. His skin whitened as both detectives had seen all too often.

Michaels saw Sarro with her head down, still crying. "I know who your victim is," he told Dredge.

Dredge took the freshly lit cigarette from his mouth and looked at Michaels. He could sense something was wrong. "Who is it?"

"He's the Army CID investigator I've been working with on the Schumaker case. He was the one investigating the attempted rape."

Dredge blew smoke from his mouth. "Do you think this has something to do with your case?"

"Yeah, I do and so does someone else. Remember that Army Major I told you about? The one prosecuting Schumaker?"

"Yeah. The real hard ass one?"

"Yes. Your victim's name is Lenny Athas. He was on his way to the Driftwood Inn to meet Major Sarro. He had just served Army Captain

Weinman with a subpoena for their case. He told her he saw something. He said she wouldn't believe whatever it was he saw, and it involved Weinman and our suspect Schumaker. He was going to tell her when he got to the bar."

"It looks like someone didn't want him to get there," Dredge exclaimed.

"Exactly. This guy's a cocky fucking asshole. God, I hope he did this. I'd love to see his arrogant ass in cuffs," said Michaels.

"Where's she now?" Dredge asked.

Michaels nodded in Sarro's direction. "That's her standing on this side of the tape. Come on, I'll introduce you."

Sarro wiped her eyes and brushed back her hair in a half ass attempt to get herself together. "Major Sarro, this is Detective Dave Hart. He's another one of our homicide detectives."

Sarro shook Dave's hand. "It's nice to meet you Detective Hart. I'm sorry, this whole thing caught me off guard. Lenny was on his way here. I know that bastard had something to do with this. He had to. Lenny saw something."

"Do you have a car here?" Dredge asked.

"Yes, it's on the lot at the Driftwood."

"Can you meet me at our office? We're in the Criminal Investigation Division building in Crownsville. It's about 15 minutes from here."

"Absolutely, but what about Lenny? Who's going to tell his commanding officer? What about his family?"

"Can you help me with getting in touch with his CO?" Dredge asked.

"Yes, I have Lieutenant Lindner's cell number. I can assist if that would help. He's going to be devastated."

"What about his family? Are they local?" Michaels asked.

"No, I believe they're from South Carolina, but we can have one of our clergy from a local base assist on that end."

"That would be great. Thanks Major."

"Please call me Dawn. Listen you guys. I can't believe a high-ranking officer would get involved in something as big as this. Killing a CID agent? This is unfuckingbelievable. What the hell could Lenny have seen that would cause this? We have to find out. Whatever it is you need from the Army, just say the word. We will, correct that, I will, do whatever it takes to put the asshole behind bars who did this."

"Thanks. Look, I have a few more things to do here before I can leave. Ronnie, can you stay here with Jeff until he's done and wait for Doc Jones?"

"Yeah, no problem buddy. Jim and I will catch a ride back with one of the uniforms," Michaels assured him.

Dave jotted down the address to the police department's CID and handed it to Sarro. "Major, I'm sorry, Dawn, can we meet at my office in an hour?"

"Sure. I'll see you there, Detective." Sarro climbed back under the tape and wormed her way through the nosey crowd, many who were now paying close attention to her. Standing outside her driver's door, she fumbled through her purse for her keys and struggled to open the door. She rested her head on top the steering wheel and cried loudly while the tears streamed down her face. Her freshly applied mascara streaked from her eyes. Everything was so surreal. *This couldn't be happening,* she thought. What was going to happen now with the Army's case? Athas was the primary investigator, and he knew all the players. After a few minutes, Sarro straightened herself up and anger set in. She knew it would be up to her to prosecute the Army's case with every ounce of fight she had. Then she would do whatever possible to assist the county with the murder of her friend. "I got this Lenny. We'll get whoever did this."

Dredge hung at the scene a few minutes longer, talking with the initial reporting officer and Jeff. Several fingerprints were recovered from the exterior roof and both doors. Once at the morgue, Jeff would collect Athas' fingerprints to be used as comparisons to those lifted from the car. A few minutes later Tommy, Dredge and Donald returned to the Crown Vic and started to the office to meet Sarro.

"Detective Michaels, what do we have here?" Standing near the car, Michaels and Jim turned to see Doc Jones carrying his trusty Polaroid One-Step camera.

"Hey Doc, how's it going?" Michaels inquired. You remember my partner, Jim Rzepkowski?"

"Yes, how could I forget. We met at the sporting goods store in Glen Burnie. Good to see you Jim," he said shaking his hand.

"You too Doc,"

"I take it there's a body underneath that trauma blanket?" asked Doc Jones.

"Yeah, Jeff put it over him. The fucking press showed up and you know how those vultures are," said Jim

"Are they still here?" the Doc asked.

"No. Once they realized they wouldn't get to see a dead body they fly out of here," Michaels said.

Doc Jones slowly lifted the silver trauma blanket from the body. "You all done here?"

"I believe Jeff has everything he needs, except of course the car," Michaels told him.

The Doc snapped off several close ups of the bullet holes. "I count at least four holes Ronnie, is that what you have?"

"I wasn't sure how many were in his chest because of all the blood," Michaels said in a somber tone.

Doc Jones retrieved a pair of rubber gloves from his pocket, snapped them on and examined the bloody shirt. "Yup, there looks like one hole in his mid-section, a second in his neck, a third in his face and the fourth directly in his forehead. Man, this was an execution." Doc Jones turned and noticed Michaels had walked away. "What's up with him?" he asked Jim.

"The victim is an Army CID agent that we've been working with for the last few days. He was a real good guy."

"Oh, that explains why he wasn't on my ass about my camera. That makes sense. Any idea who may have done this?"

"Supposedly, he had just been with an Army captain, and saw something so important he was about to tell a major who was waiting for him in that bar," Jim said, pointing to the Driftwood Inn.

"What did he see?" the doc asked.

"No one knows. He never made it."

"Damn. Let me get his information and then he's ready for the morgue."

By now the van from the morgue had arrived. The geeky young man who Michaels dressed down at the gun store, was allowed into the crime scene. He wheeled the gurney toward the car when he noticed Michaels. His first thought was the bizarre detective holding the dead man's head up like a trophy buck. "Excuse me Detective, are you ready to move the body sir?" the hesitant young fella asked.

Michaels looked at him, then at Jim. "Jim, are we ready?"

"Yeah brother, Doc Jones said he had everything he needed. I'll help get him out Ronnie."

Michaels let out a deep sigh. "Thanks Jim, oh and Jeff said he'd run us back to the office."

With Sarro's interview complete, Dredge and Donald had the full unadulterated opinion of Weinman. Totally enraged, Dawn was off to notify Lieutenant Lindner. Dredge and Donald were on their way to meet Captain Weinman. Since Weinman was one of the last to see Athas, it was only logical to speak with him first. The captain's address was off base in a modest middle class community. When they pulled up, the house was lit up and Weinman's SUV was parked in the driveway.

After one ring of the doorbell, the detectives were greeted by a middle-aged white female, dressed in business attire like she had just arrived home from work.

"Can I help you?"

Dredge held his wallet up with his badge and credentials displayed. "I'm Detective Hart and this is Detective Hauf with the county police. Is Stanley Weinman here?"

"Yes he is. Can I ask what this is about?" the woman said, taken back by their presence.

Donald was quick to speak. "Yeah, there was an Army soldier killed. Can you get your husband please?"

"I'm sorry, yes come in…Stan," she called out. "Come in gentlemen. He's reading the paper in the living room."

Dredge and Donald followed the woman through the nicely decorated home. Weinman was seated in a recliner holding up a newspaper, covering his face. "Who's at the door?" he asked.

"Honey, there're some detectives here to see you."

"That's nice. Get their card. Tell 'em I'll call them tomorrow," he said with the newspaper still perched in front of his smug face.

"No, we need to talk to you now," Dredge said, surprising the captain.

Weinman lowered the paper barely enough to see his entire face. With a pair of reading glasses canted on the bridge of his nose, he lowered his head and looked at the men. "Darling, go in the kitchen, I got this," he said in a condescending tone. The woman cowered from the room. Weinman watched until she disappeared. "Who are you and why are you in my house?" His conceit was offensive, and Dredge was in no mood for his shit.

Dredge cleared his throat. "We're detectives with the county police. We need to talk to you about a soldier who was killed tonight."

Unfazed, he held the paper in his hands. His eyes dashed back and forth, inspecting the men's appearance. "Well surely it must be one of my men for you all to barge in my home and bother me like this."

Dredge and Donald both wanted to yank the arrogant fuck from the chair. Thoroughly pissed, Donald stepped closer to him. "Put the fucking paper down asshole and talk to us. Did you hear what my partner said? There was a soldier killed tonight and you were one of the last to talk with him."

Weinman laid the newspaper onto his lap. "Is that better Detective? And I suggest you watch your tone." Weinman began to raise his voice. "I know you're just a civilian, but you don't know who you are talking to." He pulled the glasses from his face like he was about to fight.

Dredge nor Donald could believe their ears. Both moved closer to him.

Weinman eyed up Dredge and Donald, each standing on both sides of the chair. "It's time for you to leave my home. I'm done with you."

It took both men everything they had to keep from beating the snot out of the obnoxious fuck. Dredge bent down close to Weinman and put his finger inches from his face. "You listen to me. We're not done with you. Trust me." Dredge was looking for a reason to arrest the piece of shit. He hoped that Weinman would take a swing at him. Donald was waiting to pounce on the wiry framed man, posturing like a boxer in his chair.

Weinman's jaw muscles clenched, and his teeth ground together. "I want a lawyer. Leave my house now."

Donald looked at Dredge, he knew something was about to happen. "Come on partner, let's go. We'll be back asshole, guaranteed," Donald said.

Dredge started his way from the living room behind Donald when Weinman spoke. "What did you say your rank was?"

Both men stopped and turned toward him only to see the glasses back on his nose and the paper lifted halfway up. "Detectives. Homicide detectives," Donald said.

"That's what I thought. Next time I expect you to address me as sir. Be sure to close the door on the way out," Weinman said snapping the paper before lifting it in front of his face.

Donald and Dredge stormed from the house, leaving the door wide open. They walked to the car not saying a word. They both lit up when they got inside.

"Are you fucking kidding me?" asked Dredge.

Donald started laughing. "Dredge, when I saw your finger come out, I thought for sure the shit was on. I said to myself Dredge is gonna open up a can of whoop ass on this guy."

"Donald, you don't know how bad I wanted him to touch me. I wanted to snatch him from that recliner. We're gonna get him…trust me."

"I hear ya Dredge. He killed him, no doubt whatsoever. Now we just got to prove it," said Donald.

Chapter 29

Katie hollered from the kitchen hearing Michaels' keys land in the ceramic bowl next to the door. "Is that my favorite detective in the whole world?"

"Dr. Esterling, I presume?"

"Yes it is. Change your clothes honey and come sit with me. I'm making us chicken Caesar salad and I got us a bottle of red wine. I hope that's ok with you."

The two met in the middle of the living room where Michaels was stunned when he laid eyes on Katie. Wearing only one of Michaels' white long sleeve shirts, the two hugged and kissed. "Wow, you're a sight for sore eyes."

Katie took a step back and swirled. "You like? I hope you don't mind. I took it from your closet."

"Hell no I don't mind. Shit, I'm going to wear it tomorrow just so I can picture you in it all day. No wine for me tonight. I'm going to fix a rum and Coke."

"Ut oh, been one of those days?"

"Remember that guy I told you I liked over at the Army CID? The one investigating the attempted rape on base?"

"Yeah."

"He was murdered tonight. Somebody put four bullets in him. Doc Jones called it an execution style murder."

"Get out of those clothes. I'll put the wine away and fix us a drink, and you can tell me all about it. Boy Babe, I'm sorry to hear that."

For the remainder of the evening Katie listened and prompted Michaels to unveil his feelings. The night progressed and so did the cocktails. They talked before dinner, while they were eating and afterwards. Her innate ability to keep things from being couped up inside Michaels was healing.

"Who's doing the death notification to his family?" Katie asked.

"Major Sarro is going to have the military clergy from a base in South Carolina take care of that. I'm sure Dredge will be in contact with his family tomorrow to fill them in."

"It's Dredge's case, not yours?"

"Yeah, but you know how these things work. We all end up working together. The military Court Martial hearing against Schumaker for the attempted rape begins tomorrow. I don't know how it will go without Lenny."

Chapter 30

It was 8:00 a.m. and Dawn had already been in her office for an hour finishing final trial preparations. Flipping through her case folder it was all she could do to hold back the tears when she came across Lenny's notes and reports. She tried her best to channel her feelings of sorrow into anger towards Schumaker. She disliked him now more than ever and wanted to see him fry in court before the county police had their way with Weinman and him for killing her colleague and friend. Pressing firmly down on her pen, she drew lines through her notes and underlined others. She could hear footsteps walking at a fast pace toward her office.

It was Michaels and Jim. "Christ, how long have you been here? Did you spend the night?" asked Michaels.

The two stepped into her office. Though neither had been subpoenaed for the military trial, they wanted to be available if help was needed. Sarro walked around her desk to greet them with a hug. "You got to solve this. I know either Schumaker or Weinman did this."

"Hell, with my old partner, Detective Hart, as the primary and the rest of us on this, you couldn't ask for a better team," Michaels assured her.

With her eyes filled with tears, Sarro let her arms drop from around Michaels and took a half step back. "God, I hope so. Lenny was just doing his job. That fucking weasel can't get away with this."

Michaels placed his hands on her shoulders. "We got this Dawn, but first you need to bury the first sword into Schumaker today. Tell us how we can help?"

She took a deep breath and exhaled. "Thanks guys. That means a lot. I just hope my victim shows. Without her, I have no case. Lenny was supposed to make sure she got here and now, well....you know."

Jim didn't like what he was hearing. "No Dawn, we can't just leave this to a hope and prayer that she'll show. I'll go get her."

"I really appreciate that. I just haven't been thinking straight. I keep waiting to see Lenny walk through that door. We'll meet you at the military courthouse."

"See you guys shortly," Jim said.

Sarro sat at her desk. "Ronnie, give me five more minutes and we can drive over to the courthouse together. When we leave, could you carry one of the boxes next to my desk and I'll grab the other?"

Michaels rested his hands on the front edge of her desk and leaned forward. "Listen to me

Dawn. We are here to help you with anything you need. You and I both know Lenny wanted this asshole held accountable, put in jail, hung up by his balls....so that's exactly what we are going to do. If you need something, just ask."

For the last time Sarro flipped through the pages of her legal pad. Her passion was obvious. Her focus was intense. She snapped the last page over and lifted her head. "Ok. I got this." She stood up and threw down her pen. "Let's break it off in this bitch."

Michaels could feel his phone vibrating in his suitcoat. "Detective Michaels."

"Hi, this is Chrissa Lyons from the Remington Corporation. I spoke to you yesterday."

Michaels was glad to get the call back. "Yes, hi Ms. Lyons, thanks for the call."

"Sorry it took so long, but our computer finally came back up. That lot number you gave me was shipped from our warehouse in Madison, North Carolina to Severn, Maryland in May of last year."

"So that makes them roughly eight months old?" Michaels asked.

"Yes sir, that's correct."

Michaels smiled and thanked the lady for the call. He knew Schumaker's claim the bullets were as old as he was, was total bullshit. Now it was confirmed.

Michaels told Dawn about the call, then helped her get the boxes to her car. The military courthouse where the court martial hearing would take place was a short drive from the JAG Office. When they arrived, the parking lot was partially full, with courthouse support staff, jurors and the handful of military personnel presiding over the day's hearings.

"Look who it is. The murdering rapist himself decided to show," Dawn said, watching Schumaker standing outside of his Honda Civic, putting on his Class A blouse.

"Wilkes County, Georgia," Michaels blurted out, reading the tag displayed on Schumaker's vehicle. When the two stepped from the car, Schumaker looked in their direction. Nervously he shut his car door and walked toward the courthouse.

Rebuilt in the 1950's, the red brick courthouse stood apart from the other military buildings by the four majestic columns that extended from the steps to the overhang covering. The appearance alone embodied the concept of justice and was intimidating for all who entered. Dawn parked in the spot reserved for *JAG Personnel* and she and Michaels made their way into the doors, each carrying a box of files needed for the case.

With court not scheduled for another half hour, Captain Weinman, Sergeant Schumaker and his attorney, Major Joshua Barnes, stood in the hallway outside the courtroom's tall mahogany doors.

Dawn leaned over to Michaels. "I don't know who I hate more, Weinman or Schumaker."

Michaels kept a straight face and stared ahead. "I know exactly what you mean counselor."

"Good morning Major," Barnes uttered in his unique factious tone.

"Good morning counselor," Dawn said with her stone hard game face on.

Standing behind Dawn, Michaels watched as the three men moved from the doors. Schumaker shuffled to the side with a sheepish look on his face. Major Barnes went back to speaking with Weinman also cloaked in his Class A's. Michaels couldn't help to notice the cocky look smeared across his mug.

"I see Major Sarro has a new secretary. A little out of your jurisdiction, aren't you Detective?" Weinman stated.

Michaels could feel his anger pumping through the veins in his neck. Dawn turned around, just as Michaels was about to spar with Weinman. "Detective Michaels," she asserted. "I'd rather you didn't." Michaels could sense her strong desire for him not to engage, at least not right now.

Michaels fired a look at Weinman and continued behind Dawn into the courtroom. He took a seat on the dark wooden bench directly behind the prosecution table. Like a soldier on a mission, Dawn removed the lids from each box and systematically pulled the files needed for her attack, knowing all along the most important thing she could not do without, was Mrs. Kim. "Ronnie, can you call Jim and find out his status?"

"I was just getting ready to. Let me step into the hallway."

"Promise me you won't get into it with Captain Needle Dick. We can't afford having him pulling strings with one of his buddies and have you removed from the building."

Michaels let his smirk be seen as he stood from the creaky bench. "You have my word counselor. I'll refrain for now." Michaels pulled out his phone and dialed up his partner as he made his way from the courtroom.

Chapter 31

Jim sped to the Kim address where he parked his unmark cruiser in the empty space reserved for their address. This, he thought, was a good sign, thinking perhaps they had already left for court. He flung open his door and made his way toward the residence. He noticed the black charring still on pieces of the wood above the front window where the Molotov cocktail erupted. Something he wasn't expecting got his attention. He could see through the window, there were no curtains. He leaned close to the dirty windowpane. There was no couch. No television. No tables. No lamps. It was barren. "Fuck," he uttered in disbelief. Just then he could feel his cell phone vibrating. It was Michaels. "You're not going to believe this."

Michaels didn't like what he was hearing. "Let me guess, she's not coming."

"Well, it appears that way. This place is vacant."

"Vacant?"

"Yup. And it looks like they left in a hurry."

"Dawn's going to shit. Dredge gave me an address where he dropped her and her son off after taking their statements, but that was only going to be for one night. She's got to be staying with one of her relatives, but who knows where that could be."

"What about the dry cleaners where she works?"

"Great idea Jim. Do you have the address?"

"Isn't it right on route 175, near the NSA?"

"Yes, exactly. It's in that little strip mall next to Latella's Liquor Store.

"I'm on my way. I'll let you know," Jim said.

Chapter 32

By the time Michaels had finished with his call, the hallway had emptied and court was about to begin. He charged in and Dawn jumped from her chair. "Is she there? Is she coming?"

"This isn't good Major. Her townhouse is empty."

"What?"

Michaels looked over at the defense table. To no surprise, Major Barnes, Captain Weinman and Sergeant Schumaker were listening the best they could. He turned his back and lowered his voice. "They moved. They don't live there anymore."

She looked up at the ceiling and let out a big gasp of air. "We're fucked. Without her, we have no case and he'll walk," she whispered.

"I know. Jim's checking out one more thing and I'll let you know."

Sarro grabbed Michaels' wrist not realizing how hard she was squeezing. "I'll try and delay this as much as possible, but they can see she's not here. You got to find her. Do whatever it is you do, just find her, please."

The door next to the judge's bench opened and out walked a middle aged heavy-set African

American woman carrying a folder. She took a seat at the court clerk's desk. The door behind her opened again, she stood along with the 15 plus military personnel who had now begun filling up the gallery. "All rise. This court is now in session, the Honorable General Bruce Masters presiding."

General Masters was decked out in his full Class A uniform. Assigned to the Ft. Meade detachment five years prior as a Colonel, the tall handsome African American 55 year old had made his way up the ladder to an impressive two star general. His pants and blouse were freshly pressed, with each crease crisp and sharp. The metals on his chest were stacked neatly on top of each other, filling the entire left side of his blouse above his pocket. Every piece was polished and glistening from the bright overhead lights. Those military personnel in the courtroom could identify the significance of his Ranger insignia and sniper medallion. His chiseled face showed no emotion as he took a seat in the tall black leather chair behind the elevated crafted dark wood. "Be seated," he commanded with his deep voice. Sitting higher than the rest he scanned the gallery, then drew his attention to the representing attorneys sitting at their respective tables. "Good morning counselors. Are we ready to begin?"

Major Sarro and Major Barnes both acknowledged they were ready.

"Very good," he said. Both Sarro and Barnes returned to their seats. "This is a Court Martial hearing whereby Sergeant Wesley

Schumaker of the United States Army has been charged by the Office of the Judge Advocate General with Attempted Rape, Assault with the Intent to Rape, Assault in the 1st and 2nd Degree and Conduct Unbecoming."

Both counselors stood once again to address the court. "That is an accurate account of the charges General," Sarro attested.

"I concur General," Barnes stated. "General, I'd like to enter a motion to dismiss these charges, based on the fact that, well as we all know, because of the untimely death of Staff Sergeant Agent Lenny Athas from the Army's Criminal Investigation Division. Without Agent Athas' testimony, Major Sarro will be unable to provide any clear or convincing evidence this was anything more than a dedicated Army soldier caught up in an obvious case of mistaken identity. Clearly, there are cultural and ethnic differences between the alleged victim in this matter and my client."

Still standing, Major Sarro was eager to speak. "General, if I could...."

General Masters interrupted Major Sarro in midsentence. "Major, let me save you the trouble." The General looked at Schumaker standing at the defense table. "I'll dismiss your motion and allow Major Sarro the opportunity to show me how she intends to proceed without our lost comrade."

A smile came across Sarro's face. "Thank you General."

Still stone faced, the General bent forward in his chair and stared down at the smiling Sarro. "I wouldn't thank me yet counselor. Is your victim here?"

Trying her best to sound convincing, she looked back at Michaels sitting behind her and then back at the awaiting general. "Ah, well yes....yes sir, currently detectives from the Anne Arundel County Police are assisting with getting our victim to this court your honor. Apparently, she was having transportation problems." Sarro knew her shit was weak and how she sounded was anything but believable.

"Well Major Sarro do you have any of your witnesses here? Or should I reconsider Major Barnes' motion after all?"

Fearing the worst, she looked behind her when she saw the courtroom doors open. A huge relief came upon her when she saw Army CID Agent Horn enter the courtroom along with the two MP's and paramedics who assisted Suk on the evening of the attack. Agent Horn nodded at Sarro as they took their seats.

"Why yes sir General, the government is ready to proceed when you are."

Feeling the tension lift briefly, Michaels felt the vibrations from his phone. He stood and made his way into the hall. It was Jim. He moved to the end of the hallway away from any would-be listeners. "Yeah buddy, go ahead."

"We are enroute," Jim said with conviction.

Michaels was dumbfounded. "What? Do you have her? You have Suk? Are you fucking kidding me?"

"We're on our way." Michaels could hear the faint sobs of Suk in the background.

"Good job Jim. I can't wait to hear your story."

"Oh, it's a good one. See you in a few."

By the time Michaels made his way into the courtroom, four men and two women also dressed in their Class A uniforms were seated in the jury box. This seemed strange to Michaels. He was used to a jury in state court consisting of 12 members, not six like in the military courts. While General Masters was giving instructions to the jury, Sarro looked at Michaels to get a read on him. Sporting a slight smile, he nodded his head once and winked. She knew what that meant. Her shoulders relaxed, thinking she now had a chance.

"Counselors, you may begin your opening statements. Let's keep them brief please, I don't want to keep these jurors here any longer then needed," the General instructed. "Major Sarro, you may begin."

"Thank you General, and I promise to keep this brief," Sarro remarked while moving with her pad from behind her table to stand in front of the jury box. The prepared Sarro began her rehearsed opening remarks.

Michaels made his way through the witnesses now huddled in the hallway to wait for Jim and Suk. A few minutes later, Michaels saw Jim's car from the window overlooking the parking lot. He watched Jim open the passenger door but noticed Suk did not emerge. Jim knelt next to the passenger seat and could only imagine what he must have been saying. Michaels could see Jim place his hand on her shoulder and move closer. *This wasn't looking good*, Michaels thought to himself. After a few painful minutes, Jim helped Suk from the car. Her head slumped down while being assisted across the lot.

Jim and Suk appeared from the elevator, and she was escorted down the hallway. "Bring her down here," Michaels said, motioning toward an empty bench at the end of the hallway. Still sobbing, it was obvious she was scared and reluctant to be there.

"Have a seat here Suk. I'm not going to leave you. I need to talk to my partner," Jim assured her.

Jim and Michaels moved down the hallway, far enough where Suk could not overhear them. "Great job brother," Michaels said with enthusiasm. "What happened? How'd you get her here?"

Jim took a deep breath. "It wasn't easy....I'll tell you that. She read about Lenny's murder in the newspaper and her mind was made up. What I had to do Ronnie was fucked up."

"What Jim?"

"I told her if she didn't come, I'd have to arrest her as a material witness and handcuff her. I even pulled out my handcuffs. I figured, I had to do something, because I knew without her, Dawn didn't have shit. God, I feel like crap. Like she hasn't been through enough and now this."

Michaels put his hand on Jim's upper arm for reassurance. "You did the right thing brother. In this line of work, sometimes you gotta do what you gotta do for the sake of justice. Good work. Now, we have to get her calmed down so she's in the right frame of mind to testify."

Inside the courtroom, the counselors from both sides had concluded their opening statements. Even though both paramedics were present, Sarro decided to only call Paramedic Heather Fox. Through careful and deliberate questioning, Paramedic Fox described the brutal nature of Suk's injuries, the sheer obliteration of her clothing, her excruciating pain, and the degradation of her wellbeing. Her testimony was so meaningful and impactful, not only did the witness tear up, but so did the courtroom clerk. As expected, Major Barnes refrained from questioning this witness any longer than necessary, knowing it was best to get her off the stand and out of the juror's minds as soon as possible.

Oddly, during her testimony, both Michaels and Sarro noticed Barnes lean back and say something to Weinman who darted from the courtroom. Neither knew why, at least not right away.

Before General Masters recessed for lunch, both attorneys sparred like swordsmen with one another as Military Policemen Dinko and Astle were called to testify. Each had conflicting recollections of the crime scene, one painting a slightly different picture than the other. Even with the trial prep Sarro had done with them, Barnes was still successful in twisting their testimony to sound unsure and confusing. He was good.

With court scheduled to reconvene in an hour, Michaels joined Sarro at the prosecution table. "Good job Dawn."

She stuffed her notes into a box and let out a big huff of air. "We'll see," she said, noticing Captain Weinman strutting into the courtroom with an obnoxious sneer. Weinman joined with Schumaker and Barnes still seated at the defense table muttering to one another and randomly looking over at Michaels and Sarro. Michaels and Sarro gathered her boxes and made their way to the hallway.

Sarro could see Jim consoling Suk still seated on the bench. "How in the hell did he get her here?" Dawn inquired.

"Do you really want to know?"

Dawn looked at Michaels. "Oh God, is it that bad? Never mind...forget I asked."

Jim stood from the bench as Sarro approached. "Hi Suk. Thank you so much for coming. How are you?" Dawn said, putting her arm around Suk's shoulders.

Suk's eyes were filled with tears. "I can't do this Ms. Sarro. I can't be in the same room with him," Suk said, revealing her shaking hands. "He scares me so bad."

Sarro looked at Ronnie and Jim. "Suk, these guys are not going to leave your side today and when you're on the stand testifying, I want you to look at me and only me. Even when the other attorney is asking you questions. No one else…..ok?" Suk nodded her head.

"Listen, you only have to look at that horrible monster who did that to you once, and that's it."

"Why would I have to look at him?"

Dawn paused. She knew Special Agent Lenny Athas was the only witness for the U.S. Army who could testify about Schumaker being identified in the physical line-up by Suk. Without his testimony she only had one other option. "I'm going to ask if you see the person who attacked you that night, and you just have to point at him and tell the judge where he is seated. He'll be sitting at the defense table next to his attorney, and then you never have to look at him again. Can you do that for me Suk? We need you to put this bastard in jail. You are our only hope." Suk paused and wiped her eyes with the balled-up tissue in her hand. The three waited anxiously for her response. Dawn did not dare want to call Suk to the stand and treat her as a hostile witness. She knew that would never fly.

"I guess so," she mumbled.

Eager to get Suk from the courthouse so not to run into Schumaker, Dawn quickly thanked Suk, and asked the detectives to get her over to her office as soon as possible. Michaels and Jim huddled around Suk and swiftly shuffled her down the hallway, following closely behind Sarro. Weaving through the large number of soldiers dressed in their Class A uniforms, the four approached the doors to the courtroom. Acutely alert, Sarro caught a glimpse of Weinman opening the courtroom door leading to the hallway. Like an instinctive linebacker she nonchalantly extended her rigid arm onto the opening door, causing it to knock Weinman and Schumaker into one another. There was no way she was going to let her victim be intimidated or frightened away, not after all they had gone through. With a smile on her face, the four skirted to the steps leading to the ground level where they brought Suk to Jim's car and followed Sarro to her office.

Michaels laid the box he was carrying next to Sarro's desk while Jim sat with Suk in an interview room located a short distance away. Out of breath, Sarro carried her cardboard box and flopped in her chair. "I really appreciate your help Ronnie."

Michaels stood behind Dawn's desk looking out the window. "It's the least we can do Major. But frankly I wish we were helping Lenny with all this."

Silence came over the room. "God, I miss him. Any leads yet?"

"The last I heard, Dave was waiting for camera footage from various traffic intersections near the scene and local businesses. With no witnesses yet and only one good projectile as physical evidence, this is a tough one. It's early though." In order to keep Sarro on track Michaels shifted the topic. "Tell me counselor, who's next on your witness list?"

The major gathered herself. "Let me check my attack plan." She pulled her legal pad from her briefcase and flipped to the second page. "Ah yes, just who I thought. Suk's treating physician, Dr. Debbie DiMartina is next. I'm telling you Ronnie, her testimony, on the heels of the paramedic's, will plant an unforgettable picture in the minds of the jurors."

"I don't know what she looks like. Was she sitting in the hallway today?" Michaels asked.

"Now that you mention it....no I don't remember seeing her. I was so focused on everyone else. Let me give her a call." Dawn searched through her witness list and found two telephone numbers for Dr. DiMartina. She called her cell number but was surprised when it went directly to voicemail. She put her phone on speaker and placed a call to the hospital.

"Emergency Room, this is Kelly."

"Hi Kelly, my name is Major Dawn Sarro with the Army JAG Office. Is Dr. DiMartina available?"

"Hi Major, no ma'am she just went into surgery. Can I help you?"

Dawn was caught off guard. "Surgery? She was supposed to be in court today. She received a subpoena and we've talked several times. How long is she expected to be?"

"She should be tied up for most of the day. I'm sorry Major, but she was notified an hour ago she wasn't needed. In fact, I took the call."

Dawn could feel her face redden. Furious, she stood from her chair. "An hour ago? What?" she raised her voice. "Did the person identify themselves?"

"No, but it was a male. He had a deep voice and said he was with the Army. He just said Dr. DiMartina was excused from court and she wouldn't be needed. He said to tell her thanks for her help. I didn't know. He sounded legit."

"No, it's not your fault. You didn't know. Tell her I'll be in touch. Thank you." Dawn ended the call. "God damn it."

Michaels walked to the front of Dawn's desk. "Who the fuck would have done this? Maybe, you can ask for a postponement. You have to get her on the stand."

Dawn sat in her chair. "Wait a minute," she paused. "Remember when Paramedic Fox was on the stand, and she was testifying about Suk's torn underwear?"

"Sure, how could I forget?"

"That's when Barnes said something to Weinman, and the little weasel practically ran from the courtroom."

"That makes sense and it was an hour ago too, just like she said."

"That little bastard. But what I just can't figure, is where does this allegiance for Schumaker come from? Is it just because it's one of his men? That doesn't make sense," Dawn questioned.

"Here's a crazy thought." Michaels looked at the doorway to ensure no one could hear what he was about to say. He looked at Dawn.

"What Ronnie?"

"Maybe, they got something going on. Maybe Lenny saw something the night he was murdered...just saying."

"Holy shit Ronnie. That might not be too farfetched. He said he had something real important to tell me. He was emphatic about whatever it was, but he said he didn't want to tell me over the phone." Dawn leaned back in her chair. "Son of a bitch."

"Major, excuse me, she's getting a little jumpy out here," Jim said appearing in the doorway.

"Bring her in please Jim. Man, Ronnie I don't have a good feeling about this," Dawn exclaimed.

Over the next half hour Dawn sat with Suk attempting to ease her anxiety. Her tears subsided, and Dawn's confidence increased. Systematically, she went over her testimony and reiterated again what to expect. By the time the remainder of the lunch hour was over, Dawn felt comfortable her victim was ready.

"Hey guys, I'll take Suk with me if you wouldn't mind taking my things to the courthouse," Dawn asked.

"Yes ma'am Major, no problem. We'll meet you in the lot," Michaels told her.

By the time Michaels and Jim arrived at the courthouse, they noticed more cars parked on the lot than earlier. "Damn, what the hell are they giving away here?" Jim exclaimed sarcastically.

Dawn arrived with Suk and the three escorted her into the courthouse and through the peculiarly large number of young soldiers gathered in the hallway. Luckily, Schumaker was nowhere to be seen and Michaels and Jim were able to hide Suk on the bench at the end of the hallway.

"Man, what are all these guys doing here?" asked Jim.

"There might be another trial unless they're all here for Schumaker. It sure would be nice for them to see him hauled away in cuffs," Michaels added.

Michaels joined Dawn in the courtroom. They noticed Schumaker sitting two benches behind the defense counsel table talking quietly to Captain Weinman. Major Barnes was seated alone looking down intently at his notes.

Still pissed from the news regarding the doctor, Dawn couldn't resist the opportunity to confront Barnes. "Major Barnes."

Barnes turned in his chair to face her. "Yes, what can I do for you?"

Weinman and Schumaker looked over at the two. Dawn was standing like she was about to punch Barnes square in the nose. "I learned during our recess that someone, a male as a matter of fact, called the hospital an hour ago and cancelled my next witness. You wouldn't know anything about that would you?" Dawn looked at the smiling Weinman.

"What a shame counselor. Sorry, I know of no such thing. Someone from your office must have got their wires crossed," Barnes said.

"You do know that would qualify as witness tampering, obstruction of justice and I'm sure a few more things that could land someone in the brig," she stated.

Barnes turned back in his chair and spoke while looking down once more at his legal pad. "If you don't mind counselor, I don't have time to deal with your trivial mishaps." Weinman let out a halfass chuckle.

Dawn fired him a look. "Maybe I'll subpoena some phone records and see if I can find out who made that call. What do you think Detective Michaels?"

"I think that's a great idea Major," Michaels chimed in.

"All rise," the court clerk said. To no surprise General Masters resumed court promptly at 1:00 p.m.

"Major Sarro, are you ready to proceed?"

"Yes sir your honor," she said eagerly.

"Major Barnes?"

"Your honor, before we proceed, can the court ask Major Sarro who her next witness will be?"

General Masters looked at Dawn. "Major Sarro?"

"General, I want to bring to the court's attention that I intended to call the treating physician in this case as my next witness, but during the recess, we learned that a male who identified himself as being from the Army got word to our witness that she was excused from court. Because of that, Dr. DiMartina has become temporarily unavailable."

General Masters wheeled his tall black leather chair closer to the bench. "Major Sarro, is there a point to all this?"

Doing her best to maintain her cool, Dawn kept eye contact with the General. "Yes, your honor there is. No one from my office made such a call, and frankly it stinks of impropriety on behalf of the defense, or someone associated with them." Dawn peered over at Captain Weinman.

Barnes stood quickly. "Your honor, I object and would ask the court to caution Major Sarro with making any more offensive accusations regarding some imposture, which, I might add, could ultimately lead to her own court martial." A haze of tension blanketed the courtroom.

"I have to agree with Major Barnes. Major Sarro let me remind you as an enlisted officer, there are sanctions for accusing another officer of the Army of unsubstantiated misconduct. Please tell me you have more than just a hunch here, because not I, Major Barnes, or the distinguished members of our jury feel like wasting our valuable time while you play these meaningless games." Dawn could clearly see the distain on General Masters' face. "Is there someone in particular from the defense team you are accusing?"

Dawn stood looking at the General. The courtroom was silent while everyone awaited her answer. She knew without more concrete evidence the odds were against her if she accused Weinman. She pondered whether to ask for a subpoena seeking records to Captain Weinman's cell phone. She knew then she would have him red handed. She stood there with all eyes on her.

"Well, Major Sarro?" the impatient General asked.

Dawn cleared her throat. "Your honor I would like to request a postponement to have ample time to get Dr. DiMartina in. I believe her testimony is critical."

"Your honor, so not to waste any more of the court's time, I would agree to stipulate to the hospital records as opposed to postponing this matter any further," Barnes espoused.

Dawn was enraged with Barnes' strategy. He knew just as she did, the Dr.'s testimony would be much more impressionable to the jury, than simple records. Like the paramedic's account, the Dr. could describe Suk's condition in a more personable fashion rather than bland, confusing, medical records. "Your honor, I'm not agreeable to this, I…"

General Masters cut Sarro's objection short. "Well, I am. We're not delaying this court any more than necessary, therefore I am denying your motion to postpone, and I'll allow the hospital records to stand on their own if and when they are entered into evidence. Now, can we begin?"

"Your honor, may we approach the bench?" Barnes asked.

"Come on up," the General ordered. Major Barnes and Sarro walked to the front of General Masters' bench. Clueless to what this was about, Sarro took her pad with her. General Masters placed his hand over the microphone. "What is it Josh?" the General asked Major Barnes. Dawn noticed how the General referred to her opposing counsel.

"General, given your latest ruling, can you ask Major Sarro who her next witness will be? If it's who I think it is, I have a request sir."

The General turned to Dawn. "Well Major?"

Unsure of Barnes' angle, she paused. "I'll be calling Suk Kim, the victim in this case."

"General, though I'm extremely sympathetic to the victim in this matter, I believe this is a clear case of mistaken identity. Because of that, I don't want my client to be saddled in a chair next to me, where he is presumed to be the defendant."

"What are you proposing?" the general asked.

Barnes could feel Dawn's eyes drilling into him. "That my client be permitted to sit elsewhere in the courtroom sir. Of course, in plain sight of the victim, just not at the defense table."

"Your honor, really? That's ridiculous," Sarro exerted.

"He does make a good point. I'll allow it, so long as he's not hidden and can be seen by the victim. Are we clear?"

"But General," Sarro pleaded.

"Save it counselor, I've made my decision, now let's get this over with," the judge demanded.

Barnes hurried back to his table after first motioning to Weinman. Weinman rushed to the hallway and within seconds 25 Army soldiers, each dressed in their Class A uniforms identical to Schumaker, filled the courtroom. Weinman waved Schumaker towards the farthest seating area in the rear of the room. Schumaker sat between five soldiers who had already taken their seats.

Dawn and Michaels stood and watched as Weinman corralled the soldiers like penguins and strategically placed them in their seats. "Are you fucking kidding me?" Michaels uttered in amazement.

Seeing all his chess pieces now in place, Barnes straightened his dress blouse and stood facing the judge. "Ready when you are your honor."

"Call your witness Major Sarro."

Michaels went to the hallway and signaled to Jim. Dawn greeted Suk and walked her to the stand. The courtroom was silent. Once sworn in, Dawn was sure to treat Suk with kid gloves considering her fragile state. As she began telling her story, the judge instructed her repeatedly to keep her voice up. Her soft spoken nature made it difficult sometimes to hear. Her story was nothing short of heart wrenching. Several times Dawn provided her with tissues while she relived the night's events. Tears poured and her body shook while she described being drug from the sidewalk by her hair, punched in the face and her clothes ripped from her body. The earlier commotion in the courtroom subsided. Everyone's attention was now on Suk.

Barnes watched the jurors focus on the crying woman. He turned in his seat to see the entire gallery engulfed in her undeniable testimony.

By the time Suk had described her attack and her crawl across the school grounds, you could hear a pin drop in the room. Her words were compelling. Dawn knew it was time. It would be the defining moment in the trial, placing Sergeant Wesley Schumaker at the scene, savagely ripping the clothes from the helpless woman lying on the ground in his vile attempt to rape her. She knew she had to ask the question. Dawn prayed the evil face of Schumaker was still clear in her mind. She thought of a tactic that could possibly help her identification.

"Mrs. Kim, did there come a time a few days following your attack that you participated in a physical line-up with myself and Special Agent Lenny Athas from the Army Criminal Investigation Division?"

Suk took another tissue from the box in front of her. "Yes," she said softly.

"Mrs. Kim, let me remind you to keep your voice up. These proceedings are recorded and sometimes it's difficult for the microphones to record everything," Sarro reminded her.

"I'm sorry. I will."

Dawn rolled right into her next question. "And in that line-up of eight men, did you in fact see the man that did all that you just described and then tried to rape you?"

Suk sunk in her chair. "Yes."

Dawn pulled a file from the box sitting on the table and pulled out a photograph. Barnes was watching her closely and knew what she was about to do. He stood from his chair. "Your honor, it appears that Major Sarro is about to show Mrs. Kim some pictures regarding this so called line-up. I'd object to this line of questioning. It's my understanding these were taken by Agent Athas, who we all know unfortunately is unable to testify, therefore they must be ruled inadmissible."

"Your honor, I was present during the line-up when these photos were taken by Agent Athas."

"Major Sarro, since I don't have a crystal ball like Major Barnes, are those your intentions?

"Yes General, but…"

The General interrupted and rocked back in his chair, resting his hands on his chest. "Major Sarro, unless you want to recuse yourself from this Court Martial as the prosecuting JAG officer and testify, I'm not going to allow your witness to see any photographs from a line-up, yet to be established. Now please move this along."

Suk sat bewildered, wondering what was happening. "Mrs. Kim, I know this is hard for you, but I want you to think back when you were laying on your back that night and for the first time you got to see the horrible man doing this to you. I want you to picture his face, just as you did when you picked him out in the line-up we did together. Can you do that for me?"

"Yes ma'am."

Dawn could feel her blood racing through her body. Michaels watched Suk. The courtroom was silent. Dawn took a seat. "Mrs. Kim, please take a deep breath, take your time, and look at everyone in this room and tell me if you see your attacker."

Both Michaels, Dawn and Barnes all turned in their seats. Weinman had a smile beaming across his face, which infuriated the detective. Schumaker sat like a statue between the other soldiers. Dawn noticed the relaxed look on Schumaker's face disappear, causing a frown to wrinkle his forehead and his eyes to close somewhat. He looked much meaner. This, she thought, was good.

Michaels watched Suk. Without consistency her eyes panned the room. Michaels and Dawn could tell she was overwhelmed with the number of soldiers dressed the same. Neither liked what they were seeing.

"Take your time Suk. Start at one side of the room and look at each person's face," Dawn suggested, trying to instill some type of plan to her.

"I object your honor. We don't need Major Sarro influencing the witness," Barnes asserted.

"Sustained. Major Sarro let your witness do this on her own. Ma'am, do you see the person in the courtroom?" the General asked.

Dawn was pissed. She didn't like how the general was rushing her witness. "Your honor," she snapped. "I'd appreciate if the court would allow the witness to do this at her own pace."

"Watch your tone Major. The last I checked this was my courtroom."

Dawn could hear Weinman snicker. She didn't acknowledge the general's comment. "Suk, please continue. Take your time."

Dawn watched Suk's head stop moving. One by one tears flowed from her eyes.

Dawn had seen that same look on her face when she saw Schumaker in the physical line-up. Dawn's heart beat faster. She knew she finally had him by the balls.

"I don't see him," Suk said in a submissive tone.

Dawn felt the life being sucked from her body. She could hear the loud clapping noise of Weinman's hands along with an arrogant remark. Major Barnes stood up. "Mrs. Kim could you repeat that please?"

She leaned toward the microphone on the witness stand. Her crying persisted. "I don't see the man. I'm sorry Ms. Sarro."

"General, I move for a judgement of acquittal and that all charges against my client be dismissed. Just as indicated in my opening statement, though this is a horrible and tragic crime, it unfortunately is a sad case of mistaken identity against a dedicated Army soldier."

"General," Sarro said.

"Save it counselor. I don't care to hear anymore from you. I'll grant the motion and hereby dismiss all charges against Sergeant Wesley Schumaker of the United States Army. This Court Martial is adjourned. Members of the jury, I'm sorry for wasting your time. Everyone is free to leave."

Jim joined Michaels now standing with Dawn at the prosecution table. Barnes, Weinman and Schumaker huddled around the defense table, gloating over their victory.

Dawn was shocked. "He fucking got away with it. I can't believe it. You can't let him get away with murder Ronnie. Not her daughter's or Lenny's. I know that slimy fuck is involved too," she uttered.

Dawn turned and drew her attention to Suk, who stood slowly from the witness stand. Tattered with emotions, she looked at Dawn and began walking toward her. Suk's eyes pleaded for forgiveness. In mid-sentence with Michaels, Dawn stopped herself and walked toward the front of the courtroom to comfort Suk. The two wrapped their arms around each other and embraced. Crying, Suk laid her head on Dawn's chest. "I'm so sorry Ms. Sarro. I just couldn't do it."

With tears cascading down her own cheeks, Dawn leaned back to look at her. "Suk, don't you worry. I understand completely. Now you listen to me." Dawn paused and pushed her own tears away. The two starred at one another. "You're a very strong woman who's been through a lot, but now you need to stay strong for your family. Before you leave today, I'm going to give you my cell number. You call me anytime you need someone to talk to. I don't care what time of day it is. I want you to call me. Us women need to stick together. Ok?"

Dawn's words were uplifting to the battered Suk. "Thank you. That means the world to me," said Suk.

"Jim, would you mind taking Suk home or wherever she wants to go?" Dawn asked, while she wrote her telephone number on piece of paper and handed it to Suk.

"Yes ma'am, no problem," Jim said.

Michaels which as Jim and Suk walked toward the courtroom doors. "Partner, be sure to get her new address and tell her we'll keep her up to date on her daughter's case."

"You got it buddy. See you tomorrow," Jim said, with Suk following him from the courtroom.

Chapter 33

Less than an hour later, Michaels was back in the CID sitting at his desk when Sergeant Tommy Suit appeared from his office. "Shithead, how's the military trial going?"

Donald and Dredge sat at their desks. Dredge sipped the hot coffee from a styrofoam cup while he watched the angry Michaels about to speak. The look on Michaels' face said it all.

"He walked. He fucking walked. You talk about looking out for their own. This judge, general, or whatever the fuck he was, didn't give the prosecutor the time of day. The whole thing just seemed to be fixed. Like they were not going to tarnish the Army's reputation by convicting one of their own." Michaels lit up a Marlboro and threw the box across his desk. "Shit happened in there that would never happen in our courts," he said with smoke pouring from his mouth. "No fucking way. And that Captain Weinman is a piece of work. It was everything I could do to keep from punching that little motherfucker in the mouth."

Tommy stood smoking near the open back door. "Tell him what you found Dredge."

Michaels looked over at Dredge, who wasn't saying much. "Well, spill it, you big dick motherfucker."

Dredge moved slowly. First, he lit up a cigarette, then took a sip of his coffee. His typical slow pace was killing Michaels. "I got these from the State Highway Administration cameras." Dredge handed him a folder. Michaels held up the first page which was a frontal picture of a car. "About three minutes before the murder, that picture was taken at the intersection of Reece Road and Route 170, about a quarter mile from where Lenny was killed. If you look close enough, that's Lenny in the second car and the car behind him is Weinman's SUV with a passenger. You can't make out the passenger because his head's down. The next two pictures verify their tag numbers," Dredge said, now smiling.

"Maybe the passenger's loading a gun. Oh my God...fucking A Dredge, you big bag of fuck...this is perfect," Michaels said excitedly.

Dredge took a long draw on his Merrit. "Flip a few more pages. Five minutes later, at the intersection past the crime scene you'll see Weinman's SUV again, and no Lenny in front of him. This gives him or the passenger, plenty of time to stop, kill him, and drive away."

"I think we still need more before we question him," Donald interjected.

"Fuck yeah, but now we can put him near the scene at the time of the murder. What I want to know is who was in the SUV?" Tommy added.

"He could be the trigger man," Dredge said.

"Are there any cameras between those two intersections?" Donald asked.

"There's a business complex across the street owned by Saint John Properties," Dredge said.

"Ed Saint John is a good guy. He's real cop friendly. If you need anything, I have a contact number if you want it," Michaels offered.

Michaels searched through his phone and jotted a number onto a sticky pad and handed it to Dredge. "Thanks Shithead. Yeah, I'll give him a call."

"Besides what happened at Fort Meade, this was a good day. Come on boys, hop in your cars. Let's go have a cocktail at Kaufman's," Tommy ordered. "Shithead, where's Jim?"

"He was taking Suk home after court."

"Call his ass up and tell him I said to join us. It's a mandatory unit meeting. Period," Tommy declared.

In under an hour Tommy had assembled his entire unit at their local hangout, indulging in their favorite beverages. It's one thing he did instinctively and that was bring his troops together to celebrate an achievement or provide them a large dose of motivation before it was too late. He was the master of keeping his men on track, even if it called for more sleepless hours than the average person could endure. In a quick two hours, the effects of alcohol had settled into each guy causing their voices to raise, their glasses and bottles to tilt, and their stogies to burn.

"Hey guys, listen up, I'd like to make a toast," Michaels said with his Miller Lite bottle held high. The guys turned to listen. "Even though things didn't work out today for the Army's case, I want to toast Jim, for doing what he did to track down Suk and get her to court, even against her will. Today, he proved he belonged in our unit, because we all know when it comes to delving out justice, we don't give a fuck what it takes, how long it takes, or who we fuckin run over in order to make it happen. Today Jim did just that. Way to go brother." The group tapped their beverages together and joined Michaels in his cheer.

Talking a touch louder than the rest, Tommy had more to add. "Listen guys, we got two open homicides and we need to start digging up leads and busting our asses. Every one of you motherfuckers are the shit and you all know our motto..." he slurred. "We gotta hellava team. I love you guys."

By 8:00 p.m. the boys began making their way to their cruisers and headed home for the evening. Once again in his own unique way, Tommy achieved his goal. His team had joined together, bonded, and were given strict marching orders...solve the open cases.

Chapter 34

Katie waited anxiously for Michaels to arrive home, eager to hear how the military trial was going. Her daughter was sound asleep in her newly decorated room. With dinner warming in the oven, she sat in the living room swirling the Merlot in her crystal glass.

"There's my man," Katie said as Michaels came in.

"Hey beautiful." The two kissed and hugged. "How was your day? I missed you terribly," Michaels asked.

"Let's just say it was unusually productive. I smell beer. Did you guys go out after work?"

"Yeah, Tommy was in one of those moods. I think he's getting pressure from the brass for having two open homicides, so he used tonight to kick us in the ass but was cool about it. Now, tell me about your day Dr.."

"Oh…I made some good progress on a patient that's been going through a lot of depression. Instead of crying, today I saw smiles and heard her laugh for the first time. Other than that, I caught up on paperwork and client notes all day, but what about you?" Come on, tell me….how'd it go?"

"It was fucked up. The whole day was. First, the victim, Suk, didn't show up and Jim had to practically lock her up to get her to court. Then the defense team took advantage of the fact Lenny wasn't around to testify and they pulled off a shell game, bringing in a shit load of soldiers all dressed alike into the courtroom then placing Schumaker among them."

"She picked him out, didn't she?"

Standing in the kitchen, Michaels poured himself a glass of wine. "Nope. She said she couldn't do it. You know, I was watching her eyes and she seemed very scattered. She never seemed to scan the room with any rhyme or reason. Her eyes were all over the place."

"Ronnie, that's because she didn't want to."

Surprised, he looked at Katie confused. "What do you mean?"

Katie served dinner and the two sat at the kitchen table to continue their conversation. "I'm just saying, given the fact she had no intentions of showing, and then her obvious reluctance to pick out anyone, even the wrong person, tells me she wanted to abandon that part of her life, regardless of the consequences. It's a normal response I see often when a person is confronted with reliving or going forward with a traumatic event. But sadly, it only serves as a temporary wall which will eventually haunt them. She has a lot of issues to deal with, or she's going to have long term problems."

Michaels drank from his glass. "You know, that makes sense. She had no intentions of picking Schumaker out. Shit, when I was watching her, she never even looked in his direction. She knew exactly where he was. Son of a bitch. So now, he's free to do whatever he fucking pleases. Great. I know he or Weinman killed Suk's daughter. Now we just have to figure out how to solve it. That bastard has got to pay for what he's done."

Katie and Michaels enjoyed the evening together talking and eating her delicious meal. Using her unique unobtrusive techniques, Katie was able to calm Michaels and assure him he had the talent to solve the case so long as he stayed focused.

Chapter 35

The next morning Jim and Michaels met early at the office, both invigorated to get back on their case. Reflecting on the observation Michaels made yesterday of Schumaker standing in the courthouse parking lot, Michaels had an obscure, farfetched idea. After a brief search, he located the telephone number he was looking for.

"Wilkes County Sheriff's Office. Is this a 911 emergency?" the female said with a strong southern accent.

"Hi, my name is Detective Michaels with the Anne Arundel County Police Department in Maryland. How are you today?"

"I'm just peachy Detective. How may I help you sir?"

"Yes ma'am, I'm investigating a murder and I was wondering if you have a detective or a supervisor in your Criminal Investigation Division I could speak with?"

The lady on the other end chuckled. "Oh no, we're not one of those big fancy Sheriff's Offices, but you can talk to Deputy Sheriff Jesse Williams. He investigates cases, lifts fingerprints, and does all that kinda stuff. Do you want me to see if he's in the back?"

Michaels smiled. "Ok, that would be great."

"Hold the line sir, I'll check." Faintly the woman was heard yelling *Jesse, are you back there?* After a few seconds she picked up the phone. "Detective, hold on one second and I'll switch you."

"Thank you, ma'am."

"My pleasure sir. You have a great day now."

A young sounding male with a twangy drawl answered the phone. "Deputy Williams here."

"Hi Deputy Williams, my name is Detective Ronnie Michaels. I'm a homicide detective with the Anne Arundel County Police Department in Maryland."

"Good morning Detective, how are you this fine day sir?"

"I'm doing good, and please call me Ronnie."

"You got it Ronnie and I prefer Jesse."

"That sounds good. Listen, I was wondering if I could ask a big favor."

"Fire away sir. I'd be glad to help any way I can."

"This is actually an off the wall crazy thought, but I'm investigating a murder and I noticed yesterday my suspect drives a car with a tag registered in Wilkes County, Georgia."

"I follow ya."

Michaels continued. "I was wondering if you wouldn't mind checking your local gun shops to see if he ever purchased a handgun. I know you're probably real busy, but I'd really appreciate any help."

"Hell yeah, I'd love to give you a hand, but we ain't got any gun shops in town. I'll do some looking around for ya. What's your suspect's name?"

"His name is Wesley Schumaker. He is a white male, 25 years old. His tag comes back to an address in your county."

"I copy that. We don't have caller ID yet, so can I trouble you for a number where I can reach ya?" Michaels provided Deputy Williams with his contact information and thanked him for any assistance he could provide.

"Have a great day Detective. I'll be in touch."

"You too sir, thank you," Michaels said, ending the call.

Jim watched and listened while Michaels was on the phone. "Is he going to check?"

"He sounded interested, you know, he had that southern hospitality thing going on, however he did say there were no gun shops in town. Oh well, it's worth a try."

"Shithead," Tommy shouted from his office.

Michaels grabbed his notebook. "On my way." With both feet propped on his desk, Tommy had just hung up his phone. "That was Jeff Cover. He's on his way to the FBI Lab in D.C. to pick up your Molotov Cocktail. From the glass fragments gathered at your scene, they were able to reassemble the entire bottle, all but 3 small pieces. Jeff said from the photo they sent, it's an exact match of the one you got from Venessa's trash can."

"I fucking love it," Michaels exclaimed.

"I thought you'd like that. What do you guys have planned today?"

"I want to track down the witness who told Officer Falls she saw someone acting weird in front of the Kim's residence just before all hell broke loose."

Chapter 36

Doctor Esterling's secretary answered her phone. "This is Dr. Esterling's office, may I help you?"

The man on the other end of the phone cleared his throat. "I was wondering if I could make an appointment and come in today?"

"Let me check for you sir. Have you been seen by the Dr. before?"

"No I haven't, but I'd like to get in as soon as possible."

"Ok sir. Will you be going through your insurance company or your employer?"

"Neither. I'll pay cash."

"Ok sir. Each session last one hour, and her rate is $180 an hour."

"That's fine. When can I get in?"

The young secretary could hear the pushy sound in his voice. "Let's see here. She has an opening today at 11:00 a.m."

"Ok. I'll see you then," the man said in a hurry to end the call.

"Sir, can I have your name?"

"Brian." The man paused. "Brian Delray."

"Ok, Mr. Delray, we will see you then. Do you know where..." Before she could finish her question, the phone went dead."

Chapter 37

Michaels and Jim drove to the witness' home who had seen a man in front of the murder scene moments before the chaos. Located a few doors down from where the Kim's once lived, Michaels knocked on the door.

A Hispanic woman in her early 20's greeted them with a baby in her arms. She was surprised to see the two detectives wearing suits and ties standing in her doorway. "Can I help you?"

Michaels opened his wallet and displayed his badge and credentials. "Good morning, I'm Detective Michaels and this is Detective Rzepkowski. We're looking for Andrea Fernandez."

"I'm Andrea."

"Hi. We're investigating the murder that happened the other evening and we wanted to talk to you about what you saw that night. May we come in?"

The young girl seemed cooperative and welcomed the men into her home. "I'm babysitting for my cousin. Excuse me, let me lay her down in her crib. Have a seat here and I'll be right back." The woman returned and took a seat on the couch next to Jim. "I was wondering if anyone was going to contact me."

"Sorry we've been extremely busy, but we're very interested in what you saw. I know you told the officer that night, but can you start from the beginning and tell us?"

"I guess it was around seven o'clock and I was out walking my dog. I was on my way back and I remember thinking how dark it was. Somebody broke our streetlight the night before and it was hard to see. It was strange because no one was outside. Normally there are people, mostly kids, or whoever milling around, but there wasn't anybody except for this one guy."

"Where did you first see him?" Jim asked.

"He was standing in the street behind a car parked in front of the house that was bombed."

"Go ahead," Michaels said.

"When I got closer on the sidewalk my dog saw him standing between the cars and she stopped and growled, which she never does. The guy seemed weird."

Michaels looked up from his notebook. "What do you mean?"

"I don't know. It's hard to explain. He was just acting strange…like he didn't belong…like he was up to no good. He didn't say hi…he just looked at me and Megs, that's my dog, then walked away."

"You told the officer that night he was wearing a long coat?" Michaels asked.

"Yeah, it was a long black dress coat with a light colored fabric mixed in, like a tweed look."

"Have you ever seen this guy before in the neighborhood and can you describe him?" Jim asked.

"I've never seen him before. He is a white guy, I would say mid-20's with short dark hair, regular build, with wire rimmed glasses."

Michaels knew from Lenny's reports that from all accounts she was describing Suk's attacker, Sergeant Wesley Schumaker. "Could you tell if he had any facial hair?" Knowing all along Schumaker had some half ass peach fuzz on his face he called a mustache.

Andrea looked down in thought. "I'm not sure. It was dark, and it all happened so quick.

"If we showed you some photographs, do you think you could pick him out?" Michaels asked.

Not confident, she shook her head back and forth. "I'm sorry. I really don't think so, but I could pick out the jacket…that's for sure."

Michaels thanked Andrea for her help and gave her his business card. "My cell number is on the back, if you remember anything else or you hear of anyone who saw something, please give us a call."

"Yes sir I will. Thank you," she said, watching the detectives get into their cruiser.

"I've never done a line-up with a jacket before, but if we ever get our hands on one that belongs to Schumaker, we'll show her. What the fuck right? Why not?" exclaimed Michaels.

"Yeah, it would be just another piece that puts him at the scene," Jim said.

At the office, Michaels noticed a phone message on his desk. It was from Deputy Sheriff Jesse Williams. "Hey look, our boy called from Georgia. That didn't take long." Michaels dialed the number.

"Deputy Sheriff Williams here."

"Hey Jesse, Ronnie Michaels here from Maryland. What's up brother?"

"I think I may have what you're looking for partner."

"What'd you find?"

"Well, from the looks of it, your suspect, Schumaker, paid a visit to the Wilkes County Pawn and Gun Shop here in town. The owner remembered him coming in because they went to high school together. He said he never cared for him much."

Michaels was undaunted by the news thus far. "Did he buy anything?"

"No, he didn't, but his friend did. You see it was your suspect's birthday, and your fella picked out the gun he liked, and the guy with him bought it. The owner, Mr. Kent Wright, recalled the entire transaction like it was yesterday by golly."

"Please tell me it was a fucking handgun they bought."

"Ahh yes sir, it was a 9 millimeter semi-auto Taurus, with a 15 shot magazine. Kent said they even bought a box of ammo to go with it. I got a copy of the receipt if you need it. Should I mail it to you?"

Michaels couldn't believe what he was hearing. *It was the fucking news of a lifetime* he thought. "That is outstanding Jesse! You are the man! Thank you so much. Great work brother. No, you're not mailing it, I'm coming down to get it." Michaels was smiling ear to ear. Overhearing part of the conversation, Jim was standing close by, puffing on a Black & Mild cigar like a chimney.

"You mean you're coming to Georgia?"

"Hell yeah. Once I get approval, my partner and I will be on our way. Before I forget, did the owner know who was with Schumaker that day?"

"No, he didn't, but he's the one that bought the gun and ammunition, not your man. Kent said they seemed really close, if you catch my drift? It could have been family though. He purchased everything using his credit card. I have the receipt right here."

"You're right it was probably a family member. Go ahead with his name," said Michaels.

"Hold on their partner, I got it right here in my shirt pocket." Michaels could hear paper rustling. "Let's see here, his name is...Stanley Weinman."

Michaels dropped the pen he was holding. "We're on our way."

Chapter 38

The man opened the frosted glass door and walked in. The 45 year old seemed squared away. He wore a pair of neatly creased black pants, a heavily starched white buttoned-down oxford shirt and freshly shined loafers. "I have an appointment at eleven," he said to the receptionist.

"You must be Mr. Delray."

"I am."

"It's very nice to meet you." She handed him a clipboard containing some forms. "Have a seat and fill these out. Dr. Esterling will be with you in a moment. I see in my notes you said you'll be paying in cash?"

"That's correct," the gentlemen said, reaching into his pocket while eyeing up the waiting area. "It's one eighty, right?"

"Yes sir."

The man removed a one-hundred-dollar bill and four twenties from a money clip and handed them to her. "Thank you, sir. I'll get you a receipt."

"I don't need one," he said abruptly, taking a seat. A lady in her mid-60's came out of the office adjacent to the secretary's desk, dabbing her eyes with a tissue. Mr. Delray watched her walk by and out the front door.

Dr. Esterling appeared from the same room. Mr. Delray was shocked when he laid eyes on her. She was wearing a black skirt, black heels, and a pink cashmere sweater. Her shiny dark swirling hair hung down past her shoulders.

"Hi Mr. Delray, I'm Dr. Katie Esterling. Have you been waiting long?"

"No. I just got here."

"Ok, take your time and fill those out the best you can. When you're done give them to Brenda and then I'll need a few minutes to read them."

Over the next hour, Katie talked to Mr. Delray about a host of things, ranging from his upbringing, his marriage and what brought him there. Though she was accustomed to a wide variety of personalities sitting on her couch, she detected something peculiar about this patient. He said what had brought him to her was the loss of his mother, someone he was close to. His concerns seemed sincere, but during his session he kept examining the room, as if he was looking for something. With this only being their first conversation, Katie was unsure if what she was seeing was a nervous trait, indicative of a person suffering from paranoia or something more.

Katie's office was furnished with a comfortable leather couch, a polished oak end table and a matching chair situated directly across from the couch. At the other end, was her desk, where she kept her calendar book, office phone, desktop computer and two stacking trays with folders. Everything on top, including a stapler, decorative pen holder and a 5"x7" framed picture of her and Michaels was organized and evenly spaced apart.

"In mid-sentence while Mr. Delray was speaking about his mother's prolonged sickness and eventual death, he stopped. "Is that you and your husband?" he asked looking at the framed picture on her desk.

"No, that's my boyfriend," she answered in a courteous manner, not interested in discussing her personal life any further. Before she could ask him another question, he persisted on.

"Do you live together?"

Katie felt uneasy. "Mr. Delray, let's stay focused on you please."

For the remainder of the session, Katie felt an emptiness in her patient's dialogue. His words, his feelings weren't sincere, but she wrote it off as a feature of his personality make up. She knew if he was willing to continue with counseling, in time she would be able to sift through his idiosyncrasies and get a better read on him. By the end, a second appointment was scheduled for the next day and Katie knew she'd continue with his diagnosis. As quirky as it seemed, she enjoyed such a challenge. At the close of their meeting, Katie walked Mr. Delray to Brenda's desk. "It was nice meeting you Mr. Delray. I'll see you tomorrow at 4:00."

Mr. Delray pushed the door open halfway then stopped. "What time do you close?"

Another strange question, Katie thought. "I like to take my last appointment at four, but I can make exceptions, if necessary." Without another word, Mr. Delray walked out.

Katie and Brenda looked at one another. "That was weird," Katie said.

"Dr., I know we get all kinds in here, but he was creepy," said Brenda. "Dr., your line is ringing, do you want me to get that?"

"Yes, please, if you don't mind."

"Dr. Esterling's office."

"Hi Brenda, it's Ronnie."

"Hey there Mr. Michaels."

"Brenda, how many times do I have to tell you? It's Ronnie. You make me feel old."

Brenda laughed. "Ok, hold on."

Katie sat at her desk and picked up the phone while looking at their picture. "How's my hot looking man doing? You must have been reading my mind. I was about to call you."

"I'm doing fabulous. How are you? And why were you about to call?" Michaels asked.

"I just missed you, that's all. I had some strange guy in here I just finished with."

Michaels laughed. "Did you say a strange guy? Babe, you're a psychiatrist, isn't strange a prerequisite to walk through your door?" he snickered.

Katie grinned. "You may have a point detective. What are you up to?"

"You're not going to believe this Babe, but Jim and I are headed to Georgia."

"That sounds like fun. What happened in Georgia?"

"On a hunch I called the local Sheriff's Office in my murder suspect's hometown to see if he ever bought a gun there. Well low and behold, this Barney Fife sounding deputy found a pawn shop where not only did he pick out the same caliber gun used in my murder, but that obnoxious, asshole captain I've told you about is the one who bought it. Can you believe it? He bought the gun with his credit card. The gun that I'd bet was used in our murder. Isn't that great?"

"Oh my God Ronnie, what a break. No wonder you're so happy. Ok, I have some paperwork to do before I get out of here. How long will you be in Georgia?"

"We'll be back late tomorrow night. I just want to get the original receipt, see what type of ammunition he bought, and interview the store owner."

"Alright honey, be careful driving. I love you Ronnie."

"I love you too Katie. Good-bye."

Chapter 39

Michaels and Jim took turns driving two-hour intervals to Georgia as fast as they could. Hitting speeds of ninety plus, they buzzed through Virginia, North Carolina and mostly through South Carolina when they ran into a slight snag...flashing police lights. "Fuck," Michaels mumbled.

"What's going on?" Jim asked, hearing the siren squelching behind them.

"We're getting pulled over by a Mustang 5.0," Michaels said maneuvering his way to the left shoulder. He pulled out his billfold, removed his driver's license and exposed his badge and ID.

The approaching officer homed in on the prominent shield displayed in Michaels' hand. "Good evening. Where you boys headed in such a hurry?" the uniformed South Carolina Trooper asked.

"Sorry sir, we're homicide detectives out of Maryland and we're on our way to Georgia. We just got a big break in a case we're working," Michaels said.

"Roger that sir. You got a patch wich-ya?" he said in his southern twang.

Michaels looked at Jim, hoping he might have understood the officer. Jim had a blank look. "I'm sorry, come again sir?" Michaels asked.

"A patch," the officer said pointing to the one sewn to his uniform shirt. "Do you have one of your patches wicha?"

"Oh, I gotcha." Michaels laughed. "No, I don't, but if you give me your card, I'll mail you one when we get home."

The officer lifted his Velcro shirt pocket and pulled out a business card. "Here you go sir. You boys be careful now," he said, and he turned and walked away.

"He was cool. We can't forget that when we get back," Michaels said.

"I'll remember. It's been about two hours. You wanna switch now?" Jim suggested. They made the switch and for the next several hours they raced down I-95 like they were running on a call.

Just shy of 11:00 p.m., Michaels and Jim pulled into a Holiday Inn located just outside the rural town of Wilkes County, Georgia. Once checked in, they sat at the hotel bar drinking rum and Cokes until it closed. By 2:00 a.m. they were both happy and wasted.

"I hope…God I hope we can put handcuffs on Weinman and Schumaker. That would be so fucking sweet," Michaels said.

"Can you imagine if either one of them resisted?" Jim said with a Joker like look on his face.

"Oh yeah, I'd like to split both of their heads wide open. A good ole fashion wood shampoo," Michaels exerted.

"Fucking A Ronnie. C'mon, lets hit it, I'm drunk and tired and besides, we should get there early tomorrow?" Jim said. The two raised their glasses, tapped them together and gulped the last of their cocktails. It was the end of a good day.

Chapter 40

By 9:00 a.m. the next morning Michaels and Jim were drinking coffee with their new best friend, Deputy Sheriff Jesse Williams. The building he worked in was small. It resembled an old red brick post office, converted into a Sheriff's building. Inside the front entrance was a half wooden door with a ledge built onto it. On the other side, was their Communications Room, operated by a single dispatcher, who did everything from answering phones, greeting people, dispatching calls and booking arrestees, most of who she knew. Jesse didn't have an office. His old grey metal desk was situated against the wall next to six pigeonhole mailboxes and various bins full of police forms. It was like being thrown back in time 30 years, but neither Jim nor Michaels cared.

Jesse provided them with a copy of the sales receipt for the 9mm Taurus and box of ammunition. Michaels briefed Jesse on the entire case, including the significance of Weinman buying the weapon. He was intrigued and understood the importance of his discovery.

"Jesse, you don't know how happy this makes us. When you're ready, we can go to the Pawn & Gun Shop."

"Sure partner," he said, pulling out his holstered Smith & Wesson 5 shot revolver from his bottom desk drawer and sliding it on to his waistband. We'll take my cruiser."

Parked on the main drag in front of the Sheriff's Office were two older marked Sheriff vehicles, both with their driver's windows down. This was odd both detectives thought. As they approached one of the vehicles, they could see a shotgun mounted to the dash next to the radio console in plain view of the public.

"You all don't worry about leaving your shotgun in here with your windows down?" Jim asked.

Jim opened the unlocked driver's door. "Oh no. It's ok. Nobody will mess with it."

Both detectives looked at each other as they climbed into the car. "This is a whole different world down here," Michaels said.

On the way to the pawn shop, Jesse stopped at the local convenience store. The girl working inside, along with a fella pumping gas in his truck, all knew Jesse by name. The three men grabbed a coffee and Jesse was sure to pour an extra one, along with a box of donuts for Kent. Less than a mile away, Jesse pulled his cruiser up to the Wilkes Pawn & Gun Shop. "That's Kent there, opening up his store," Jesse said pointing to the well-groomed African American man in his late 40's unlocking the barred-up front door. Wearing an off white colored cowboy hat, blue jeans and a black T-shirt with his Glock prominently displayed on his side,

Kent looked the part of a true southern pawn and gun shop owner.

"Good morning Kent," Jesse said managing two coffees in his hand while he got out of the car.

"Good morning gentlemen," Kent said, tipping the brim of his hat down to greet his guest.

"I brought you a coffee. Let me introduce you to Ronnie and Jim. They're the homicide detectives from Maryland, I told you about."

"Good morning Kent. I believe these are for you," Michaels said, handing over the donuts.

"Thank you," he said with a big smile on his face. "Boy, coffee and donuts with the sheriffs. Ain't this something. Come on in fellas."

Inside, Kent laid the box of donuts on the glass countertop. The men drank their coffees and helped themselves to the cream filled breakfast. In their strong accents, Jesse and Kent talked about some mutual friends and local gossip. Jesse told Kent about the homicide investigation in Maryland and the value of the weapon purchased by Weinman.

Kent easily recalled the transaction a month earlier involving Schumaker and Weinman. He described the sale just as Jesse had relayed. His recollection was spot on. The detectives knew he'd be an excellent witness. Kent retrieved the original receipt and handed it to Michaels. The name Stanley Weinman was embedded in dark ink on the paper. Michaels knew what was in his hand was golden. A piece of evidence never expected to be found.

Having been the one who discovered the shell casing at the crime scene, Jim distinctly remembered the impression on the base. "Do you have another box of the same ammunition you sold them?" Jim asked.

"I sure do. It's one of my biggest sellers." Kent walked to a back room and returned carrying a red box of Winchester 9mm ammunition. "Here you go. You can take this with you if it'll help."

"Stand by, I'll tell you in one second." Jim scurried to open the box. He slid out the tray of brass to inspect the base of a bullet. "Bingo."

"Well, talk to me Jim," Michaels inquired.

"It's the same. The same as the one at the scene. Hot Damn," Jim said excitedly. Jim shoved the last morsel of his glazed donut in his mouth. "These fuckers are going down. Are you ready Ronnie?"

"You guys just helped us solve a murder. Thank you. What do we owe you for the ammo?" Michaels asked.

"Nothing Detective. My treat. Always glad to help law enforcement. I can't believe Wesley would have done the things you told me," Kent said.

"Jesse, how far is the Schumaker address from here?" Michaels asked.

"Heck Ronnie, remember this is Wilkes County, if you blink, you'll pass right through. His plate is listed to a street in the sticks about 5 minutes up the road. You need me to run y'all over there?"

"If it wouldn't be too much trouble?" Michaels asked.

The men said their goodbyes before they gathered themselves back into the cruiser. Jesse had the address written in the notebook he kept in his back pocket. They traveled down a few backroads until they saw the address on an old brown rusty mailbox next to a gravel driveway.

"Man, you weren't kidding. They do live in the sticks," Michaels pointed out.

The driveway extended through a long strand of Georgia Loblolly Pines, to an old rancher style home. Parked out front was an older, grey Silverado pickup and a dark blue minivan. The living room curtains pulled to the side, and someone looked out. "Looks like somebody's home," Jesse announced. "I'll knock on the door, introduce myself and then you guys can have at it."

"Let's do this," Michaels said. The men approached the home when the front door opened. A Caucasian male in his late 50's stood in the doorway.

"Good morning deputies."

"Would you happen to be Mr. Schumaker?" Jesse asked politely.

"Why yes, that would be me," the man responded.

Jesse shook his hand. "Good morning Mr. Schumaker. How are ya sir?" Jesse said in his best friendly drawl.

"I'm doing just fine deputy. Is everything ok?"

"Everything's just peachy sir. Can we step inside and talk?" Jesse suggested.

Michaels and Jim greeted the man with a smile and a handshake.

In the living room sat Mrs. Schumaker, with a breathing apparatus attached to her nostrils. A three foot high green oxygen bottle was propped next to the end table close to where she was seated. "This is my wife, Jeanette. Honey, these deputies want to talk to us. Are you feeling ok? Sorry, gentlemen she has asthma, and some days are worse than others and today is one of those bad days."

"I'm fine. What's going on? Are my boys ok?"

Michaels spoke up. "Folks, my name is Detective Ronnie Michaels, and this is my partner, Jim Rzepkowski. We're not with the Wilkes County

Sheriff's Office, we're with the Anne Arundel County Police Department in Maryland."

"What brings you gentleman all the way to Georgia?" Mr. Schumaker asked.

Michaels unleashed an ingenuous idea he devised on the drive over. Jim and Jesse stood by like patrons watching a Broadway show. "We are investigating a minor shooting back home involving the gun Wesley bought at the Pawn & Gun Shop here in town." Concerned, the Schumaker's looked at each other.

"Wesley told us he left the gun here," Michaels hoped to spark a supportive reaction for their son, and it worked.

"Detective, I haven't seen that gun in a long time. Hell, let me check the gun cabinet in the basement," Mr. Schumaker said leaving the room.

Jesse engaged in small talk with Mrs. Schumaker while they waited for her husband to return. Michaels could hear the faint sound of Mr. Schumaker's voice coming from downstairs. He was talking with someone.

"Mrs. Schumaker, you asked if your boys were ok. Is your other son here, or anyone else?" Michaels was trying to determine who her husband was speaking with, fearing it may be Wesley on the phone.

Mrs. Schumaker wrestled to project her voice. "No....no, James lives in Virginia."

Mr. Schumaker returned to the room with a befuddled look. "It's not there." He looked at his wife without speaking. "It must have been stolen," he said.

Michaels knew he must have been talking with Wesley on the phone. His entire mannerisms had changed. Michaels passed over his claim of theft and changed the topic. "Mr. Schumaker, driving up to your house I noticed you have a nice set of woods around here. Do you hunt rabbits? I saw a nice set of briars running up the left side of your driveway."

He smiled and looked at Michaels. "I sure do. We have a lot of rabbits here and some nice size bucks too."

"So I have to ask you…do you use rabbit dogs or do it the old fashion way? Kick and shoot."

Mr. Schumaker chuckled. Michaels knew he had relaxed him. "The old fashion way of course."

"Ha ha, now there's a man after my own heart. I'll bet you're a good shot, aren't ya?" Michaels said, massaging his ego.

His grin grew and his chest pushed out. "I'm not too bad. That's how I grew up hunting. It's how my Dad taught me. We couldn't afford no hunting dogs."

Michaels knew he had him right where he wanted him. It was time to throw the fishing line in the water. "Hey, did you shoot the gun Wesley bought?"

Mr. Schumaker couldn't see the hook he was about to be impaled by. "Yeah, we all did. It was a smooth shooting handgun."

"You say y'all shot it. Who else was here?

"His captain. I never got his last name, but he went by Stan."

"Did you shoot it here on the property?"

"Yeah, right out back. As you could see there's no houses for quite a spell from here."

Michaels was hell bent on overdosing him with compliments and bullshit. "You guys have a beautiful piece of land here. I'd die to be able to have a place like this, where I could hunt and shoot anytime. Can you show me where you guys shot the gun?"

"Absolutely Detective. Let's go out back. Hun, are you ok? We're going to step outside." Mrs. Schumaker nodded her head. Michaels knew he had a big fish on his line and this one wasn't about to get off.

"Ronnie, if you don't need me, I'll stay inside with Mrs. Schumaker," Jesse offered.

"That's awful kind of ya sir. Thank you," said Mr. Schumaker.

Jim and Michaels followed the gentleman into the backyard. He walked about 30 yards from the house until he stopped near a dingy, yellow, five gallon bucket. He pointed at two large tree stumps nearly 40 yards away. "There...right there. We set up coffee cans and a couple of milk jugs on those rotten stumps."

Acting surprised, Michaels continued his fishing expedition and Grammy performance. "You could hit them from here? Damn, you must be one hellava shot. Where were you guys standing? Christ, I'm a good shot, but I can tell ya I would have had a hard time from here."

"Not everyone could," he said looking down. "Here, here...yup this is it. We were standing right here," Mr. Schumaker said.

"Could everyone hit the targets this far away?" Michaels asked.

"Wes and I could, no problem, but Stan had a heck of a time."

"Stan couldn't shoot too good huh?" Jim asked.

Mr. Schumaker laughed. "No, I guess he wasn't an infantry man, probably stuck behind a desk most of his career. Wes grew up shooting. I had a gun in his hand since he was old enough to hold up a Daisy Red Rider."

The hook had been set. They could now put the gun in both Wes and Weinman's hands, but there was one more thing he wanted. Michaels looked down in the wet grass and saw several spent shell casings. He reached down and grabbed a few to inspect them. He noticed there were several 9mm casings scattered among the far less .22 caliber ones.

Squatting above the find, Michaels kept their friendly conversation going. "Mr. Schumaker, these probably won't be worth anything, but do you mind if I take these? I'll just throw them away when we're done, if that's ok."

Mr. Schumaker wasn't prepared for Michaels' question. So not to appear uncooperative with law enforcement, he stuttered to answer. "Uh, well, I guess. I reckon there'd be no harm in that." The words were magic to Michaels' ears. He knew without consent he would have to endure the laborious process of writing a Search and Seizure Warrant and present it to a judge in a strange rural town. Neither he nor Jim felt like dealing with that bullshit. The easy way was always the best way.

Michaels wasted no time and scooped up the entire compliment of casings and shoved them in his front pocket along with slivers of grass and dirt. Realizing what his partner was doing, Jim had the foresight to distract Mr. Schumaker, persuading him to walk to the tree stumps where the targets were. Gathering his treasures, Michaels fought back the urge to smile. A snippet of the investigation highlight reel played in his head. He could see himself in a courtroom, testifying to the fact he had gathered all the casings, indiscriminate of the caliber of gun which fired them.

Michaels stood. The Georgia dirt covered his hands. "Mr. Schumaker, we really appreciate your kind southern hospitality, but we've taken enough of your time. We're going to have to get back on the road." The detectives could hear the muffled sound of a phone ringing in Mr. Schumaker's pocket. Michaels feared it was Wesley and perhaps if told, he might convince his father not to allow Michaels to take the shells he had gathered. *That could not happen*, he said to himself. He pulled out the phone and looked at the screen with a troubled frown. He pressed the button to take the call, turning his back to Jim.

With his pocket bulging, Michaels and Jim walked at a fast pace toward the home. Inside Jessie sensed something of urgency was happening. "C'mon Jessie we gotta run," Michaels uttered.

The back door of the residence opened. "Detectives, Detectives," Mr. Schumaker called out.

"Come on, come on, let's go," Michaels urged. They rushed out the front door and beelined to the cruiser.

"Detectives, wait, wait…," Mr. Schumaker yelled.

"Go, go, go Jesse," Michaels shouted.

Jesse had no clue what the rush was about, but he slammed the car in reverse and peeled backwards. Dirt and gravel flung up into the wheel wells. He slammed the gear selector to drive and stomped on the gas. In the rearview mirror Mr.

Schumaker stood outside his doorway with his phone in his hand.

No one said a word until they cleared the driveway and the three began to laugh. "What the hell was that all about?" Jesse asked.

Michaels turned and faced Jim in the back seat. "Oh my fucking God. I can't believe this. They all have Luger 9mm stamped on them Jim."

Michaels told Jesse of his discovery and how the casing he just scooped up matched the same casing found at the murder scene. It was the type of success only a cop would understand. It was one of those unique occasions when a missing piece of a puzzle is found.

"Jim, look in my crate. Grab one of those brown paper evidence bags," Jesse suggested.

Jim retrieved one and handed it to his partner. Michaels reached into his pocket and emptied the contents into the bag. There were over 20, 9mm shell casings and much fewer .22 caliber shells. It was brilliant police work, and all based on a hunch stemming simply from the tag displayed on their suspect's car.

Chapter 41

Brenda stood inside Dr. Esterling's office doorway and interrupted her from the report she was working on. "Dr., it doesn't look like your 4 o'clock is going to show."

"Can you call him? Maybe he's running late."

"I looked on his paperwork and he left the phone number section blank."

"Let's give him a few more minutes and we'll get out of here."

By 4:20 p.m. Katie and her secretary said their goodbyes. Katie started her freshly detailed Mercedes. From the corner of her eye, she caught a glimpse of a man leaning against an SUV at the far end of the sparsely filled lot. He resembled her 4 o'clock appointment but she couldn't be sure. She dismissed the idea and started home. Driving the heavily travelled road, Katie kept a haphazard watch in her rearview mirror. Behind her she noticed an SUV, similar to the one in the lot, but paid it little attention. She changed lanes and increased her speed. The SUV did the same. She could feel her heart race. Her gut feelings about the man who had questioned her the previous day in her office was troubling. She jerked her car from lane to lane to lose her follower, but the driver was persistent. She was being followed and she was scared.

She snatched her phone from the console and placed a call to Ronnie.

Michaels answered his phone. "Hey baby. I was just about to call you. You won't believe what we found down here," Michaels said, eager to share the news.

"Ronnie, I can't talk about that now. I'm being followed."

Already on their way back to Maryland, Michaels sat up in the passenger seat. "What, what Katie? What do you mean you're being followed? By who?"

Katie continued her speed and darted between cars, adjusting her mirror to watch behind her. "I think it's that guy," she said frantically. "The patient I had yesterday...the one who was asking questions about me and you and what time I closed."

Michaels' hands began to tremble. His pulse increased. "Who Babe? Tell me his name."

"He said his name was Delray...Brian."

"What's he driving? Can you get his tag number?"

"No, no I can't see his tag, but it's a dark green SUV. I think a Ford. I'm not sure if it's my patient. This guy looked like he was wearing Army fatigues."

Michaels' heart skipped a beat. The lump in his throat made it hard to swallow. "Oh my God Katie it's Weinman. It's Captain Weinman. You have to get away from him."

"Weinman? Isn't that the Army Captain?" she yelled. "Why in the hell would he be following me?"

"I don't know, but I don't trust him. Chances are he knows I'm not home."

"How, how Ronnie? How would he know that?"

"It's complicated Babe. We think our suspect, Schumaker, and his father spoke on the phone while we were down here. Where exactly are you?"

"Come on, get out of my way!" Katie shouted, swerving through traffic.

"Tell me where you are?"

"I'm north on Route 97. I'm coming up on Benfield Road. He's right on my ass. Christ, Ronnie he's trying to hit me. Oh my God, he just bumped my car!" she screamed.

"Jim, get dispatch on the phone. Weinman's behind Katie. They're north on 97, near Benfield. Get units there quick, tell them he's trying to kill her. Katie listen to me…"

Katie maneuvered across three lanes nearly striking cars. Her Mercedes was much faster and handled the abrupt turns better than the trailing SUV. "I think I'm losing him," she said.

"Take the Benfield exit Babe," Michaels yelled. "Head toward the police department."

"I can't...I can't. I've already passed it. Jesus Christ Ronnie there he is. What do I do?" she yelled.

"God damn it Jim, where the fuck are they?"

"They should be coming up on her now."

"Babe, do you see police lights behind you?"

Katie gripped the steering wheel. Tears gushed from her eyes. "Yes, I do...yeah. I think he's backing off Ronnie. He took the Crain Highway exit."

"Jim, tell dispatch the suspect is driving a green SUV and he took the Crain Highway exit, traveling north."

"Babe, did you get a look at the driver's face, or get a tag number?"

"No, I was driving way too fast and trying to avoid hitting cars. The police are behind me now. I'm pulling over. I'll call you back." The phone went silent.

"They better get that son of a bitch," he said striking his fist on the dash. "What are they saying Jim?"

"He gotta jump on them. It sounds like one unit stayed with Katie and the other two are on Crain Highway," Jim said.

"Fuck! He better not get away," Michaels bellowed. "Let me get Dredge on the phone."

"Shithead," Detective Hart answered.

"Dredge. Listen to me. Weinman just tried to run my girlfriend off the road. Marked cars are looking for him now on Crain Highway. You know where he lives, can you go to his house? Find out where he was. See if there is any paint transfer on his front bumper? He rammed her black Mercedes and I want him locked up," he demanded.

"Donald and I are in Annapolis, but we can start that way. Did she get a good look at the driver or get a tag number?"

"No. Let me know what you all find."

"Ok, I appreciate your help," Jim said to the dispatcher. "No luck. He had too much of a lead on them," Jim told Michaels.

"And I'm four fucking states away. Fuck. I'll kill him Jim. I'll put a bullet in his fucking scrawny head if he hurts her."

Michaels answered his phone. It was Katie, crying. "I've never been so scared in my life

Ronnie. God, I'm shaking so bad. I was trying to get away and keep from wrecking. I'm sorry, but I really couldn't see his face."

"It's ok Babe. I'm just glad you're not hurt. Was there anything unique about the SUV? Anything....spots on the paint, a dent, a sticker in the window?"

Katie's nerves got the best of her. She couldn't control her tears or trembling hands. "I don't know. I'm sorry," she cried. "I can't remember Ronnie. What am I supposed to do? Where will I go until you get home? I have no place to go. He probably knows where we live. When will you be here? God, I need you."

Michaels' eyes filled with tears. "Step on it, Jim."

Jim grabbed the portable blue emergency light and threw it on the dash, then jammed the power cord into the cigarette lighter until the light began oscillating. He reached to the box mounted below his radio console and switched on the siren. The car jerked forward when he stomped on the gas pedal. Jim looked at his partner. "Fuck it...let's go."

"Katie, we are running lights and siren. I'll be there as fast as I can. Stay where you are with the officer. I'll call you right back." Michaels scrolled through his cell phone and called the number he was searching for.

"Hey Detective, how's it going?" the woman on the other end answered.

"Dawn, it's me. God I'm glad you picked up."

"Of course…you don't sound right. What's wrong? Is everything ok?"

"No. I need your help. I need a favor."

Dawn could hear the panic in his voice. "Yeah Ronnie, anything. What do you need?"

"It's Katie, my girlfriend. She thinks Weinman followed her from work tonight and rammed her car on Route 97."

"Are you fucking kidding me? What do you need me to do?"

Michaels was upset and spoke very fast. "Jim and I are on our way back from Georgia. I know this is asking a lot, but can Katie come stay with you until I get home. She's got no place to go and she's a total wreck. Christ her mom's dead and her sister lives in California. We should arrive in Maryland later tonight."

"Oh my God, absolutely. Where is she? I'll go get her."

"Give me your address. I'll have her come straight to you and have the police follow her."

"I'll text you my address…that way you can send it to her."

"Perfect. Thanks Dawn. I owe ya."

Michaels called Katie's cell and she answered right away. "Hey, I'm going to text you Major Dawn Sarro's home address. You've heard me talk about her."

"Isn't she the military attorney?"

"Yes. I want you to go to her address. She's waiting for you. Jim and I will be there as soon as we can. Give your phone to the officer. I want to talk to him."

Katie handed her phone to the assisting officer. "Sergeant Kulez here."

"Kenny…This is Ronnie Michaels."

"Ronnie, what's happening man? I haven't talked to you since that Signal 13."

"Hey bud, that's my girlfriend you're with. Thanks for helping. Would you mind following her to an address not too far from where you are?"

"Sure, anything for you bro," he said, handing the phone back to Katie.

"You're in safe hands honey. You'll really like Dawn. She's a tough one and she can't stand Weinman. I'm texting you her address now. The sergeant with you is going to follow you to her home."

Katie released a big sigh. "Thank you, Ronnie, hurry home and be careful."

"I can't tell you how careful I'll be, the way Jim's driving. We're already out of Georgia and halfway through South Carolina."

"Tell him he better not hurt my man. You're all I have."

"Jim, she said she'll fuck you up if you get me hurt," Michaels joked.

Focusing on the road, Jim smiled. "This will be the longest emergency run in the history of our PD. Tell her, I got this...we're on our way."

Forty-five minutes elapsed before Donald and Dredge arrived at the Weinman residence. In front was a red Audi A4 and a dark green Ford Explorer situated in the driveway.

"Hood's still warm," Donald said, resting his palm on top.

"See anything on the bumper?" Dredge asked.

Donald bent down. It was dark and difficult to see. "Dredge, did you say her car is black?"

"Yeah."

"I can't see shit, since it's black on black," said Donald.

Dredge walked toward Weinman's front door. "Let's go see what this asshole has to say."

"Without an ID, a tag number or evidence of paint transfer, we'll need a confession on this one. I swear to God I'm not in the mood to take any of his shit," Donald professed.

Dredge held his badge prominently in his hand when the woman opened the door. "Yes ma'am. I'm sure you recognize us. I'm Detective Hart and this is Detective Hauf. We need to speak with your husband."

The woman had a worried look. "He's sleeping detectives. He's not feeling well."

"That's too bad. Go wake him up. We need to talk to him right now," Dredge said pointing his index finger at her.

Mrs. Weinman was astonished by Dredge's aggression. She was unsure what to do. Nervously she spoke. "He told me not to wake him. He'd be very mad if I did. I'm sorry gentlemen," she said, closing the door.

"What the fuck? That little weasel," Donald said in disgust.

The two sat in Dredge's car and kept watch on Weinman's home for a few minutes. They could see what few lights were on, were now off.

"Ronnie's going to be pissed," Donald said. "I better call and let him know what happened."

Michaels answered his phone. "Tell me he's in handcuffs."

"No brother. His wife won't let us in. She said he doesn't feel good," Donald said.

Michaels was infuriated. "Fuck him," he shouted. "What about his vehicle? Any signs of black paint on the bumper? Did you tow that motherfucker?"

"You can't see shit on the car Ronnie. His bumper is black too."

"Fuck!"

"Is she sure she couldn't make his face out? I'll get an arrest warrant right now for the dickhead," Donald offered.

"No, I asked. The first time she saw him, it was low light, and he was far away. When she was driving, she never got to see his face. Ok Donald, thanks for everything. I'll talk to you later."

Chapter 42

Out of uniform, dressed in blue jeans and a pink Tommy Hilfiger pullover, Dawn sat on the front steps of her 3-story townhome. She could hardly wait to hear the story, hoping she would see Weinman go down. She was totally oblivious to the discovery made in Wilkes County.

Katie parked her car and thanked Sergeant Kulez. "Hi Katie, I'm Dawn Sarro. I've heard so much about you. Your boyfriend has been such a big help since Agent Athas' death."

"Yeah, he's one of a kind. Are you sure I'm not intruding? I can get a hotel."

"You stop that girl. Come on in. Can I get you a glass of wine?"

Katie laughed. "A glass? I'm gonna need more than that."

"Oh, don't you worry, after what I've experienced lately, my wine rack is full. I can see you and I are going to hit it off. Make yourself at home and tell me what the hell happened."

Katie and Dawn kept the red wine flowing while Katie recapped the bizarre events involving a man she only knew as Brian Delray. From her description, Dawn was emphatic it was him. As the evening progressed, the girls kept the libations pouring.

Dawn lowered the wine glass from her mouth and swallowed. "Detective Michaels, I, I mean Ronnie," she stuttered, "never told me how you guys met. Now of course I don't want to violate any patient confidentiality stuff," she snickered.

"It's all good, but it's really not a good story," Katie offered, taking a large taste from her crystal.

Dawn didn't know how to respond, so she watched and waited.

"My mother was killed by a sick deranged fuck. Listen to me, and I'm a damn psychiatrist?"

"Oh my God, I'm sorry I didn't know. We don't have to talk about this."

"No, it's ok. Ronnie was one of the detectives investigating her case. He was the one who notified me of her death." Katie finished her beverage. "Any more left?"

"I gotcha honey." Dawn made her way to the kitchen to refill Katie's glass. "I am so sorry to hear that. God, I can't imagine. That must have been horrible. Please tell me they made an arrest in your mom's case," Dawn said returning to her loveseat.

The alcohol and days events took hold. Katie began to well up. One by one tears emerged.

"I'm so sorry. I didn't mean to...," Dawn said handing Katie a box of tissues.

"It's ok. It's been a rough day. Yes, they did find him, but they didn't arrest him."

"What do you mean they didn't arrest him? I don't understand."

"You see, the guy was a serial killer and before my mother's death, he killed another lady on the B&A trail, miles from where my mom was killed. Come to find out, he killed other women in another state before he brought his crime spree to Maryland."

"I remember reading about that. Oh my God. I didn't know your mom was one of them. Look we don't have to talk about this Katie."

"No, it's ok," Katie said, dabbing her eyes.

"Well, the first woman killed had a son, a retired Marine, some bad ass, one of those Special Forces guys. Put it this way," she paused, wiping her tears. "He killed the piece of shit who killed his mother and mine, before he took his own life."

Dawn leaned forward. Her eyes bugged out. "What? How….how did he know who it was? I mean, how did the Marine know who to kill? Shit, I never read that."

The thought of telling Dawn her dark secret loomed in her mind. Having been a seasoned attorney who cross-examined hundreds of witnesses, Dawn detected an odd look on Katie's face. Something wasn't right. "What is it, Katie?"

Tears streamed down Katie's face. Keeping her secret pent up had taken its toll, and the day's events didn't help. Katie took a deep breath. She stared back at Dawn hoping to sense some type of trust. "Let's just say he found out." Katie took a big sip from her glass, overcome from her new found relief. "God, I can't believe I just told you that."

"Damn, good for him. I'm glad he found out," Dawn said.

"I never thought he'd kill himself," Katie confessed. "I never thought he'd do that. He was probably dealing with some PTSD issues." She took another swallow and finished the last in her glass. "That's why I never told Ronnie."

"Wait…." Dawn moved to the edge of the couch, taking hold of her glass with two hands. "Are you telling me you told the Marine who the suspect was?"

Nervous, Katie cleared her throat. "I saw the pictures of my mom in Ronnie's case folder one day when he went to the store. I couldn't believe what that monster did to her. He cut off parts of her body for God's sake. I can't imagine what he actually did to her. Sick bastard. I wish I could have killed him. I never had such a feeling in my life until I saw the pictures." Katie cried harder.

Dawn joined her on the couch and held her. "My God Katie, I had no idea. I'm so sorry for bringing this up. Jesus."

Katie appreciated the hug and sobbed more on Dawn's shoulder. She then leaned back to look at Dawn. "Ronnie doesn't know this. I know I should tell him, but I don't want him to think bad of me. I can't imagine what you think of me now…What have I done?"

"It's ok Katie. It's ok. This is between us girls and we've been drinking. Can I tell you a secret?"

Both women were wiping their tears. "Sure, go ahead," Katie said.

"People like that don't deserve to live. Period. People like Schumaker and Weinman, the ones who I know killed Lenny, and whoever did this to you, doesn't either. Fuck him. Assholes like him…no, let me rephrase that…narcissistic manipulators, like that fucking dirt ball need to go. I'll just leave it at that."

After several hours and four bottles of Merlot, Dawn and Katie were drunk. The two career oriented, well educated women bonded and were now cloaked in one another's secrets. Throughout the evening they laughed, cried, and shared stories of their childhood and similar drives to succeed. The two were very much alike. The hours passed by when a knock sounded at the door.

Dawn attempted to focus on the figure through the peephole. "It's Ronnie and Jim."

Katie ran to the door. She wrapped her arms around Michaels and cried. "Are you ok honey?" Michaels asked.

"Yeah, I was so scared. Dawn's been great. I love her. We got drunk," she giggled.

"I see that." Michaels kissed Katie and looked at the table next to the couch. "Ah yeah, I guess so, I can see all the bottles over there. Dawn I really appreciate you doing this."

"Oh no problem. We had a blast. Any luck arresting Weinman?"

"Fuck no. He wouldn't answer his door and Detective Hauf couldn't see any paint on his bumper. Since she never saw his face, we don't have shit."

"If there's anything I can do, just say the word. You know how much I hate that little prick."

"You're gonna love what we just found," Michaels said with a grin.

"What?"

"We just returned from Georgia where we discovered that Weinman bought a handgun for Schumaker. And it's a 9 millimeter."

"No way."

"Stand by, it gets better...we paid a visit to the Schumaker home where I found several spent shell casings where they both fired the gun. And get this, the base of the casings has the same stamp on them as the one at our homicide scene." Michaels couldn't contain his smile.

Dawn slapped Michaels a high five. "Great work Detective. You got to promise me I can be there when you arrest them."

"Done counselor. Done. It's late, Jim you can cut out buddy. I'll see you in the morning. I'll take this gorgeous woman home. Good work brother."

"You too Ronnie. I'll see you at the office."

Chapter 43

Sergeant Suit was seated in Captain Donoho's office along with Lieutenant Tank for the morning briefing. Tommy relayed the news of the find in Georgia, which was music to their ears. Based solely on an instinctive gut feeling, it was a break they needed badly, but now what was concerning to everyone was the imminent threat to Katie.

"What are we going to do about Michaels' girlfriend? How certain was she it was that Army Captain?" Donoho asked.

Tommy was overly protective of his troops and their families. His proactive nature came to no surprise to his bosses. "It was him. I've already arranged for periodic checks at their house and her office indefinitely, especially when she gets off."

"Ok, good. What about the two murders? What's next?" Donoho inquired.

"Dredge and Donald canvassed the businesses in and around the scene where Athas was murdered. They came up empty. They also put up *Information Sought* signs in most of the complexes in the area. As you know, we've put out a press release and a $10,000 reward through Metro Crime Stoppers, but so far, nothing."

"Anymore camera footage?" Lieutenant Tank asked.

"Dredge met with Ed St. John, the owner of St. John Properties. He's having his security team download footage from his businesses around the time frame of the murder. We should be getting that today. As for the Kim case, Ronnie is reaching out to Brazil to see if they can send us measurements of the lands and grooves of the gun purchased in Georgia. Jeff Cover said the projectile taken from Seo-Yun's arm is in perfect condition. He also recovered a good projectile from the seat of the car driven by Agent Athas. It was a round that grazed his neck. Now we have the spent casings Ronnie recovered from Georgia to compare to the casing at the first scene. But strangely enough, there were no casings recovered from the Athas scene, but the FBI Lab did confirm a 9 millimeter caliber bullet was used. We'll see how this all pans out."

"Do you think someone may have taken the casings from the scene after shooting the agent?" Tank asked.

"They must have." Tommy said.

"Good work," Captain Donoho said. "I'll get word to the Chief's Office. Sergeant Howes said Chief Russell wanted an update first thing this morning."

In the homicide squad room, Michaels and Jim sat at their desks drinking coffee, enjoying a morning smoke. Following the command briefing,

Tommy joined them. "Shithead, did you make that request to Brazil yet?"

"Fucking A, I did. I had to email some dude named Masimo Tamfogliospa. He's the owner of the Taurus Arms Corporation. Hopefully, it won't take too long to get them. Jeff said the FBI still has the projectile."

"How's Katie doing? Is she going to work today?" Tommy asked.

"Reluctantly...she's pretty scared. Just for your 10-43, Jim and I are paying a visit to dickhead Weinman today. We're gonna have us a little chat."

Tommy looked away and puffed on his cigarette. "Be sure to cover your ass. That's all I'm gonna say."

Chapter 44

Katie took the phone from her bedroom dresser. She didn't recognize the strange number. "Hello."

"Good morning. How's your head? Mine's killing me," the hung-over Dawn Sarro asked, laughing.

Katie took a breath and rested her hand on her forehead. "I know. My head is pounding. I guess we had too many grapes."

"I just wanted to say I enjoyed myself last night and if you ever need anyone to talk to, call anytime. Even if you are, you know, a psychiatrist."

"What a night. Boy, that wine sure did hit me. I think I might have said a little too much."

"Not at all. We'll keep last night between us girls," Dawn assured her. "Are you working today?"

"Yeah, Ronnie's got the police department checking on me throughout the day and one of them will be following me home for the next few weeks."

"That's good to know. This is my cell number, so don't be a stranger. Give me a call sometime."

Dawn's call brought a smile to Katie's face. "I will Dawn, thanks."

Chapter 45

Michaels was hot. "Come on partner, let's drive over to Fort Meade and drop in on Captain Dicknuts. He ain't getting away with this. No fucking way," The two got in Michaels' car and started toward the base.

"Can Dawn see Weinman's building from her office?" Jim asked.

"Yeah. It's across the street. Why?"

"Give her a call and see if she can see his vehicle."

"Good idea brother." Michaels pulled out his phone and put a call to Dawn.

"Hi. I just hung up with your girl. She's not feeling too good today either. I think we had a little too much last night."

Michaels laughed. "Yeah, she looked like she was hurting when I left this morning. Considering the circumstances, I really don't blame her. I appreciate you doing that last night."

"No problem, glad to help. I like her. You got a real firecracker there Ronnie and a smart one too."

"Yes she is. Hey, can you see Weinman's office from your window?"

Dawn spun in her chair. "Yep, sure can. He's about 350 yards away. Why's that?"

"Outfuckingstanding. Jim and I are going to do a little, how shall I say?...Community Policing, with him."

"Good old Community Policing. A long-forgotten art. God, I wish I could be there. Let's see, yeah, his green SUV is in the lot. Would you mind calling me when you're done? I'd love to know what he says to you."

"Will do, thanks."

Michaels and Jim parked next to the dark green Explorer in the reserved spot marked *Commander*. The two walked to the front of Weinman's truck. "This has been freshly cleaned," Jim pointed out.

Michaels bent down to get a closer look at the bumper. "Yup, it definitely has. That son of a bitch."

Watching through his office window, Weinman flung open the front door and stormed toward Michaels and Jim. "Get the hell away from my government vehicle. What the hell do you think you're doing?"

Michaels welcomed Weinman's belligerence, hoping he'd get the chance to punch his teeth out and lock him up. "I'm conducting a fucking investigation, that's what I'm doing. Back off." Michaels moved uncomfortably close to

Weinman's face. "I need you to tell me where you were late yesterday afternoon."

Dawn stood at her window and watched Weinman engage the detectives.

"Must I remind you, you're on a United States Army base, Detective? You're not conducting any such investigation. You're nothing but a peon civilian here. I suggest you leave," he said pointing toward the road.

"Listen you fucking asshole. I said, where were you yesterday?"

"I don't have to tell you shit. You're all alike. You remind me of that spineless pussy Army agent that was killed. Poor bastard. I guess you were too much of a coward to join the Army. Gotta hide behind that badge huh?"

Michaels looked around to see if anyone nearby was watching. He looked at Jim, who knew the shit was on. Michaels clenched his fist and was about to knock him flat when the door leading to Weinman's office opened. It was his secretary.

"Captain, Major Barnes is on the phone for you," the woman yelled.

Not breaking his stare down with Michaels, Weinman spoke. "Tell him I'm being harassed by the county police and I'll call him back."

"Is everything ok?" she asked.

"Go back inside Margaret. I can handle these civilians."

Dawn watched with excitement from her 4th story window. She could plainly see how close Michaels was standing to Weinman and their aggressive gestures.

Michaels stuck his finger inches from Weinman's nose and gritted his teeth. "Let me make something very clear you pompous arrogant prick. If I ever see you around my girlfriend or my home, I'm going to put a nice shiny .40 caliber bullet between your eyes." Michaels lowered his finger and poked Weinman in the sternum. "Got it asshole?"

Weinman looked down at Michaels' finger and then at Jim who was now inches away. He knew he was outnumbered. "I trust you civilians are not armed on a federal installation?" he asked with spit spraying from his mouth.

Michaels slid his coat to the side revealing his Glock. "You mean this? I don't leave home without it, Dickhead."

Weinman glanced down at the weapon. "You're gonna pay for this," he said, turning and walking toward his building.

Michaels and Jim got back in their car and sat for a few seconds. "Partner, I must say, I think he got the message," said Jim.

Michaels lit a cigarette while he started the car. "Ya think? Fuck him." Michaels pulled his vibrating phone from his suit coat. It was Dawn. "Counselor."

"Ronnie, you're not going to believe this, but I just got word the MP's are looking for you and Jim."

"What do you mean?" Michaels asked.

"There's an MP standing outside my office making an appointment with my secretary and I just overheard your name and the description of your car come across his radio. Something about being a civilian armed on a military base."

Michaels laughed. "So, what's wrong with that?"

"That's just it. There's nothing wrong with that. He doesn't know what the hell he's talking about, but I'm afraid you're gonna get arrested by one of these young gung-ho MP's. You have concurrent jurisdiction here, he obviously doesn't know that, nor will the MP's. You might want to leave base until I can get this straightened out."

"No…I know just who to call. Do you mind if we hang in your office for a bit?" asked Michaels.

"Sure, no problem." Fearful, the MP in the building might act on the lookout broadcasted, Dawn came up with an idea. "Go to the back of my building and I'll let you in through the employee entrance. Hurry, and try to avoid any MP cars."

"See you in a sec," Michaels said.

Michaels scrolled through his phone while he jockeyed his car to the rear of the JAG building.

"Hello Ron," Ray said on the other end.

"Dad, is your friend Bill Boilin still a big wig at the Fort Meade Army base?"

"Yeah, he's a full bird Colonel. Why?"

"I was wondering if he could help me. You know the Kim homicide I'm working?"

"Yeah."

"Well, I got an Army Captain over here, that's either a suspect or an accomplice in my case whose got a real hair up his ass for me."

"What do you mean?"

"We believe he followed Katie home from work yesterday and tried to run her off the road, and now he's trying to get Jim and I arrested for having our weapons on base."

"What's wrong with having your guns with you?"

"There is nothing wrong with it, but he's put a look out on Jim and me. He's trying to get us locked up."

"What an ass. Wow, let me call Bill."

Dawn waited at the back of her building holding the door open. She saw Michaels speed onto her lot and skid the car to a stop. "I can't fucking believe this," Michaels said barely out of the car.

"From my view, it looked like it was getting a little heated over there. What did the moron have to say?" Dawn asked, closing the door before she took one last glance into the parking lot.

"I came so close to decking him. I wanted to flatten his face, but his secretary was eye fucking us through the window. He likes to pray on people he can intimidate," Michaels said taking his jacket off and looking out the window towards Weinman's building. "Damn, you do have a good view from here. With binoculars you could probably see into his office."

"You're right," Jim said joining him.

Dawn took a seat at her desk and opened a large green three ringed binder, marked *Memorandums of Understanding* on the front, along with several surrounding jurisdictional seals. "What I plan on doing is providing our Military Police Chief, the Colonel and Weinman copies of the Memorandum we have with the Anne Arundel County Police which provides you concurrent jurisdiction on base." Dawn flipped briskly through the pages until she found what she was looking for. She browsed down with her finger. "Here. Right here. Clear as day."

Michaels answered his ringing cell in his hand. "Yeah Dad."

"Where are you?"

"Jim and I just got to the JAG building on base. Why?"

"Stay put. Bill's hot. He just heard about the lookout himself."

A big smile covered Michaels' face. "I love it. Thanks Dad and tell Bill I said thanks too."

Jim and Dawn saw Michaels' glowing look. "Well, come on, what was that?" Jim asked.

"Since my Dad and Bill Boilin are drinking buddies at the Elks Club..."

Dawn interrupted. "Boilin? You don't mean Colonel Boilin do you?"

"Yup. The colonel, his wife and my mom and dad have been close for years."

"Holy shit. That's great," Dawn said.

"According to my dad, he's on fire about trying to get us locked up." Michaels looked at his ringing phone once more. "It's Katie. Are you ok Hun?"

"Yes, we're fine. There's been a cop sitting in our parking lot all morning. He even came up and introduced himself to Brenda and me. He said he was a good friend of yours...a Sergeant Speake?"

"Ah, Richard...yes. Yeah, he's a good dude. That's very nice of him."

"Yeah, I told him we're treating him to lunch today. How's your day going?"

Michaels chuckled under his breath. "Oh, just a boring ole day for Jim and I running from the law. In fact, right now we're fugitives, taking refuge from the MP's in Dawn's office."

Katie recognized Ronnie's sarcasm. "What are you guys up to now?"

Michaels could see his dad's number on his cell. "Long story Babe. I'll tell you tonight. I gotta run." Michaels ended the call and connected with Ray. "Hey Dad. What's up?" Michaels switched his phone to speaker mode so Dawn and Jim could overhear.

In his deep, unexcited voice, Ray relayed the news. "You're captain buddy is being ordered to report to the base commander's office, who I believe is a three-star general and Bill's going to be there also because he falls under him. They're going to rip him a new ass and I believe a transfer to some far away cold place might be in line."

"Ain't the fucking beer cold," Michaels said high fiving Dawn and Jim who were jumping around the room like they had just won the lottery. "Thanks for your help Pop. I think the crew here wants to buy you a beer. I'll talk to ya later."

Jim raced back to Dawn's window. "Look, look," he raised his voice. "There he goes. Look how fast he's walking. I should take a picture of his ass, because he isn't gonna have one in about ten minutes." Jim laughed as the three watched Weinman's vehicle pull onto Mapes Lane.

Chapter 46

Dredge and Donald returned to the CID building and took a seat with Tommy in his office. Simultaneously the three lit up. The room quickly filled with smoke. "Any word from Mr. St. John?" Tommy inquired.

Dredge opened the manila folder in his hand. "We have two more pictures of what looks to be Weinman's SUV less than a block from where Athas was murdered. They're only side shots, but you can definitely see two people in the green SUV following behind Athas."

Tommy took the pictures and examined them. "Damn, it's a shame it's so far away. I'd love to know who's with him."

"Fuck Tommy, I'd bet my right nut it was Schumaker, especially after what Ronnie found in Georgia," Donald surmised.

Finally, back at the office, Michaels and Jim joined with the rest of the boys in their sergeant's office. "Jim, Shithead, what's going on?" asked Tommy.

"You're looking at a couple of federal fugitives here," Michaels said smiling.

"Oh Christ, now what?" Tommy asked.

"After a friendly chat with asshole extraordinaire Captain Weinman, he tried to get us locked up for having our guns on base, no wait....or as he called it...*a federal installation.*"

"Are you fucking kidding me?" Donald piped in.

"Nope, but it just so happens dear old Dad is close friends with a colonel over there…..and as we speak the captain is getting a serious attitude adjustment by a three star general and a full bird colonel. Let's just say, it's not a good day for him. What about you boys?" Michaels said looking at Dredge. "Got any good news?"

Tommy handed Michaels the folder. "Is that our buddy following Lenny's car?" asked Michaels.

"Looks like it," Dredge mumbled.

"Shithead," Tommy said. "Jeff Cover called and said he's got the measurements of your victim's projectile from the FBI."

"Good, let me see if I got an email from Masimo yet." Michaels took a seat at his desk and searched through his emails. "Bam, here it is…fingers crossed they're the same." Michaels opened the email, then the attachment. It was a cross section diagram of the gun barrel purchased at the Wilkes Pawn & Gun Shop, sent directly from Taurus Arms in Brazil. Next to each land and groove were finite measurements that served as a distinguishable, unique fingerprint for that weapon and no other. "Fuck. I've never seen such small dimensions. Let me send this off to Jeffrey and see if they compare to the impressions left on the projectile taken from our victim's arm. Let's hope for the best partner."

Jim flicked his lighter and toked on his cigar until it was lit. "I'll smoke to that."

Michaels stood and joined Jim for a smoke. "I can promise you one thing, we're getting fucking drunk if this comes back a match."

"No shit. Just think if it matches the projectile from Lenny's case too. Fuck," Jim said, letting the fragrant smoke trickle from his mouth.

Michaels desk phone began ringing. "Homicide, Detective Michaels, may I help you?"

"Shithead," the man on the other end shouted.

Michaels recognized the voice. "Jeff Cover, Jeff Cover, Jeff Cover," Michaels said as fast as he could like always.

"Are you sitting down?"

Michaels took a big drag from his cigarette. "No, I'm standing. Why?"

"Is your dick in your hand?" Jeff asked, sarcastically.

"Um, yes, it is now," Michaels shot back.

"It's a match. It's a fucking match. The gun they bought and fired in Georgia killed Seo-Yun

Kim in Severn. The ejector marks on the shell casings found in Georgia matched the markings on the casing found at the Kim murder. And the impressions on the projectile from your victim are the identical size of the lands and groves from the gun they bought. No question about it. Congratulations Shithead."

Michaels dropped the phone on the desk. From his facial expressions, Jim knew what he was just told. Michaels jumped up and down and clapped his hands yelling, "it's a match…it's a match…it's a match. Fucking A. Can you believe it? We got these motherfuckers now. Yee fucking haa!"

Tommy, Donald and Dredge poured from Tommy's office. "Congratulations boys," Tommy said, slapping Michaels' and Jim's hands.

"Another one bites the dust," Donald shouted. "Way to go guys," he said sharing hugs with Michaels and Jim.

The last in the receiving line was Dredge who had been distracted from the celebration by his desk phone ringing. "Homicide, Detective Hart." Dredge covered his opposite ear to muffle the noise of his comrade's jubilation.

"Dredge, it's Jeff."

"Hey."

"From the noise in the background, I guess you've heard the news. Tell Shithead he left me hanging on the phone." Dredge let out a short scratchy laugh.

"I didn't want you to feel slighted, but yours is a match too. The same gun used to kill Seo-Yun Kim was used in your case also. Congratulations brother."

Dredge eased out a small grin. "Good, good," he said showing no overt signs of excitement from the news. He looked at Tommy, Michaels and Jim who were still chatting with gleaming smiles. "Thanks Jeff. I'll see ya," he said hanging up the phone and firing up a stogey. Dredge walked nonchalantly to the front of his desk where the rest stood. He reached out and gave a hearty handshake to Jim, then Michaels, but this time he held onto Ronnie's hand squeezing it tightly, looking at him. "You ain't the only one happy boy," Dredge paused. "Mine's a match too," he said rendering a rarely seen smile.

"Oh my God. I can't fucking believe this," Michaels yelled. "Guys, Dredge has a match too in his case. We're not solving just one, but two homicides from this," Michaels bolstered, wrapping his arms around Dredge.

"Holy fucking shit," Tommy said in amazement.

For the next several minutes the small tucked away Homicide Unit in the rear of the old CID building turned into an unanticipated celebration. Jim turned on the radio and cranked up the volume when he heard Bon Jovi singing the most fitting song, *Living on a Prayer.* The other detectives from the Sex Crimes and Robbery Units heard the commotion and watched the dancing detectives from down the hall.

Tommy stood in the middle of the Homicide Squad room with his men and raised his voice over the noise and jocularity. "Everyone climb into their cars. Let's go figure out what's next. Drinks are on me. I'll see everyone at the 4100 Club."

"Not me brother. As much as I want to, I can't leave Katie alone. You guys let me know the plan tomorrow." Michaels returned to his desk to answer his ringing cell. It was Katie. "Hey pretty lady."

"Hi Ronnie. Sorry to bother you, but you told me to call when I was about to leave the office."

"You're not bothering me. Guess what? I just got great news."

Katie could hear the exhilaration in his voice. "What honey?"

"We just received confirmation that the gun Weinman bought for Schumaker in Georgia was the same weapon used to kill Suk Kim's daughter and the Army Special Agent."

"Oh my, that's outstanding. No wonder you sound so happy. Now what?"

"I'll tell you at dinner. Is there someone there to follow you home?"

"Sergeant Speake is sitting here in our waiting room. He's been talking to Brenda for hours. He's a real hoot. He's had her laughing most of the day."

"He's still there? Wow. Tell him I said thanks. I'm leaving here soon too. I'll see you at home Babe."

"I'm so happy for you Ronnie. I love you."

"Thanks Hun. I love you too. See you soon."

"Bye Ronnie."

Tommy and the boys got their coats on. After a brief stop to fill in Donoho and Tank of the latest development, they beelined to their cars. Still elated from the news, Michaels reached out to Dawn, who would be equally thrilled.

"Hi, Detective Michaels," she answered.

"Counselor did I get you at a bad time?"

"No of course not. I'm in my office with Lieutenant Lindner. We're talking about the shit Weinman started today. Have you heard from your dad?"

"No, he hasn't called, but I do have something you guys are going to love to hear."

"Let me put this on speaker…ok, go with it," she said.

"Good afternoon Lieutenant. How's it going sir?" Michaels asked.

Lindner chimed in. "I couldn't be happier Detective since I heard the news about Weinman. I wish I could have been a fly on the wall when they ripped his ass."

"Me too, but I do have something that may be even better."

"We're all ears," Lindner said.

"We just got confirmation from the FBI Laboratory, the same gun was used in the murders of Mrs. Kim's daughter and Agent Athas. I don't know if you heard, but we determined Weinman was with Schumaker in Georgia, where Weinman purchased a handgun. Afterwards, they went to Schumaker's parent's house and shot the gun. That's where we gathered a shit ton of casings. Isn't that outfuckingstanding?"

There was complete silence. Lindner looked at Dawn. "I can't believe it. My prayers have been answered," Dawn said.

"Thank God. His family is going to be so happy." The lieutenant wiped his eyes. "So now what? Who's going to be arrested?" Lindner asked.

"We have to lay everything out first and put our game plan together," Michaels explained.

"Ronnie, if there's anything you need, just give us a call," Dawn said.

"Okay guys, I'll be in touch."

On his way from the CID building, Michaels was called into Captain Donoho's office where he and Lieutenant Tank sat. "Shithead, get in here," Tank said. "Good job man."

Donoho slapped Michaels' hand. "Way to go Shithead. Good job."

"Thanks. I don't know what made me call Wilkes County Sheriff's Office. Something just hit me when I saw the county name listed on his tag."

"That's good detective work. It's when experience, intuition and gut feelings come together. It becomes instinctive when you've been in this line of work long enough. You have a gift son," Donoho said in admiration.

Now overdressed in accolades, Michaels felt uncomfortable but happy. "Well, thank you. I appreciate that, but it's not over yet." Michaels turned and walked from the building to start home.

Chapter 47

It was 7:30 a.m. the next day when Tommy rolled onto the CID parking lot in Crownsville only to notice Michaels' Malibu already there. Nursing a Vodka hangover, Tommy strolled to the squad room with a large black coffee. "You're in here awful early," Tommy said to Michaels, typing vigorously on his keyboard.

"Did you fellas have fun last night?" Michaels asked.

"Fuck yeah. What are you doing?"

Michaels pushed himself back from his desk. "I'm typing an Application for an Arrest Warrant charging Wesley Schumaker with the First Degree Murder of Seo-Yun Kim. It's time to lock him up."

"We were talking last night. We think, well most of us think, you have enough to charge him, but not enough for Weinman. Donald thinks you have enough to charge Schumaker with murder and Weinman with conspiracy, but the rest of us don't think so," Tommy explained.

Michaels fired up a cigarette and leaned back in his chair. "The more I think about it, the more I realize just how much we have. First, I got big time motive. Just days before Schumaker is set to be court martialed, his accuser's daughter is murdered, which was either done to intimidate her not to testify, or the wrong person was killed. Then I have the identical bottle used for the Molotov Cocktail at the murder scene found in the trash where Schumaker lives, along with a receipt showing two were purchased days before the crime, but only one bottle could be accounted for. Next, let's not forget, I got that chic walking her dog who observed a man fitting Schumaker's description standing outside the crime scene minutes before the murder." Michaels flipped through the pages of his notebook..."What else? Here it is. I have witnesses who seen Schumaker just minutes after the murder of Seo-Yun at the GI Party looking all disheveled and shit. Then let's not forget I got Schumaker picking out a gun for his birthday, that Weinman bought for him in Georgia. And....not only did they buy a gun, but they bought the same ammunition they used to shoot at cans...which I might add, just happens to have the same manufacturers stamping, ejector and firing pin markings like the casing discovered outside the window where the fatal round was shot. Did I mention we can forensically show the projectile that passed through Seo-Yun's body and Lenny's, was fired through the very barrel of the weapon purchased at the Pawn & Gun Shop in lovely Wilkes County, Georgia? BAMM!" Michaels took a big drag of his cigarette and blew it out hard. "With all that, I'd say Schumaker's fucked and maybe his asshole buddy too."

"Sounds good enough for me. Let me see what Commissioner is working today. This would be worth a few bottles of wine if Commissioner

Wolfe is in Annapolis. Tommy retreated to his office to start making calls. He didn't want Michaels' Warrant Application to land in front of some rookie Commissioner who didn't have a fucking clue what he or she was doing and deny his warrant. Tommy knew all too well the value of a phone call and a few bottles of spirits. It was a small slice of justice never spoke of, and another way Tommy looked out for his men and their victims.

"Shithead," Dredge said entering the squad room also carrying his coffee as if it was an oxygen bottle keeping him alive. "What are you doin?" he said in his deep voice.

"Dredge...you big bag of fuck. What's going on? I'm typing my dick off over here so we can lock up asswad today."

Dredge sat in his chair, rocked backwards and laughed. "Which asswad would that be?"

"Um, that would be one Wesley, no walking the dog, Schumaker."

"Yeah, I'm going to start writing mine up too. Can you give me the info on the gun and the shell casings?"

"It's in the folder I put on your desk, along with Schumaker's info."

Chapter 48

Also an early arrival at work, Dawn sat at her desk touching up an opening statement she had mapped out. It was a cut and dry assault case where one soldier went a little overboard when he walked in on his girlfriend and another soldier, entwined like snakes banging the fuck out of one another. Though he didn't lay a hand on his whoring girlfriend, he did hurl all her belongings on the street and beat the fuck out of his so called, comrade. The Army didn't take to kindly to his actions. Dawn could hear her phone vibrating in her briefcase. It was Katie.

"Good morning Dr.."

Katie laughed. "Good morning Ms. Judge Advocate General Attorney person." They both laughed some more. "What do I owe the honor for such an early phone call?"

"I only have a handful of appointments in the morning and my afternoon is free. I wanted to see if I could take you to lunch, since I still haven't returned the favor for what you did for me."

"Katie, you don't need to do that, but I would love to go to lunch with you. I have a short trial starting at 9:00 a.m., which may turn into a plea and then I'm stuck here the rest of the day starting at 1:00 p.m. as the duty attorney."

"Then lunch it is. How about I meet you at your office? There's a restaurant called The Grill we can go to. They have great food. You'll love it. Would 11:45 be too early?"

"That sounds good. I should be done by then. This will be fun."

Chapter 49

By 10:00 a.m. the first step of the day was done. Dredge and Michaels had crafted their separate applications charging Wesley Schumaker with two counts of murder and personally delivered them to their handpicked Commissioner, Stephanie Wolfe. Michaels' finished masterpiece was a whopping four pages long, chock full of motive, witness info and indisputable forensic evidence. Dredge's, on the other hand, was two pages of creative writing, combining circumstantial information, along with the intricacies of gun barrel and projectile measurements. Because the probable cause in each were starkly different, the plan was to first present Commissioner Wolf with the most compelling evidence, three bottles of expensive red wine Tommy had secured at the nearby Harbour Liquor Store. After that, her first warrant application would be the gem Michaels prepared, persuasive enough to lay a convincing foundation of guilt. It was thought once her emotions were spiked and the first warrant was issued, she'd be more likely to rubber stamp the second, which was Dredge's.

As expected, their strategy came to fruition. In less than 45 minutes Dredge and Michaels were on their way back to the CID with two murder warrants. It was now time to hunt down Schumaker.

Tommy and Donald waited in the squad room for Dredge and Michaels. Smoked swirled in the room from the breeze blowing through the open back door. As the two entered the building, like old times, Michaels had to restrain his excitement and walk at a snail's pace next to his old partner. "Could you walk any slower Dredge? Christ, they're liable to repeal the death penalty before we get to our desks," Michaels said sarcastically. Dredge paid no mind to the young spry detective.

"Well Shithead?" Donald yelled from his desk.

Michaels' smile was telling enough. "BAMM," he said loudly. "We got both. Tommy, she loved the wine too and said thanks."

Tommy was ecstatic. "Ok listen up…we'll take two cars. Jim's already surveilling Venessa's parking lot and Schumaker's car is there. Let's get this show on the road and close two homicides. I want the gun and I want the goat and I want it now," Tommy exclaimed.

"What the fuck did you just say? Did you say goat?" Michaels clamored.

Tommy laughed. "I meant coat. I want the gun and the coat. You know, that long coat he was wearing that night?"

"Alright boys, you heard Tommy he wants the gun and the goat," Michaels said, chuckling as they gathered their things.

Chapter 50

Michaels led the way up the stairs to Venessa's apartment with the rest of the squad behind him. With his right hand gripping his Glock, he pounded hard on the metal door. "I hear movement," he whispered. The peephole darkened. "County Police Wesley, open the fucking door or I'll smash it in," Michaels said firmly. The door opened just a few inches and Schumaker peaked his head out. Michaels placed his gun inches from his forehead. "Put your hands up real slow so I can see them." Michaels pushed his way into the foyer and took control of the suspect. "Get on the ground," he ordered. Wesley laid face first on the living room carpet, wearing a blue t-shirt, black sweatpants and socks. "You know the drill, put your hands behind your back." Michaels holstered his weapon and towered above him holding shiny dangling handcuffs.

Venessa heard the commotion and walked from the bedroom, slipping on a robe. "What's going on?" she said, shocked to see her boyfriend on the floor, surrounded by the men.

Tommy made it a point to intercept her so she couldn't get too close. "He's under arrest."

"For what?"

"Two counts of murder, that's what," Tommy said.

"Two counts of murder? I didn't kill anyone. Captain Weinman killed them," Schumaker blurted out.

Intrigued from what he just heard, Michaels yanked Schumaker from the ground and put him on the couch. The guys were surprised from his comment and looked at one another. Michaels knew the importance of taking advantage of a talking suspect and he wasted no time questioning him. "What do you mean Weinman killed them? Killed who?"

"Shouldn't he have a lawyer?" Venessa said moving toward Wesley.

Jim wasn't in any mood for Venessa's advice. "Hey," Jim said with his finger pointing toward her. "I'll tell you what he needs. He needs you to shut the fuck up."

"It's ok V," Schumaker said. "I didn't kill anyone. Stan, you know, Captain Weinman, shot that girl. I only threw the bottle."

"Wesley," Venessa said shocked from his words.

"What the fuck did I just tell you?" Jim said raising his voice to Venessa.

"Can you take her back to the bedroom? I need to talk to you guys," asked Schumaker. He watched Tommy and Jim walk Venessa down the hallway and out of sight. Michaels could tell there was something he didn't want to say in front of her and he appeared eager to talk. "And he killed that agent too. He made me go with him. He just opened his car door and started firing, like he was crazy."

Michaels looked at Dredge and Donald and turned back to Schumaker. "Why...why?"

Schumaker looked toward the hallway to be sure Venessa couldn't hear. He scooted to the edge of the couch and looked down at his socks. "We," he paused..."We had a thing and the agent caught us, you know...Also, Stan didn't want me to end up in jail. He said he would take care of everything."

"Where's the gun he used?" Dredge asked.

"I'm not sure."

"What happened to the fucking shell casings where Agent Athas was killed?" asked Donald.

"He told me to pick them up, something about getting rid of the evidence, but I hid one, just in case something like this would happen."

Michaels looked at Dredge and Donald. "What do you mean?" Michaels asked.

"I took one of them out of my pocket when we were driving away and stuck it in the passenger seat of his truck. It's probably still there."

"What did you do with the rest of them?" Michaels asked.

"I threw them out the window."

"Where?" Donald asked loudly, getting frustrated.

"Umm" Schumaker thought for a moment. "I think we were across from the firehouse. I remember seeing trees."

Donald was getting pissed with his halfass answers. "What firehouse?"

Schumaker thought for a second. "The one in Odenton."

Michaels had an epiphany. "Wire. That's it." Michaels clapped his hands together. "You're going to wear a wire." Now besides Schumaker's testimony, Michaels knew Dredge needed more evidence to convict Weinman. Schumaker looked at Michaels who continued with his ingenious idea. "We'll send you into Weinman's office and get him to talk about the murders. Maybe even..."

"But..," Schumaker interrupted.

"Shut the fuck up," Donald said, he's talking.

Michaels continued. "Talk about the gun and the shell casings." Everyone could see he was thinking through the strategy without even once asking Schumaker if he was willing to carry through with his plan. "You can ask him if he took the shell casing from the first scene…yeah, and then ask him how many times he shot the second guy, because you're not sure how many casings you picked up."

Michaels scratched his head and began looking around the room while he thought some more.

"Get him to talk about what you're supposed to do or say if you get locked up?" Donald suggested.

"Fuck yeah. I like it," Michaels agreed.

"Do I have to do this?" Schumaker meekly asked.

Michaels grabbed Schumaker by the arm and jacked him off the couch. "Put it this way motherfucker, you ain't got a whole lot of choices here Chief. This may be the only thing that keeps you from the electric chair. Ready when you are Tommy," Michaels shouted.

"Grab my coat Babe," Schumaker asked Venessa.

Tommy and Jim followed behind Venessa to the living room. She took a dark overcoat, mixed with a light tweed thread from the foyer closet and draped it over Schumaker's shoulders. Jim shot Michaels a look. It was the missing jacket.

Michaels grinned. "Looks like we got the goat Tommy."

Chapter 51

At the CID building Michaels scrambled to get ahold of a surveillance body wire set from the Narcotics Section. Not taking any chances, he replaced the battery in the device with a fresh 9-volt. Jim started on the Search and Seizure Warrant for Weinman's SUV, while Dredge coordinated with Jeff on the phone so they could search for the casings, once Schumaker pointed out where he dumped them.

Michaels taped the cigarette box size unit to the small of Schumaker's back. He snaked the microphone cord around his mid-section and secured it to the middle of his chest with duct tape. He wanted to be sure every word would be captured. "Now listen. Act like none of this is here. Just talk regular. We don't want him to get hinked up. You hear me?"

Schumaker was nervous. His palms were drenched with sweat. "What do you want me to say again?"

"Jesus Christ. You're a real bad ass when you're trying to rape a little Asian lady huh?" Michaels fired a look at Schumaker and grabbed him by the throat and shoved him against the filing cabinet. "You're fucking doing this whether you like it or not. He ain't getting away with this. No fucking way, not on my watch. Remember...you're concerned he left a bullet casing behind at the first scene, and you're not sure that you got them all at the second scene. Ask him how many times he shot the agent. Then flat out ask, what are you supposed to say if the police come to your house again. That should get him talking."

Michaels cuffed Schumaker in the front. "Sit down. We'll be leaving in a little bit."

Schumaker took a seat in the chair next to Michaels' desk. "Would it be possible to have one of your cigarettes please?" he asked Michaels.

"What do you think this is, The Make a Wish Foundation? Fuck off. Jim, are you about done?"

Jim walked to the printer and snatched the sheets that dropped into the tray. "Yup, all done. Let's go get this bad boy signed. Weinman's going to have a heck of a time explaining why a shell casing that killed a U.S. Army federal agent is in his truck." Jim stood in front of Schumaker while he put his coat on. "You're sure you put that in his seat?"

"Yes sir," he mumbled.

"Enlighten me Wesley, if you're banging this guy, what made you decide to leave evidence in his truck? That doesn't make any sense," Jim asked.

"I'm not sure. He was so controlling, and it kept getting worse. He had all these crazy plans for him and I when he retired. I just figured if it came down to it, he'd throw me under the bus. I put that in his seat as my life insurance policy."

"I'll call Judge Williams' office from the car and tell him we're on our way to his chambers," Michael said.

"Ronnie, let me know when you're headed to Fort Meade. Donald and I will meet you at the Odenton Fire Department. That way, he can point out where he threw the casings before you send him in and I'll get Jeff's crew to see what they can find," Dredge said.

"Will do brother. Come on," Michaels said to Schumaker. Michaels stopped briefly in front of Tommy's doorway. "We're off to Annapolis to get this Search Warrant signed and then we'll be dropping in on Weinman."

"You taking him with ya?" asked Tommy.

"Yup, he and I will wait in the car while Jim's in with the judge."

"Ok. Do you need me to go?" Tommy asked.

"No. There'll be four of us in two cars. That'll be plenty. There shouldn't be any problems. I'll give you a call."

"What's the plan Ronnie if he incriminates himself on the wire?"

Michaels looked at Schumaker standing between he and Jim. "Once he comes out and is secured in my car, the boys will go in and lock his ass up."

Schumaker piped up. "What will happen to me?"

"I'll tell you what Wesley. If you get him to admit his involvement in these murders, I'll give you all the cigarettes you want. Fuck, I'll even buy you a sub and a coke when I take your statement."

"Statement?" Schumaker had a confused look on his face. "Aren't you supposed to read me my rights?"

Michaels started walking. "Yeah, we'll get right on that, just like you did to that little girl before you put a bullet in her. I'd suggest you just shut you're fucking mouth. Come on Jim."

Driving like a bat out of hell, in just 20 minutes, the three arrived at the Circuit Court in Annapolis. On the way, Michaels threw a phone call alerting Judge Williams' secretary of Jim's arrival time. Cuffed and belted in the back seat, Schumaker remained in the car with Michaels, while Jim hurried to the judge's chambers.

"Go on in Detective, he's waiting for you," the secretary said.

Carrying a folder with three copies of the Search Warrant, Jim walked in with confidence. "Good morning your honor."

"Good morning. So, you're in the Homicide Unit now?"

Jim smiled. "Yes sir Judge. Wow, what a change of pace from working B&E's to this."

Judge Williams looked over his reading glasses at Jim. "I'll bet it is. I thought my secretary said Detective Michaels called a little while ago."

"Yes sir. We're partners now."

"I really like him. He's a good man," the judge said taking the folder from him. "Let's see what you have here." He opened the folder and began reading. Judge Williams raised his head while he turned the pages. "That was very intuitive of the co-defendant to leave a shell casing behind. That's more like something a victim would do, not an accomplice."

"I know, we thought that was strange also, but we're glad. I just hope it's still there," Jim answered.

Judge Williams took the cap off his Mont Blanc pen and began scratching his swooping signature on the Search and Seizure Warrants. The detectives were now authorized to search Stanley Weinman's Army issued green Ford Explorer. "Please tell Detective Michaels I said hi."

"He's outside right now sir, babysitting our suspect. I'll be sure to tell him."

The judge stood at his desk. "Be careful and happy hunting."

Jim shook his hand and smiled. He never heard a judge say that before. "Thank you sir."

Chapter 52

Dawn answered her ringing cell phone. "Hey girl."

"Are we still on for lunch?" Katie inquired.

"Yes but take your time. The defense attorney has been granted a mini recess to talk to her client about my plea offer. How does 45 minutes at my office sound?"

"That's perfect. I'll finish some of my paperwork then be on my way. See ya soon."

"Bye bye now," Dawn said.

Chapter 53

Michaels and Jim sped from Annapolis to meet Dredge and Donald at the Odenton Fire Hall. As they neared, Michaels instructed Schumaker to be on the lookout for where he chucked the casings from the window. Michaels took it slow down Route 175.

"Here, here," Schumaker said, motioning his head toward the side of the road. "This looks like it. It's different because it's light out, but I remember that small clump of trees."

"How certain are you?" asked Jim.

Schumaker continued to look out the window. "I'm pretty sure that's it, cause there's no other trees around and I remember it was just before the fire department."

Michaels pulled into the fire house lot next to Donald's car. Smoke was billowing from his open windows.

"How'd it go?" Dredge asked.

Jim held up the folder. "All signed and ready to go."

"What's the plan Shithead?" Donald asked.

"I'm going to let him out down the street and have him walk up to Weinman's office. We can park on Mapes Lane not too far away. That way we'll be close enough to hear the wire and still have an eyeball on the front door." Michaels turned to face Schumaker. "You got your lines, right?"

"I think so."

"Ok. I'm going to drop you off by the guard shack. When you're done, that's where we'll pick you up. Don't forget you're still under arrest for 2 counts of murder. If you decide to run, we will shoot you."

"I'm not gonna run. I didn't kill anybody…he did."

"Good, then get him to tell you that," Michaels insisted.

Michaels and Jim drove Schumaker to the guard shack a block from Weinman's office, while Dredge and Donald took up surveillance 100 yards from the small aging office that once served as a single-family dwelling for commissioned officers. The front of the building had two windows and a flimsy warped oak door. The larger window was to the left of the front door, when facing the building from Mapes Lane. It once provided a view from the living room, but now casted light into Weinman's office as did the window on the side of the building. Previously a bedroom, the smaller window on the opposite side of the front door belonged to the office occupied by the Captain's secretary.

In a small lot adjacent to the guard shack, Michaels and Jim went through last minute preparations with Schumaker, ensuring the wire worked and could be clearly heard from the briefcase resting on Jim's lap in the passenger's seat. He could be heard crisp and clear. The mission was a go.

"One last thing. If I text you with a bunch of explanation points, that means leave, like get the fuck out of there and meet us at the shack. Got it?"

Schumaker nodded his head. "Exclamation points mean abort. Roger that."

"Ok, let's do this Wesley. Start walking. We'll watch from here then we'll set up out front where the other detectives are when you're inside," Michaels informed him.

Jim called Donald's cell. "Ok brother, Schumaker is headed your way. Is Weinman's SUV there?"

"Yup. He's here. His secretary's parking spot's empty."

"Fucking A. We'll be coming in your direction once you have an eyeball on him. Text me when you see him."

"Will do."

With just a short distance to walk, Jim received Donald's text, *we got your boy.* "Let's go brother. He's there," Jim told his partner.

Careful Weinman wouldn't recognize Michaels' vehicle, he tucked his car out of sight, behind Donald's Cavalier. Michaels dialed up Donald's cell.

"We gonna get this punk ass today Ronnie?" Donald asked jokingly.

Michaels laughed. "I hope so. I'll keep my phone on so you guys can hear what's being said over the wire."

"Dredge is nodding his head, so I guess that means good," Donald said laughing.

"He's in the door. Let's hope he doesn't fuck this up," Jim said.

Sitting at his desk wearing fatigues and talking on his phone, Weinman could see it was Schumaker who had arrived. Weinman motioned for him to lock the door.

"Damn, this is coming across clear. I can hear his big mouth on the phone," Michaels said. A veteran to surveillance, Michaels took his small set of binoculars from the glove box and glassed the building.

"What can you see?" Jim asked.

Michaels adjusted the focus. "I can see dickwad sitting at his desk. It looks like he's still on the phone. Schumaker must be off to the side. I don't have eyes on him." Michaels kept the optics against his face.

"Are you hearing this, guys?" he said over the phone to Donald and Dredge.

"We got it," said Donald.

Michaels watched Weinman hang up the phone and walk around his desk toward the front of the building. "Schumaker just locked the door. Wait....What?...You're not gonna fucking believe this. They're kissing. I mean they are going at it right in front of the fucking window." The guys heard the sounds of the men embracing. "Fuck, Weinman just closed the blinds," Michaels alerted the group.

Schumaker was afraid Weinman would feel the device taped to his back. Weinman released Schumaker from his bear hug. "You surprised me. I wasn't expecting you," Weinman said.

The voices over the wire were crystal clear. "Yeah, I, I just wanted to talk to you. I've been thinking about something. It's been bothering me," Schumaker said.

"Here we go," announced Michaels.

Weinman walked to the window, lifted a blind and perused the lot. "I thought you came over here for something else." Not waiting for a response, Weinman turned from the window to face Schumaker, unbuttoned his pants and revealed himself.

"I did, but can I ask you something first?" Schumaker was reluctant to having a ravenous sexual encounter overheard by the surveilling detectives.

"This better be good," he said stuffing his bulging genital into his pants.

Schumaker took a seat at the round table in the middle of the room. Weinman stood in front of him with his arms crossed. The young sergeant's nerves overtook him. His mouth was dry. "Stan, can I get a water?"

Weinman sensed something was not quite right. "Yeah...wow, what's wrong with you? You don't want to go down on me and now you want a water?"

"Fuck. He knows something's up. God damn it," Michael said, inhaling a big drag from his cigarette.

Schumaker walked to the small stainless refrigerator behind Weinman's desk and grabbed a water bottle. "I've just been wondering. I had to talk to you." Schumaker returned to his seat. "I'm just scared. I don't want to go to jail. I mean, I didn't shoot anybody but..."

"What? What do you mean you didn't shoot anybody?" Weinman interrupted. "Jesus Christ, you ain't turning into a pussy on me are ya? Let me tell you something boy," Weinman said, raising his voice. "You're as guilty as I am. I ain't going down for this. It was all over your crap anyway, trying to fuck that Asian bitch and all. I've been running around trying to clean up your mess. You don't know who or what you want. I mean really. One day you're bent over my desk telling me you love me and then you try and rape someone?"

The detectives couldn't believe what they were hearing. "Donald, you guys copying this?" Michaels asked.

"Yup."

Schumaker forced out an anxious cough. "No, no."

Weinman was becoming very impatient. "Spit it out. What is it?"

"Remember after you, you know, shot that agent in the car?"

Weinman was getting frustrated with the pace and direction of their conversation. "What about it?"

"You told me to pick up the bullet casings on the ground. You said something about keeping them, you know, from the police."

Weinman began pacing back and forth across the room. "Yeah, and what the fuck about it? What are you getting at? I don't like the sound of this Wes. What are you trying to say?"

"I, I was just wondering if you took the one, you know, the one, the casing from the first place where you shot that girl?"

"Fuck I wish I could see inside," Michaels said, still examining the building through the binoculars.

Weinman rubbed the back of his neck while he continued pacing. "No, I didn't. But who knows if they even found it. It was dark. There was a lot of grass. I don't fucking know, but why are you so concerned about this now? You've been watching too much TV, now get over here." Weinman began to unbutton his pants again and move closer to Schumaker.

"Is he pulling his junk out again?" Jim asked.

Michaels nodded his head. "What the fuck?"

Donald was heard snickering in the background.

"Stan…no…Can we do this later. I mean I don't feel like it right now. What am I supposed to say if those detectives come knocking at my door again? I keep forgetting what you said."

Weinman stopped in his tracks. He looked around the room like he was trying to find something. He rushed toward the window, this time carefully examining the parking lot and outskirts. Schumaker closed his eyes, took a deep breath and swallowed what little saliva he had.

Chapter 54

Dawn climbed into her car parked in front of the military courthouse. It was the first time she had been back since her devastating loss. Looking forward to her lunch plans, she rang Katie's cell. "Hey girl."

"Hi Dawn, I just got to your office. I was introducing myself to this nice lady who must keep you in line," Katie said in fun.

"Oh, my secretary Phyllis, yeah she's the best kept secret on base. You should tell her retirement isn't what it's all cracked up to be. She's supposed to be leaving me next month."

Looking at Phyllis, Katie smiled and laughed and played along with Dawn. "Tell her not to retire? Tell her you'll be lost without her? I'd be glad to Major." The three laughed. "I'll be there in less than five. Make yourself at home."

Dawn drove down Mapes Lane to her office. She was glad her case ended in a plea, one that would be good for all involved so long as the defendant stayed clear of the new happy couple.

Chapter 55

Weinman walked past Schumaker without saying a word. He looked out the side window next to his desk toward Mapes Lane and the JAG headquarters. Everything appeared to be business as usual he thought, except for his lover's behavior. Something was amiss.

Schumaker's nerves were shot. He looked at Weinman who was acting like a caged tiger. Trying to calm him, Schumaker spoke up. "Whatcha doin Stan?"

"Oh, everything is just fine. I'll be right there," he said in his best phony voice.

"It's been awfully quiet. What do you think's going on?" the inquisitive Jim asked.

"I didn't like the sound of that," Dredge said referring to Weinman's dismissing comment.

Turning away from his guest, Weinman opened his top desk drawer and pulled out his fully loaded Taurus. He approached the waiting Schumaker from behind, then slapped his left hand across his mouth. Schumaker could feel the cold steel barrel against his temple. His body tensed. Weinman leaned closer and whispered in his ear. "Don't say a word or I'll fucking kill you. Take off your shirt."

Michaels put his head closer to the speaker. "Somebody's talking, but I can't make it out."

Schumaker was petrified. His hands shook. He didn't know what to do. He thought of shouting for help but was afraid. He knew if Weinman saw the wire on him, he would have to let him go. He would have to know the police were listening and giving up would be his only option.

"I said take your fucking shirt off," he mouthed. He repositioned himself in front of Schumaker and removed his hand from his mouth, now shimmering with sweat. He pressed the gun between his eyes. "Now."

"I don't like this Ronnie. What the fuck is going on? Did the wire die?" Donald asked.

Michaels flashbacked to when FBI Agent Smith's wire failed, and she barely escaped death. "No, it couldn't have. It was working fine. I don't fucking know what's going on. I'm going to get him out of there. I'm texting him now."

Chapter 56

Dawn emerged from the fourth floor elevator wheeling her briefcase in the direction where Phyllis and Katie sat talking. "I trust you girls are having fun?"

Katie and Phyllis smiled. "So, what's on the menu Katie?"

"How does a good Reuben sound?"

"I love them. I haven't had one in years," said Dawn.

"*The Grill* on Quarterfield Road has the best," Katie boasted.

Katie began admiring the numerous awards and plaques on the walls. She continued her examination of Dawn's achievements, working around the room, reading each accolade. "I'm impressed Major. These are some serious accomplishments. You should be proud."

Dawn laughed. "Just call me the over achiever. I didn't have a life growing up, so school was my only outlet, well except for one other," and she pointed to the trophies on the credenza behind her desk.

Intrigued, Katie walked to the trophies and began marveling over the insignia inscribed on the plates. "First Place, 10th Annual Army Sniper

Tournament, First Place, 7th Annual Army Sniper Tournament, First Place, 35th Green Beret Sniper Challenge, First Place, 18th Annual Quantico Invitational Sniper Tournament, 2nd Place, 23rd Fort Benning Marksmanship Games." Katie laid the last trophy down. "Damn girl."

"Hell, you're a psychiatrist, you can probably tell me the meaning of all this. Besides school, shooting was the one thing I really enjoyed. It was an exercise in relaxation and breathing. Each time I squeezed off a round I would erase everything in my mind, like I would escape from every worry I had when I looked through the scope, holding the crosshairs steady on my target. I don't know, in my own weird way, it puts me at peace."

Katie watched and listened to Dawn describe her passion. "There's nothing weird about that Dawn. It's good to have something healthy that comforts you. Some people achieve this at the gym, others through hiking or reading…I know Ronnie enjoys riding motocross and hunting. If you don't mind me asking, have you put your skills to use in combat?"

"No, no, I've never been on the battlefield. I did something crazy and went and got my damn law degree. I've never put my talents to use in the field. I've just been restricted to shooting boring targets of all shapes and sizes."

"Do you still compete?"

"I sure do. I practice at the range as much as I can. Like I said, it's like a sedative to me."

"What kind of gun do you shoot?"

"Would you like to see it? It's here in my closet."

"Yeah, I'd love to."

Dawn's office phone rang. "Excuse me Katie, let me get this real quick."

"No problem. Take your time." Still standing near the trophies, Katie enjoyed the view from the fourth story window.

Chapter 57

Schumaker slid his coat off onto the back of the chair. Thoughts were racing through his brain. He pulled at the bottom of his shirt to lift it off. Weinman pushed the gun harder against his skull and placed his index finger in front of his own lips, signaling Schumaker to be quiet. "Shhhh," he said.

"I just texted him the signal to get out," Michaels told the team.

With his shirt partially off, Weinman's suspicions were confirmed. He could plainly see the microphone wire. He was infuriated. With the surveillance equipment fully exposed, Weinman's face was beet red. Michaels' text went through to Schumaker's phone.

"Aren't you gonna answer that?" Weinman grabbed the phone from Schumaker's pocket and saw the exclamation points across the screen.

Michaels tapped the steering wheel. "Come on, get out of there." Michaels tapped faster. "Donald, once he comes out, we'll grab Schumaker, and you and Dredge lock up Weinman."

"Ok. What's all that noise coming over the wire Ronnie?" Donald asked.

"I'm not sure. They could be kissing again. I have no clue."

With the gun still against his head he squeezed the frightened Schumaker's arm and lifted him from the chair.

In total panic Schumaker screamed, "Help!"

Weinman tore the box from the small of his back and yanked the wire from the device. All communications were cut off. With the butt of his gun, Weinman slammed the hardened steel grip to the back of Schumaker's skull. Blood gushed from the instant gaping wound.

"Fuck," Michaels yelled. "The wire went dead. He found it." Michaels keyed up his radio. "Detective 132 to communications." The seasoned dispatcher detected the urgency in his voice.

"Go ahead Detective 132."

"Detectives 131, 133, 134 and I are at 225 Mapes Lane in Fort Meade about to make an arrest on a homicide suspect. Have the base start some MP's our way and tell them to switch their radios over to our channel 4H. It's urgent." Michaels stuffed his portable police radio in his rear pocket and unholstered his Glock. "Let's go guys." The four detectives bailed from their vehicles and sprinted toward the building.

Dawn ended her phone call only to be startled by Katie still watching out the window. "Oh my God, that looks like Ronnie. Christ, it is. It's him and the guys he works with. They're running toward that building. They have their guns out. Holy shit."

Being the youngest of the bunch, Jim and Michaels led the charge with their weapons drawn. They scaled the four steps leading to the front door, each standing on either side. Michaels grabbed the doorknob, prepared to open or kick it, when without warning a flurry of gunshots rang out. Repeated blasts came from inside. A barrage of bullets pierced through the old wooden door and adjacent wall. Michaels' weapon was struck causing it to fly from his hand making a loud thud on the top step. A second bullet penetrated Michaels' upper right shoulder, inches from his carotid artery, dropping him face down. Blood poured from his wound, soaking his starched white shirt and black suitcoat.

Katie and Dawn helplessly watched the events unfold. Dawn swung open the two barn door style windows. "Oh my God Dawn, something's wrong. That's Ronnie laying there." Tears filled her eyes.

"Shit. That's fucking Weinman's office." Dawn said pissed off.

"Whose office?"

"Weinman. The asshole that tried running you off the road."

"Ah fuck," Michaels moaned. "That son of a bitch."

Jim could see the blood spewing from his partner and the splintering holes which speckled the door. He knew they were still in danger, and they had to get out of the line of fire. "Ronnie, hurry we gotta get you away from this door. Give me your arm." Michaels stretched one arm out and used his partially incapacitated limb to grab his gun. Jim took hold of his wrist and drug him like a sack of potatoes off the steps to the corner of the building. Drag marks from the blood doused the top step.

Jim looked down at Michaels' bloody hand keeping pressure on the wound. "How ya feeling?"

Michaels lifted his hand and they both inspected the bloody hole in his jacket. Blood bubbled out like a faucet. "It's hot and stings like a bitch," Michaels mumbled, wincing in pain. "I'm getting lightheaded Jim. Shit. I'm losing a lot of blood. Fuck," he said exhaling.

Just a few feet behind when the gun fire broke out, Donald and Dredge dove for cover on the ground at the base of the building. They could hear the bullets zipping over their heads. Small pieces of wood rained around them as the projectiles whizzed by. Donald keyed up his portable radio as the sounds of multiple sirens drew nearer. "Detective 133 to dispatch."

"Go ahead."

"Detective 132's been shot. We're gonna need an ambo and the SWAT Team and fast. Notify Sergeant Suit.

To no surprise, Tommy was already on the air. "Detective 130 to Dispatch, I copy direct. Donald, how's Ronnie?"

"Standby." Donald looked toward the corner of the building. "Jim," Donald shouted. "Can you hear me?"

"Yeah."

Donald hollered out, "How's Ronnie?"

"He's lost a lot of blood. This ain't good."

Donald keyed up his portable. "Not good," he advised Tommy.

There was complete silence for a few seconds. "Ok," Tommy said. "Has anyone made contact with the suspect?" Being a trained Hostage Negotiator, Tommy knew the importance of his question.

"We're about to," Donald responded.

The men watched as two MP Jeeps came to a screeching halt in the parking lot. Each of the vehicles were occupied by two military police officers wearing camo fatigues. Oddly, in the second jeep were Dinko and Astle, the same officers who responded the night Suk was attacked. Bullets were still being shot at random through the door.

The MP's took cover behind their vehicles. "We need to evacuate the JAG Office," Astle shouted to Dinko.

"I agree. On three, jump in and I'll back us out of here," Dinko told him over the popping sounds of gun fire.

"Ready when you are," Astle said.

"One, two, three." The two men hopped in their CJ-7. "Hold on," Dinko shouted, shifting the vehicle in reverse, and backing up at a high rate of speed. He stomped his brakes and jerked the steering wheel, causing the jeep to skid around facing forward. Immediately, he shifted the vehicle into drive. The smoking tires squealed while he zipped across Mapes Lane into the front of the JAG building where it skidded to a stop.

They raced into the lobby area where the unarmed security guard sat flipping through a magazine, oblivious to the pandemonium. Luckily, because of a judicial conference in Bethesda, the majority of the building was vacant except for a handful of attorneys.

The guard stood when he saw the MP's. "What's going on?" he asked.

"We have an active shooter across the street. We need to evacuate this building, now," Specialist Astle instructed the man in no uncertain terms.

"Yes sir, there's only a few people here on the first floor, and Major Sarro and her secretary are the only ones on the top floor."

"Ok, listen to me. Have the ones on the first floor exit through the back door. Tell them to leave using the rear employee entrance way and wait in the lot of the Officer's Club until further directed. Under no circumstances are they to drive to the front of the building. We'll head upstairs," Dinko said.

"Got it sir." The elderly man shuffled as fast as he could down the hallway.

"Are you sure that's him," Dawn asked.

Katie was frantic over what she was seeing. "I'll call his cell and see if he picks up. Do you have any binoculars?"

"No, I don't," she said, noticing the two MP's in her hallway walking in her direction. She walked out and stood next to Phyllis' desk. Katie walked close behind her. "What's going on outside gentlemen?" Dawn asked.

Both men saluted her. "Good afternoon Major. Ma'am, we have a county policeman shot and there's one or two suspects inside. Major, do you know whose office that is?"

Dawn and Katie looked at one another. "Trust me, I know whose God damn office it is."

"Major, considering how close it is, for your protection we need everyone to evacuate using the rear door and back entrance way," Astle said.

"Give me your radio," Dawn demanded.

"Excuse me ma'am," Astle said, dumbfounded from her request.

"Give me your God damn radio Specialist. You guys need to leave the building now." Both MP's stood speechless. "That's an order gentlemen," she snapped. Astle handed over his radio and the two uniformed soldiers turned and hurried down the hall. "Phyllis, take the rest of the day off. Do what they asked and leave now."

"Yes Major. You all aren't staying, are you?" the concerned secretary asked.

Dawn watched Katie wipe the tears from her face. "We'll be leaving soon. Go home...I'll see you tomorrow."

"Yes ma'am." Phyllis took her purse and started down the stairs.

Katie's crying intensified. "He can't die Dawn. He can't. I lost my mother. I can't lose him. Dear God."

"Don't you worry honey. He's not gonna die." The two ladies resorted back to the window hoping to monitor the operation over the radio.

Detective Donald Hauf was the first transmission they heard. "Dispatch, find out the ETA for the ambo for God's sake. Tell them to step it up. We have an officer down."

"How you holdin up partner?" Jim said to Michaels leaning against the foundation with his eyes closed.

"Ok, I guess."

"Keep pressure on that and stay awake. You hear me?"

"Uh huh," Michaels groaned.

MP's Dinko and Astle's Jeep returned to the lot tactically positioning it to provide them with the best possible cover and concealment.

"Captain Stanley Weinman," Donald yelled at the top of his lungs. "This is Detective Donald Hauf with the Anne Arundel County Police Homicide Unit. Can you hear me?"

Now standing against the furthest wall from the front door next to his desk, Weinman had Schumaker standing in front of him, bound in a choke hold with duct tape covering his mouth and a gun embedded in his temple. "What do you want?"

"I need you to open the door and put your hands out, so we can see them," Donald ordered.

"Why? I didn't do anything. Sergeant Schumaker is the one who shot the door up. Not me. I'm not getting blamed for this," he bellowed.

"I just need you to open the door before anybody else gets hurt," Donald demanded.

"I'm not opening the door. You gun happy cops have it out for me. I'm not the one you're looking for, it's Schumaker. He played you guys. I'm not coming out until you leave. I'll bring Schumaker to you, after all, he's MY soldier. The court ordered that he be put under my care. He's mine."

"Holy fuck. He's lost it," Donald said to Dredge.

"Is there a back door?" Dredge asked.

Donald shook his head. "No. There used to be, but it's boarded up."

"Weinman, you've already shot a policeman. There's no way you're getting out of here. You need to come out now," Donald shouted.

"Bullshit," Weinman yelled.

"You shot Detective Michaels. I'm telling you to put your weapon down and both of you come out with your hands where we can see them, and no one will get hurt," Donald ordered.

"I didn't shoot anyone. Sergeant Schumaker did…and fuck Detective Michaels, he deserved it."

Dredge looked back to see Tommy's car pull behind theirs. "Tommy's here."

Dawn and Katie kept a watchful eye from Dawn's office. More sirens were heard in the distance. "I wish we could see. He's still not answering his phone. God, I hope he's all right," Katie said, still upset.

Dawn thought for a moment. "You know, there is a way."

"What do you mean? A way to do what?" Katie questioned.

"To see. You said you wanted to see what's going on, right?"

"Yeah but…" Katie said while she watched Dawn pull out a black Pelican case the size of a shoebox.

"We can look through my Gosky spotting scope. I use this in competitions to determine target distance and wind adjustments. We'll be able to see everything with this." Dawn unlatched the case, removed the high tech scope, and attached the tripod stand to the base. She slid a few trophies to the side and placed it on the credenza. "Here you go Katie, take a look."

Katie began to pan the front of the building. From the magnified view, she could see Donald and Dredge hunkered down with guns in their hands. She continued to pan when she stopped at the front door. "It's showing they are 327 yards away. Which one of these dials lets me zoom in?"

Dawn pointed to the numbered dial on the side. "Turn this clockwise and it'll enhance your target."

Katie turned the knob two clicks until the obliterated door came into view. The bullet holes were sprayed about like swiss cheese she thought. Beneath the door she could see the dark blood stain on the top step. "Oh my God."

"What is it?" Dawn asked.

"There's blood." Katie lifted her head. Her tears unleashed. She lowered her head again and examined the right corner of the building. There she was able to see Jim kneeling next to the blood-soaked Michaels slumped against the wall. Her heart practically stopped. She tilted her head up once more. "He's bleeding Dawn. It's Ronnie, he's bleeding. I can't do this. I won't just sit here and watch him die. I gotta go help him."

"We're not going anywhere just yet. Hold tight, let me take a look. Dawn pulled her gun case from the closet. She laid it carefully on the floor and released the two latches on the front. She paused for a moment and looked over the weapon before lifting it from the grey encasing foam. "If you think that spotting scope is good, you should see the view through these optics. It's made by Nightforce and this one's called the BEAST. It's one of the most state-of-the-art scopes made. I've hit eight-inch moving targets 1000 yards away because of this." The 7.62 caliber Remington was suited with a flat black synthetic stock and a customized trigger, synchronized to Dawn's touch.

"Wow, now that's a rifle," Katie said in amazement.

"Have you ever shot a gun before?" Dawn asked.

Katie rubbed her eyes and took hold of the gun. "I'm from northern Pennsylvania Dawn. I got three older brothers and a father who did nothing but hunt. What do you think?" Katie looked down the barrel through the wide-ranging scope.

Donald could feel his cell phone vibrating in his pocket. It was Tommy. "Yeah boss."

"What's the latest Donald?"

"He said he ain't coming out until we leave. And he said Schumaker is the one who shot the door. He's full of shit. Is someone coming to help us?"

"Yeah, I called for our SWAT Team, but they'll be at least 45 minutes." The squelching siren from the Army ambulance blasted. Tommy waived the driver over to his location, then keyed up his radio to contact Jim. "Detective 130 to 134...can you copy?"

"Go ahead Sarge."

The girls looked at the radio.

"Status?"

Jim looked at his partner. "Semi-alert. A lot of pain."

"Can he walk?" asked Tommy.

Michaels took a deep breath and shook his head back and forth. "He's advising no. He's lost too much blood...way too weak."

"Ok, standby. The paramedics are here. They want you to look at his pupils and tell us what they look like."

Katie couldn't keep herself from crying.

Jim inspected Michaels' half opened eyes. "They're dilated Tommy."

"Ok, hold tight, we're gonna try and get to you."

"10-4." Jim laid the radio on the grass next to him. "You hear that Shithead? Help is on the way," he said trying to lighten the moment. Michaels eked out a grin and held his thumb up.

"It's Ok Katie. You heard him. They are going in for him," Dawn said trying to calm her friend. The two continued to scan Weinman's building with the aid of their scopes. They had front row seats to a nightmare which was about to worsen.

Tommy stood at the rear of the ambulance, devising an extraction plan with Paramedics Fox and Garten. With windows on both sides of the house, and two in the front, Tommy knew they'd be vulnerable, regardless of their approach. Not knowing where the gunman was inside, they figured it best to go for the corner at an angle more toward the side of the building rather than the front. Either would be dangerous, but something had to be done, and fast.

Dawn and Katie stood by the window and watched like spectators as the emergency vehicle arrived. "Fuck, what took them so long?" the frustrated Katie uttered. "Why are they standing there? Go help him for Christ sake," she shouted.

"Katie, get a grip. They're probably figuring out the best way to get him out safely."

"I can't take this. I need to get down there and help Ronnie." Katie snatched her jacket from the chair and ran toward the door.

Dawn leaned the rifle against the wall. "Katie," she yelled, running after her. Just before the stairwell, Dawn managed to grasp her arm. "No, you can't," she shouted. "You can't go down there. You're liable to get shot. Then how are you going to help him?"

The two hugged. "He can't die. I need him. He can't. I have to do something."

They'll take care of him, and I'll tell you what. As soon as we see Ronnie being loaded in the ambo, we'll go straight to the hospital." Dawn pushed back from her hug to see Katie's face. "Sound good to you?" Katie nodded her head and the two moved back to the window.

Tommy dialed up Donald's phone once more. "Yes sir. I see the paramedics finally got here."

"We are going to get Ronnie out of here. There's no real safe way to do this. We're worried he's lost too much blood," said Tommy.

"What do you want us to do?" Donald asked.

"You guys cover the front door. We're gonna rush in from the side with the stretcher."

Donald frowned. "What do you mean, we?"

"I'm going with them to provide cover, just in case." Donald didn't like what he was hearing. Of all people, he didn't want his sergeant, mentor and friend to become the next victim. Not if he could help it.

"Boss, let me come back there. Dredge can watch the door."

"No. Stay there. They're just about ready. Standby."

Dawn snugged the stock against her shoulder and looked through the scope. She watched as the two paramedics and Tommy secured red medical bags to the top of the stretcher using the patient binding straps. "It looks like they're about to go help your man," Dawn said, lowering the weapon and looking at Katie.

Katie could see what was transpiring. "Thank God."

Tommy retrieved a second magazine for his Glock and shoved it in his pants. The plans were finalized with the two paramedics. "How this is gonna go down is, we are going in from the side like we said. We're going to push this fucking stretcher as fast as we can across the grass. I'll pull from the left side, Zach you pull from the right. Heather, you push as hard as you can from the rear." Scared, they both acknowledged Tommy. "Are we ready?" They both looked at one another and swallowed. Their adrenaline was about to take control.

"Yes, yes sir," Fox stuttered.

"I'm ready," the eager rookie Garten responded.

Donald answered his phone. "Yeah Tommy."

"We're making our move. Stay alert."

"Ok, be careful," Donald urged.

Tommy alerted Jim again on the radio. "Detective 134. Stand by and keep your eyes peeled. We're coming to ya."

Both ladies released a deep sigh.

"Standing by," Jim said, observing them whisking the stretcher across the paved lot.

Looking again, Dawn could see the medical personnel and Tommy wrestling with the cart as they entered the bumpy terrain. "They're on the move. The two from the ambo and the plain clothes guy are walking fast," Dawn reported like a play by play announcer.

Donald and Dredge reared their heads up. It was impossible for them to see in the building because of the blinds. "I can't see shit," Dredge said. "Can you Donald?"

Donald tilted his head sideways. "I see shadows and a little movement, but that's it." Donald and Dredge remained squatting beneath the window. They turned to watch Tommy.

Jim's head was now perched up high. He could see Tommy and the medical team about to embark on their mad rush to his position.

Tommy, Heather and Zach stopped less than 50 yards from the building. They were all nervous. "Lets' get this boy out of here." They both nodded. "GO," the sergeant shouted.

With their weapons at the ready, Donald and Dredge kept close watch on the front door, and what little they could make out beneath the blinds. Holding his handgun tightly, Jim alternated his attention from the small window on his side of the building, to the front door. With his firearm in his hand, Tommy and his assistants raced across the grass, guiding the stretcher uneventful to Jim's location. The three finally reached their destination, panting profusely.

Dawn and Katie were fixed on the events happening over three football fields away. The two watched intently.

"It looks like they're taking his jacket off and cutting his shirt to treat him," said Dawn.

"Is he alright? I mean, does he look ok? Can you tell if he's breathing?" Katie asked.

"He's going to be fine. Everything's going to be ok, you'll see."

For the next several minutes the paramedics cleaned and stabilized Michaels' wound. They wrapped the injured area with a sterile gauze and secured the dressing with tape. "Detective Michaels, do you remember me?" Paramedic Fox inquired.

The groggy Michaels opened his eyes and attempted to focus. "You testified in the court martial hearing," he mumbled.

Glad to see her patient's senses were still intact, she smiled. "Good memory. I heard he got off. That's so sad."

"I got movement inside. I can hear walking," Donald informed everyone over the radio.

Tommy turned the volume down and keyed it up. "Dispatch, can you advise the ETA of the SWAT Team?"

"Special Ops 1, to Detective 130," the SWAT Team Commander, Captain Bowman called over the radio.

"Tim, we got a real shit storm over here. What's your ETA?" Having known Tommy for years, he could sense how dicey the situation must have been.

With his siren blaring in the background, Captain Bowman responded. "Hold the scene as best you can. We're about 20 minutes out."

"Twenty minutes?" Katie yelled. "He'll be dead in twenty minutes."

Continuing to assess the building and grounds, Dawn focused on the window facing Mapes Lane. "Holy shit, I can see him."

"See who?" asked Katie.

"I can see Weinman. He's got tape over Schumaker's mouth."

Katie swiveled her scope to the left and could see Weinman. "I got 'em. It looks like he's handcuffing him to a chair."

"This is bad. I need to tell them." Dawn reached for the radio when Katie abruptly stopped her.

"Don't...not yet," Katie said with a cold blank look on her face. The two stared at one another. Dawn removed her hand from the radio. "Ok Katie, listen to me. I want you to be my spotter. Stay fixed on Weinman and call out his exact distance."

Pissed, Tommy shoved the radio back into his pocket. "Fuck. We don't have 20 minutes. Tommy knelt next to the barely coherent Michaels. "Listen to me Shithead, I need you to do everything you can to get your ass on that stretcher."

"I'll try," Michaels groaned.

Zach lowered the cart. Jim, Tommy and Heather helped the aching Michaels slowly to his feet.

"AHHHH," Michaels moaned. The excruciating pain jetted from his shoulder down his extremity. "FUCK," he blurted loudly. Zach pushed the cart closer. Michaels sat on the white linen covering the cushion and paused to catch his breath.

"Come on man. Grab his legs and let's help him up. Ronnie, I need you to lay back. Hold on buddy, this is going to hurt."

"AHHHH," Michaels yelled when he leaned onto the stretcher. Heather adjusted the cart to its normal height while Zach strapped in the ailing detective.

Tommy's willingness to get his man out was obvious. "Grab your shit. We'll go out the same way we came in. Jim, this time you help pull the cart. I'll get on one side, Zach on the other and Heather in the back. It's going to be a lot harder to push. I'll walk backwards and keep an eye on the building. Let's not fuck around." Heather and Zach flung their medical bags over their shoulders. Everyone was ready. "Let's do this," Tommy said.

"I wonder why he's taking Schumaker hostage?" said Dawn.

"I don't know, but we need to get ready to leave. I want to be there when they get Ronnie to the hospital," Katie urged.

With Katie still glued to the window, Dawn walked over to her gun case on the floor in front of her desk. With her back to Katie, she removed one precision loaded 7.62 bullet from the ammo box. Laying in the palm of her hand, she inspected the shiny brass casing and lead projectile for imperfections. It was flawless. She placed her right hand under the bolt action lever and lifted it up and to the rear. The well-lubed rails silenced the noise. She placed the round into the chamber. Katie turned just as Dawn slid the bolt forward engaging the bullet into the barrel. The gun was locked and loaded.

"Now we're in business," Katie said. Dawn took her position at the window.

"Go, go, go," Tommy shouted to Jim, Heather and Zach. The three struggled to maneuver the top-heavy stretcher across the bumpy terrain. At the halfway point, gunfire took over. Chunks of dirt and grass flew up around Tommy and the others.

Dawn lifted her head from the scope. "That's gunfire."

"Shit," Tommy shouted. He could see muzzle flash from a window on the same side of the building they just left. Tommy returned fire. Spent shell casings flew in the air from his weapon, while pieces of the siding around the window and glass broke apart. Donald and Dredge felt helpless. They knew if they moved from their position, they would be in Tommy's line of fire.

"Move, move," Tommy hollered to his crew. He continued shooting, taking better aim at the window. His bullets were finding their mark. He could see the glass shattering, but the relentless gunfire persisted. Jim and the paramedics continued to labor across the field.

Katie's nerves were subsiding. She gathered herself into a state of courageous calm. "I got Weinman at 334 yards, just in front of Schumaker," Katie said.

Dawn scoured the windows. "Got 'em. He keeps moving around."

Tommy turned when he heard the sounds of metal crashing and commotion. The stretcher had toppled over. The strapped in Michaels slammed to the ground. "OWE," he screamed.

"Dear God...get him up...get him up." Katie exclaimed.

The shots resumed. This time the crackling sounds originated from the window to the right of the door. Rounds skipped through the dirt, narrowly missing the extraction team. The pinging of metal sounded as bullets ricocheted off the base of the stretcher.

Dawn watched powerlessly as the bullets skirted the men. "That fucking bastard," she said, knowing it was just a matter of time until someone was struck and killed.

Donald, Dredge, Tommy and Jim opened fired on the front window. Holes filled the glass until it shattered, sending pieces everywhere.

"Dispatch we're taking on heavy fire...signal 13, signal 13, send all available units," Tommy insisted.

Jim holstered his smoking Glock to quickly assist the others fighting to upright the cart. Michaels groaned in agony. The gauze protecting his wound was saturated in blood. The shooting ceased once more.

"He's gonna kill them Dawn. They have nowhere to hide. They're sitting ducks. Ronnie's not going to make it. You gotta do something. He's at 333 yards now, directly in front of Schumaker."

Inside, Weinman uncuffed Schumaker and jerked the tape from his face. "Walk to the front door," he said poking the gun barrel in his back. "You're not pinning this all on me. If I'm going down, so are you bitch. Now move."

"They're on the move toward the front door...332, 331, 330," Katie called out.

Schumaker walked to the front door. The wood chips on the floor snapped as he stepped on them. "Tell 'em we're coming out," Weinman bellowed at Schumaker. "Now," he barked at him.

"Detectives, can you hear me? It's Wesley Schumaker."

Donald turned toward Tommy and the others. "Schumaker is yelling to us, stand by."

"Yes, I can hear you," Donald shouted.

"We're coming out. Don't shoot." Schumaker's voice cracked.

"They're coming out. Stand by," Donald told everyone.

With the stretcher now in the upright position and Michaels secured once more, each of the four-armed men fixed their sights on the mangled door.

With Dawn still affixed to the scope, she and Katie watched intensely from their vantage point.

In the background, the sounds of the whaling sirens neared. Several seconds passed, but nothing happened. Then the door creeped open. The shirtless Schumaker filled the doorway shielding Weinman standing close behind.

"The front door just opened. I see Schumaker," Dawn said.

A muffled shot sounded from inside. Schumaker's limp corpse collapsed and fell down the steps. Weinman kicked the door closed. The detectives and paramedics were astonished.

"He fucking killed him. Weinman just put a bullet in the back of Schumaker's head," said Dawn, raising up to look at Katie.

Katie didn't flinch. "331, 332, 333, 334…he's by his desk now."

The two looked at one another. "It's time," Katie said softly. "It's time."

Dawn took a deep breath and exhaled. Katie turned the dial on the police radio to the off position. The room was silent. Dawn rested her weapon securely on the window ledge. Studying her view through the scope, she looked at both windows in the front, then to the window outside Weinman's office. She could see him leaning against the front of his desk reloading a magazine.

"He's stationary at 334 yards," Katie said calmly.

Dawn lifted from the scope. She could see the tactical team gathered around an Armored Personnel Carrier preparing to rush the building. She knew the danger and peril they were about to face. She took another deep breath, this time releasing half of it as she eased herself behind her scope. She took aim at her target. The crosshair reticles held motionless on Weinman's skull. For a split second, Katie lifted from the spotting scope and looked at Dawn's trigger finger as it whitened. Without warning, the rifle discharged, making a loud cracking sound. The subsonic bullet passed through the glass and tracked between Weinman's eyes, taking with it chunks of skull, brain matter and hair. Only a small portion of his head remained intact. Just as she was trained, the shot placement was spot on, designed to render her threat incapable of any aggression. Katie jumped in her seat and focused once more through her scope. Dawn remained in position, then both lifted their heads. Dawn looked at Katie and winked. They both smiled.

"Turn on the radio," Dawn told Katie. Katie did so and handed it to her. The two stared at one another while she keyed up the microphone. "Major Sarro to all units. Target eliminated."

The End

Made in the USA
Middletown, DE
25 November 2022